Two Secret Worlds

By

Harper DePagter

Synopsis

Two Secret Worlds is a queer youth science fiction romance novel about a teenage girl named Amara (15) who is internally battling her unconscious demons that are finding ways to escape into Amara's conscious reality. Half of Amara's identity is centered around her small-town Christian community and family values. The other half of Amara's identity is being an extrovert in her imaginary world, which she created to hide and protect her queer lesbian secret. Amara's family's religious beliefs and morals initiate a building of years of a cosmic thunderstorm of confusion between her queer identity as a lesbian and her family's religious morals.

A summer crush develops between Amara and Zali (17), who is Amara's parents' farm help. As sparks fly between Amara and Zali, Amara lets her guard down more around Zali to share her queer lesbian identity. The secret of hiding Amara's queer lesbian identity was challenging when no one knew, but now, in a relationship with Zali, Amara realizes the secret lesbian relationship is more of a burden on her unconscious. Darkness creeps in to haunt Amara's unconscious as she progresses with the relationship with Zali.

Amara faces challenges along the way in her relationship with Zali to keep her queer lesbian identity hidden from the community, family, and friends. Each step in the relationship becomes more challenging for Amara as she wrestles with her reality and her imaginary world; these two worlds slowly bleed together, causing a massive shift in the universe. Amara doesn't realize that the unconscious imaginary world she created, that universe, continues to bleed into her conscious reality.

Amara is faced with her ultimate challenge when, suddenly, her hidden queer identity is exposed to the world, causing a fusion between Amara's reality and her imaginary world. In Amara's imaginary world, her love Kelly (15, 21) arrives in this new universe alive and real. The two secret worlds have become one and bring with them the antagonist Kumari (17). Amara discovers quickly that battling Kumari, her imaginary world powers are now real, and so are Kelly's. Amara's two secret worlds are now fused as one universe of existence; however, in one of the most troubling moments of Amara's life, she finds comfort in the most unexpected individual for support in her queer lesbian identity.

Contents

Chapter 1...1

Chapter 2...7

Chapter 3..12

Chapter 4..18

Chapter 5..26

Chapter 6..33

Chapter 7..38

Chapter 8..44

Chapter 9..50

Chapter 10...55

Chapter 11...61

Chapter 12...68

Chapter 13...73

Chapter 14...81

Chapter 15...91

Chapter 16...97

Chapter 17..102

Chapter 18..108

Chapter 19..115

Chapter 20..122

Chapter 21..128

Chapter 22..134

Chapter 23..141

Chapter 24..145

Chapter 25..150

Chapter 26..155

Chapter 27..165

Chapter 28..173

Chapter 29..179

Chapter 30.. 189

Chapter 31.. 197

Chapter 32.. 205

Chapter 33.. 211

Chapter 34.. 217

Chapter 35.. 223

Chapter 36.. 227

Chapter 37.. 232

Chapter 38.. 239

Chapter 39.. 247

Chapter 40.. 255

Chapter 41.. 262

Epilogue... 272

Glossary of Symbols & Motifs 277

Reflection & Discussion Question Guide 280

About the Author 282

The Acknowledgement 283

Chapter 1

Stories begin in all shapes, sizes and forms. One can never know when a story truly begins or for that matter ends. Stories, I guess never end, once someone reaches death their lives somehow, for a few generations live on. This story is an unwritten story that seems to be like a fairytale. Maybe humans wonder, do the stories have a happy ending like fairy tales? Time has not written my ending. Worlds have collided to bend and blend the fabric of time to write my story.

Faces and shapes of one person might define certain aspects but to whom one may ask does it define? Names, meanings, only are given to the object by humans; but one does not listen, see, touch, taste, smell, what is hidden inside. Think or imagine putting on goggles to observe the environment of water from a different perspective. Sure you might be able to look underwater without them but the eyes begin to hurt or possibly not see clearly. The beauty that lies underneath the water[1] is so amazing. How the sunlight is refracted differently. It is like the beauty is returned where the surface has worn down and even taints the image. The glimmer and shine of the light illuminates objects like the surface can not. The beauty of pink painted toes is amplified by ten fold. Little children's toes are seen from a lens that does not exist on the surface. These toes push water aside to move the body creating bubbles of

---

[1] Glossary of Symbols & Motifs

beauty beneath the water. This is where this story begins, underneath which no one seems to pay attention to.

Appearances can be very deceiving. For example, darkness can distort an image but that image is still the same, people just perceive it differently. Then the same goes for when someone puts their feet in the water, they know they are their feet underneath the water; but the sunlight distorts the image into rays of beauty. For me the story begins with the sight of the world that does not perceive her to be this girl at first glance. Darkness overshadows[2] the light of the water for the true inner beauty.

The summer heat and long days of hard labor end with long talks well past the dinner bell. Friendship begins to form on these summer nights. The orange and pink skies get washed away by twinkling stars. The soft summer breeze fills the air as conversations seem to never end. Secrets are not shared in these conversations but what our joy and interests are. One never knows how a friendship will start or with whom.

Us two girls spend the summer evenings reminiscing, giggling, laughing and maybe a little flirting between us. The conversation seems endless even after long days of working in the summer heat. We both enjoy the conversation so much we usually forget about the time. Isn't that the beauty and innocence of the conversation? The world changes in front of us, and how the light reflects off both of us. Each time one of us brushes our hair from our faces it creates a new beautiful image because of the color rush of the setting sun. My mind drifts to questioning if Zali notices my beauty as we talk? My hands run through my hair to brush it behind my ears so I can see her better, to hear her

---

[2] Glossary of Symbols & Motifs

better. It amazes me how her lips move with every word she speaks, because the color around her changes with every word spoken.

She laughs and finds the things I say funny. I didn't know that I am this funny. I look forward to the nights we work together so we can enjoy more conversations. One conversation we talk about is our favorite movies. I am not sure why this conversation stands out more than the others. Remember it's all about the hidden beauty within. Secrets are not shared between us friends, but will be revealed in very subtle ways. Sharing about past times and favorite movies, I am taken back when Zali asks me to a movie. Did I hear her correctly? She wants to take me to a movie. I hope I am not blushing. Hard to tell in the starlit sky. Why does she want to take me to the movies? I have had several conversations with this girl. We have laughed the summer evenings away and now Zali wants to change our setting.

I have never been out with her before but she is adamant. She is taking me as a friend. My mind races with questions and thoughts: is my secret going to be safe? Will she discover me for who I am? I can't let her know my secret. I'm scared to be alone with her. How is it any different than our evenings conversations watching the sunset, and seeing the stars appear in the sky. I can get lost in her world of words and even mine when we talk. There is so much beauty where we talk, why does she want to change it?

Context of time sometimes gets lost in translation. Numbers mean the world to me. They make sense in my head. Sometimes numbers come in visions but the meaning is not revealed. On this particular day, when she will arrive to pick me up for the movie, what will it mean for the future of my emotional state of hiding my secret from her in our conversation after work?

Nerves run through my body as I try to find an outfit to wear. She has only seen me in my work clothes. Ugh, what do I wear? How should my hair look? Why am I freaking out about going to a movie with Zali? We are just friends. Oh my god, there is no way I have a crush on her, but Zali is cute. I stare at myself in the mirror as I take deep breaths to calm my nerves. My palms are sweaty. I finish putting two braids in front of my eyes and clip them back. I adjust my bra straps to make it comfortable, possible nervous ticks as I look over my outfit. I adjust my hair a few more times, as I begin to stare in at my inner self. I can not let her know my secret. No one knows my secret. I must hide myself from her and from everyone. What would she think of me if she found out my secret? Deep breath in, count to four. One, two, three, four.

She arrives in her car to pick me up. I put my purse over my shoulder, brush the strands of hair behind my ear and slip on my sandals. I wave and smile at her as she looks at me walking to her car. She gives back a warm smile just like the one she always gives in our conversations.

"What movie are we going to see?" I ask.

"It's a surprise Amara," Zali responds.

Is Zali hiding the movie we are seeing from me because she thinks this is a date, even though she stated it wasn't? I am nervous sitting in her car and don't remember the conversations we had or songs on the radio. I find myself brushing my hair back and looking out the window. The time of day is all wrong. The sun is too high in the sky. It's to light out. When we arrive at the theater I ask again "what movie are we seeing?"

Zali replies, "you'll see, come on."

She asks for two tickets for *The Tomb Hunter* and then she turns and smiles at me. I don't know if it is the lights of the movie theater or the sun on the low horizon but I see this beauty in her from the inside to the outside. She looks cute in her outfit and that smile.

"Your outfit looks cute," I utter to Zali.

"So do you, Amara," responds Zali.

Did I say cute? Oh my, she is cute. Play it cool. Maybe I might play this one too cool, and not show excitement because I think she just asked if I am excited for the movie. Of course I am. Okay I'm now seeing a movie that I wanted to see with the actress I have a major crush on with outfits in the movie I totally want to wear. Please keep this a secret. I can not let her know this. Also, now I think my friend is cute and not in oh that's a cute outfit; but in a cute way that I like you more than a friend. There is no way she feels the same way. Does she think I'm cute tonight? Does she like girls, like I do? Oh no, please keep this secret. Secrets don't make great friends.

Zali is so excited that she brought me to this movie. She can't stop smiling. I love her smile, it just lights up the room. We take our seats for the movie and eat our popcorn and make quiet conversation waiting for the movie to begin. I want to relax, but now I'm nervous. What if she reaches for my hand during the movie and my hand? I want her to but she probably doesn't even like girls. I can't let her know I like girls. My crush is going to be on the screen soon; I need to make sure I don't let on that I like girls during the movie. My body language is everything at this moment.

The movie was fantastic. It turned out to be a wonderful evening with my friend. I did miss the conversations under the setting sun and night sky. Come to think of it, she had never seen me all cleaned up, only in my work clothes all sweaty and dirty. As we are leaving we run into some of my classmates. They were excited to see the movie they wanted to see; but my friend I came to the movie caught my attention, and I missed what movie they were going to see. Once again that smile she has on her face makes her look so cute.

We talked about the movie on the way back to my house. We said our goodbyes for the evening until the next time we worked together. Even though she mentioned this wasn't a date; I feel like it might have been after the feelings came bubbling up at the movie theater. Part of me wants her to kiss me goodbye tonight. I certainly am not going to be the one to make that move first. I need to know for sure she likes girls too. Please, just give me a kiss goodbye before I leave your car. At last, no kiss. My first kiss will have to wait, but I hope she will be my first kiss.

Chapter 2

Life is an interesting concept. How humans grow and develop through the years are a constant change but the changes are so subtle people don't notice them on a daily basis. One never knows how a person will change, grow, develop, or for that matter what lies with a person in their changes. As children we go through physical changes at a rapid pace. Our social and emotional development also accelerates. Understanding how the world works can be complex and hard to understand. Curiosity in children is endless, similar to the ever expanding Universe. Why do things look, smell, taste, feel, sound like that? It can be difficult to explain these concepts to children but they love hearing about them.

When children enter adolescence physical changes continue, but the social and emotional concepts accelerate like an Indy car on the race track. Human identities begin to form in who they want to be through influences that fit in with social and peer groups, and the relationships they form from those groups. Family members can also mold our identities if one has strong connections with them. I know religion is a major influencer affecting my own identity; however, there are so many more factors that can contribute to formulating one's own identity. Humans are social creatures in nature like most species in the world. Some of us like more insolation than others. Freedom of expression can come from isolation, but it also can cause loneliness in others.

I learned how to garden from my Grandpa Ed, as well as being a Midwestern Wisconsin farm girl. Plants, animals, growth, and life were always around me, and I love the peace gardening brings me. When a person looks at a seed, it is not much different from me or other humans. People are taught that life must come from a male and a female unless it's an organism that is asexual and can reproduce itself. The secret of life, and my own secrets are held with these seeds I plant every spring. This is where the story continues in a simple seed, and the secrets that can be unlocked from the seed.

Plants don't hold judgment against other plants. They are trying to survive just like any other creature. As a gardening girl, I learned how to grow and care for my plants. Native Indigenous people grew the three sisters of corn, beans, and squashes so they can survive together. Are plants asexual or are they not? During the hot summer days the squash plant begins to bloom. The plant produces male and female flowers. These plants are so unique that it seems like it can reproduce on its own but the plant in itself is both male and female. Without being both the plant will not survive. The buzzing of bees in each male and female flower will create new life. The insects who pollinate the plant don't care if it's a male or female flower, the insects just interact in a cohesiveness which is important to life.

Spending my summers tending to my plants I can understand my uniqueness as a human, as a girl. When I garden, I ponder how I will fit in this world like the plants I am planting. People can look at the plant and just see a squash, bean, corn or whatever; but to see the true beauty of the plant you need to pay close attention to the details. Plants and humans are very much alike, they interact in a cohesiveness that is important to life. Humans hide their true beauty from the world in plain sight.

The squash family produces a vibrant orange flower with a lush green plant. Both the male and female flowers are orange. Their outside appearance looks the same from a distance, but up close one can see fruit on the female flower. It seems like there are more male flowers than there are female flowers on the squash plant. As a gardener I must be patient. Those early flowers close to the roots are usually male, but as the plant grows its vines, the female flower begins to appear. In early stages of life this squash plant may look male and won't be able to produce life; however, as the summer heat and rains help it grow, it begins to look more female with all the fruit. There are some humans that seem to look male upon early development but as they grow, they know they are female. Their true beauty will bloom.[3]

I spend hours in the garden tending to the weeds and watering the plants. I live for the isolation of the garden. I can be me and feel connected because I really am not that much different than the plants. My Grandpa Ed always visits me in my garden to see my progress. We will chat about how his garden is growing versus mine. When I was little he guided me with the hoe to make sure the rows were straight. He taught me that I don't need a tape measure for proper spacing, just use your pinkie finger and thumb stretched out to plant corn. Next, the pinkie finger and the index finger to plant beans. I could go on and on about the things Grandpa Ed has taught me about gardening, but that's not what this tale is about. I have hidden my true beauty from so many people just like a quick glance at a garden. It looks like plants but there is so much more there.

---

[3] Glossary of Symbols & Motifs

There are some summer nights the plants in my garden are producing fruit and I share my love of gardening with Zali after work. It isn't always the hay bales in the calf barn or sitting on the hood or trunk of her car. We will chat over a handful of beans or peas. We are both hungry after work, but we enjoy each other's company and friendship more. Nothing says friendship like two girls covered in cow shit, and eating green beans in my garden.

Our friendship has only grown since she took me to the movies. We have shared many conversations since the early July night at the movies. I want her to notice me. Maybe I look like the illusion of my garden, I just look like another girl to her. I find Zali cute and adorable, does she think the same of me? As I pick beans, peas, and hand them to her, our hands lightly brush each other. There have been a few times we have said goodbye with a warm embracing hug. I enjoy those fine moments. There are nights after work I want to take her hand and walk through the corn rows; better yet take her hand and run through the corn field in the back forty. Sometimes we would sit on the grass and watch the sun set. Maybe that's all we need is peace in talking as the sky fills with beautiful shades of pink, purple, orange and reds. Looks don't matter between us; we are dirty, smelly, with strands of hair out of our ponytails or braids, but I don't care and nor does she.

She has spent most of her summer with me; however, she could be anywhere else, but she stays to talk to me. I know my feelings continue to grow for her; of course, I don't know if Zali feels the same way. Her prior dating experiences have been brought up a few times and she has mentioned the boys she has dated. This only cast doubt that she would even consider me more than a friend. Why would she be into me; someone who is so different from the rest. My secret stays hidden just like the beauty of the garden.

Remember change happens slowly without anyone seeing it happen. I can look at the garden everyday and it seems like nothing has grown but over time my mind begins to map each time I view the plants; suddenly, I realize why these plants have really grown.

People can be similar to how plants grow. Our growth is so unnoticeable that there is a sudden realization of growth, maturity that happens in us. Surprises only arise as time passes, and this story will only continue to grow. My secrets lie within my plants, and I hope she will take notice of my beauty.

Chapter 3

I stare at myself in the mirror with my hair and make up all done. My mind drifts deep into thought of my hidden secrets. I have hidden myself from my family and friends from this world. The Universe knows my secrets, but how do I talk to the Universe? When I was in kindergarten I had a crush on my best friend Emery. She and I would hang out at least once a week at each other's homes. I knew then I was different and to her I was just a friend. How can I as a five or six year old express a crush and feelings to another five or six year old girl? I am different and the world will not accept me for being different.

Besides my best friend Emery in kindergarten, I was a shy girl. I didn't make friends that easily and I liked to play by myself. I always felt left out at school, but maybe that feeling comes from being shy, and seeking isolation from others. At home I played with my siblings but I enjoyed my time to myself. As a young girl that's why I enjoyed gardening with my Grandpa Ed, and when I was old enough I started my own garden. I could be by myself hidden away from others so no one would know my secrets.

As a 15 year old girl who is shy, likes being isolated by herself, and hidden secrets makes for an interesting story. This is where the story continues. Why do we keep secrets from others? Being social creatures, one would think we would share thoughts with others. Maybe we don't want to share everything because of the fear of rejection. When I was six I had a crush on Emery. We would do all activities together in the classroom and on the playground.

One school day, I drew a picture of Emery and I holding hands. I showed my Mother, and she was so proud that I drew a picture of my friend until I said I'm going to marry her. The mood changed as fast as the wind changed direction to blow in storm clouds. No longer was she happy and proud of the picture but tried to explain to me that girls don't marry girls. That was yicky and boys and girls only marry. I didn't understand why I was experiencing the emotion of sorrow.

The seeds of a secret had been planted in that moment, and my isolation would only begin to grow. I felt like an isolated plant pot taken from its sun filled window sill then placed in a dark cabinet with no sunlight. How is it any different for a child to say I'm going to marry Mommy or Daddy? Parents find that silly and funny, but for me to say I'm going to marry another girl was wrong and not silly.

I have hidden my secret from my family for nine years. Is it hard; yes, but no. My liking and attraction to girls can be hidden, but holding in those emotions is hard. I feel like I am a rarity while my middle school classmates start forming relationships as boyfriend/girlfriend but that is common. My nature is uncommon and it's uncertain to know if another girl is like me. I can only imagine it's still hard for a boy or girl to express interest in the opposite gender, but society doesn't fully accept same gender relationships. My isolation comes, so I can stay hidden.

My emotions have been scrambled since showing my Mother the picture, and saying I'm going to marry my best friend when I was six years old. Growing up in a Christian home has made me question who I am. I have heard hundreds of times homosexuality is wrong while sitting in the pew at Church or during family gatherings. I have prayed to God to change who I am. I didn't want this sin. Why am I cursed to be different? The struggle is real, as there will be nights I cry myself to sleep. I couldn't cry loudly because I didn't want to wake my sister. Once my sister is asleep, I kneel next to the window and wrap the curtain around me to look at the night sky. I tell myself I am not from this world; I'm not even from this Universe. I feel different and out of place.

"Why am I here," I ask myself, as I stare out the window.

I gaze at the beauty of the stars twinkling, or watch the clouds pace over the moon. There must be a world where I can be accepted. These nights I feel lonely, but I know I am not because I have a family who loves me, but I still feel alone in this world because I am different.

The mind is a powerful thing. It can take emotions you might know, and hide them deep in your unconscious mind. I always feel vulnerable in many different situations to keep my secret hidden. When I have a class with a girl I have a crush on I will try not to stare, or even look at her because I am always worried someone might catch on that I like girls. I live in constant fear of my secret being found out by others and casting judgment.

The same thing applies to me looking at magazines with female models. I don't want anyone to know I think the models are cute. I became very reserved with my emotions and expressions. I know this is my mind trying to protect itself and the secret. Entering my teenage years and puberty it has become more difficult to hide my secret; but somehow my unconscious mind does it without me even knowing. The danger only lies within that.

Middle school was difficult because I would find myself styling my hair a certain way, or wearing an outfit just to see if the girl I had a crush on would notice me. The trouble I faced was that the boys noticed me more than the girls.

A few boys tried to ask me out, but I politely declined to tell them my parents wouldn't let me date anyone in middle school. The problem with being in a small community with an older brother, people caught on that wasn't true. I started telling them I don't like you that way. That must have been hard for them to hear the rejection, but my rejection would soon come too.

A new girl arrived at the start of the 7th grade school year and her name was Adelaide. Being new in a community is hard enough, but her first impression on my classmates didn't go so well. How to best describe her personality, bright, bold, and stubborn. She was the odd one left out on most partner projects, as was I. We ended up partnering up for most projects. I thought she was cute with her curly blonde hair that came down to her shoulders. We got to know each other well during those partner assignments to begin to develop a friendship. That friendship evolved into a crush for me.

We hung out a few times outside of school, and she invited me to go roller skating one night. It was a great night roller skating with her friends from her old school. Of course, I had never roller skated so she held my hand the whole time. I felt safe with her and her smile filled my heart. We laughed and had so much fun that I let my guard down. I wanted to kiss her that night. While we were skating I tried to figure out when I could kiss her. They played slow songs to allow skaters to slow dance while skating. I asked her to slow dance because I thought it would be fun since one of her friends was there with her boyfriend. It was hard for me to keep balance but she helped me stay on my feet. I remember her saying "here, you put your arms around my shoulders and I'll put mine around your waist. That way if you fall I will catch you."

She asked if I was okay because my balance wasn't great. How could I tell her I was great at the moment? I was loving this moment and didn't want it to end. I felt lost in the moment with her, and all the other skaters seemed to fade away. This was my moment under the disco lights to give her a kiss. When she turned her head to look at me I took the chance. Something about her melted me to let my guard down. I leaned in to give her a kiss, and she pulled away.

Adelaide asked "What are you doing?"

I replied, "I'm sorry"

I felt so awkward with her and my arms around each other. Lucky for me the song ended.

Adelaide told me "You don't need to apologize, I'm just not into girls and I didn't know you were."

I felt ashamed and embarrassed. My secret was out and the whole world is going to know. The rejection hurt, but as she helped me off the rink Adelaide whispered to me "your secret is safe with me. I won't tell anyone. It must be hard for you to feel this way. You have been a kind friend to me at my new school, and I can't ruin our friendship because you tried to kiss me."

I was shocked by her response. The rejection hurt, and only led me to bottling up my emotions and feelings towards girls even more. Two years later we are still friends. We have never talked about me trying to kiss her and maybe it's out of respect for me to protect my secret.

As I stand at the mirror fidgeting with my hair to make sure it's perfect. I bring my thoughts to tonight. Deep breath in. Now exhale. Zali is taking me to the movies, but she won't say which movie. It's not the calf barn sitting on the bales, or sitting in the grass next to my garden. I have to protect my secret from her. We are just friends. Deep breath in! Let the air out and it's time to go to the movies.

Chapter 4

My eyelids close to create full darkness. The night sky is filled with passing clouds as the stars twinkle between the passing clouds. The moon is rising over the treetops creating shadows across the land. The only way to understand this story is with your eyes closed. For the eyes can be deceiving. They can play tricks on you. Whether it's daylight or the night sky, but especially the night sky. Humans rely on their eyes for everything to gain perception of the world. Those without sight rely on their other senses to gain perception of the world; so I wonder what their perception of the world consists of? Do they experience things differently than those with sight? I close my eyes to try to understand the world in darkness. I can hear the cows clattering on their freestalls. The sounds of cows banging up against the neckrail to reach their feed. Crickets sing their songs on the summer night. There is a soft, rather peaceful sound of the tall grasses growing around the manure pit swaying against each other from the warm summer breeze. Sounds of vehicle tires racing on the payment of the freeway nearby. It's almost more peaceful visualizing the world by sound alone. My perception of the world can identify the sounds I hear because I'm already familiar with these sounds. If I am put into an area I am not accustomed to, will the ears deceive me like the world?

Darkness is unique in its own beautiful way, just like light is. The colors I can see in the light creates beauty like I have never seen before. Different images will create different perspectives of beauty in light. Take that light away, the beauty is still there, it's just hidden from my sight. By letting my other senses take over I can still experience the beauty as if the light is still shining. Darkness plays tricks on my mind.

Humans hide from the darkness when it arrives only to create light from fire, candle light or electrical light. These lights create a barrier to create a sensation of protection from the darkness. Those artificial lights will create shadows similar to how moonlight will create shadows. These night shadows are not the same as daytime shadows. They tell a different story to people's minds. A sense of not understanding what an object might be. Remember the beauty is still there but by allowing a person's eyes to guide them in the night, they lose sight of the beauty.[4]

The entire world is different from the environment people are accustomed to, and people don't like it and fear it because it is different. A person's mind plays tricks on them and puts them on edge. People light up the world to make the darkness different to make it look the same as light; but it will never be no matter how hard we try to change darkness to light. It will never be the same as true light.

I hide in isolation amongst the shadows of the darkness. As the artificial light chases me to turn me into something I'm not. I hop, skip, jump, dash, and sprint to not be exposed by the artificial light.[5] Why am I viewed in the light one way, but once I announce to the world I'm different, everyone views me only in the darkness? Of course, then the world wants to change me by casting that artificial light on me. Hiding from the light can create fear, and unknowing because people don't want to just close their eyes and listen. I am the breeze that rustles the

____

[4] Glossary of Symbols & Motifs

[5] Glossary of Symbols & Motifs

summer and fall leaves. That artificial light only creates images of shadows they don't understand, or for that matter never seen before.

Close your eyes and listen. I am here in those treetops rustling those leaves. I am dashing through the tall grass, shaking each tall grass as my body moves through them. Once again, I'm only a shadow[6] that frightens you. Close your eyes and listen to my cries. I know I'm alone in this situation, but finding myself in this world is hard.

How long can I hide in the shadows? Sure there is beauty in those shadows, but it's no way to live. My secrets are hidden in each chamber of those shadows. There are times I do feel alone, but there is one at this moment. When I stand here with my eyes closed, I want to come into the light. I want Zali to find me, but I am almost lost in these shadows of darkness. How can she find me? I want to reach out to take Zali's soft gentle hand so she can pull me to the light to hold me close. I don't want to live in the darkness forever. I just want Zali to close her eyes and listen for me. I am the girl who is near to her, but does she notice me? Will Zali notice? I feel she might be the one to help guide me out of isolation in this dark land I live in. I stand here listening to the sounds being lost in its beauty. I am different, but I'm beautiful too, if only she can hear me. Tonight I wish she was here with me. I want to feel her warmth draped over me as I can lean my head on Zali's shoulder. I want her to kiss me on these star filled nights. I will have to wait another day to see Zali again.

Our summer nights are coming to a close. We have had several weeks of conversations after work to grow our friendship. Like my garden, I have grown out vines of feelings for Zali. How is this night any different

---

[6] Glossary of Symbols & Motifs

than those other nights? We sit on the back of the 1986 Ford pick up truck. It is red and silver with several rust spots on it. We sit close to each other so our bodies can flirt with one another. Tonight for some reason she and I decided not to hang out right after work; but to enjoy each other's company cleaned off from the sweat and cow shit. Zali's hair is combed back but still wet from her shower. Her smile lights up the setting sky. I can tell Zali is happy to rejoin me for the evening. We decide to watch the moon rise on another beautiful summer night. I can only imagine my subconscious knows tonight is going to be different. We had to look better than our work selves. My stomach has butterflies in it while I sit next to her on the tailgate of the pick up truck. I can't contain myself only to flirt with my body and words that fly from my mouth. I have never been so sure of these feelings toward Zali. Yes my feelings are conflicting with my family beliefs, but I can't deny them anymore. I want to sit and wait for the moon with Zali, but I want her to take my hand too. I want to kiss Zali under the moonlight. I have picked up on some flirting from her. I'm still unsure. Do I take the chance and slide my pinkie on her's? I resist the temptation, so I give her a shoulder to shoulder tab in our conversation.

I find myself opening up more to her than I have to anyone else before. Those emotions of who I am have tormented me for many years. I feel lost in the stars with Zali, everytime I'm with her. Will I ever love someone, or will they love me because I'm different. My secrets can't be contained anymore. She has become my kryptonite. I share my wild imagination of other worlds and Universes. In these stories I confess I feel like I should be a part of a different Universe. She doesn't judge me, only smiles with the intrigue of my words.

Our conversation is disrupted by my brother storming out of the house with his rifle in hand. He sees us sitting on the end of the tail gate.

The shadows of darkness have crept across the Earth with only faint colors of setting sun visible. I hide myself back into those dark shadows to not let on to Markus to know how close we are sitting next to each other. The motion sensor light on the garage turns on as Markus walks gun in hand closer to us.

"Time to check the traps," he calls to me.

"Traps?" Zali responds.

"Ya, coon traps," I say with excitement.

This is something Markus and I do together a few times a summer and fall. It's about the only thing we seem to bond over. Markus has already passed us and is heading to the traps that are by the manure pit.

"Do you want to go," I asked her.

"Sure," Zali responds.

Zali hops off the tailgate and I reach to grab her hand. It is a natural thing that we have done before. I smile with delight at her. I feel like someone just pushed the pause button on the T.V. Her hand is cool and soft. Our interlocking colorful painted fingers felt incredible. Those butterflies from earlier were now gone. My hand and hers were finally interlocked, and I now feel more connected to her. She isn't pulling away. She is embracing this moment with me. All those worries that she might reject me because she likes boys are gone. I know now because she is holding and squeezing my hand back her feelings toward me are mutual. All those star filled, sun setting nights, eyes and body flirting with each other have been worth it. The darkness I have been hiding in for so long, now has light to guide me through the darkness.

We walk together, hands interlocked together, towards my brother who is now over by the manure pit. The sky is dark and the stars are out. The moon is beginning to peak over the treetops in the east. I do worry my brother will see us holding hands. I can't let go of Zali's hand now. I have wanted this moment for so long, I want to be in it forever with her. Luckily for me there isn't any artificial lighting by the manure pit. The shadows of the night are once again my friends. My mind intentionally positions itself to almost hide our hand holding. The darkness knows I have been waiting to hold Zali's hand, so the shadows work their magic to keep us hidden.

We stand several feet behind my brother as he takes aim. He tells us to stay quiet as he has a coon in his sights. Bang! The rifle fires, Zali gets startled by the gun fire and squeezes my hand tighter. I squeeze back.

"Ah shit. I missed" Markus shouts as he goes for the chase of the coon.

Markus creates distance between us as the darkness wraps its blanket around us to create a fort to hide in. The moon is bright and creates shadows. Our silhouettes creep out from our bodies. The perfection of what our summer has been. My butterflies return to my stomach as we stand there holding hands. We give a few whispering words but my mind isn't focusing on the words anymore. I want to take the next risk. If she isn't going to kiss me then I will kiss her. I have wanted to kiss her since she dropped me off after seeing the movie *The Tomb Hunter. I turn* to her nervously, my knees begin to shake. I try to breathe, even in the darkness her beautiful smile can be seen. I smile back at her. We stare at one another as I wonder in our engagement if she is thinking of kissing me too? Maybe she is waiting for me. At that moment both our hands are interlocked and I can feel her body heat radiating. A breeze blows the tall grass and tickles our legs. Who will give in first?

I take my hand and brush the hair that has blown into her face behind her ear. She embraces the touch of my hand as she cradles her cheek in my palm. I take my hand away from her face and we lock hands again. I can't wait anymore. Please just kiss me already. Then as if the darkness and wind couldn't contain the suspense any longer, we both lean in and lock lips. My first kiss, I say in my head as I smile at her with our foreheads resting on each other. We kissed again. I can feel the weight release from me as my lips are pressed against her's. My dream has finally come true. I have found a girl who likes me for being different. The darkness that I have hidden in for many years, finally brings me out of isolation. It must be fate that our friendship began as the shadows of darkness crept across the sky. My inner conflict at this moment is gone. I don't care what the world thinks of me or my family. I have found the girl of my dreams.

As the coon hunting ends we walk back to Zali's car to say goodbye. This time will be different as the night comes to a close for us. Neither one of us wants this night to end. We hug goodbye, and Zali's warm embrace is heartwarming. I can smell her shampoo she used in her hair. We kissed longer this time. It has become the night of firsts. My secret is out and my curiosity takes over as she climbs into her car. What is next for us? Is my secret safe with her? How will she react to a secret she didn't know she had? We live in an area where the secret of this relationship, that is a lesbian couple, is not accepted. At this moment she is with me in this secret and darkness. We hold hands one more time. I brush my hair behind my ears and lean in to give Zali several more kisses before we say goodbye. We smile and laugh about this moment because it's different than before all the other nights we have hung out together. This is the night of firsts and it is beautiful.

Chapter 5

Tic Toc, Tic Toc. I lie awake in my bed with my thoughts. I share a room with my middle younger sister Zoey, which is totally unfair. I should have my own room, but I guess I'm not old enough. Those are not the thoughts that keep me awake at night. It's the more disliking of myself, for who I am. At nine years old I had thoughts on and off again of who I am. My nine year old self had a hard time understanding my thoughts I had on those nights. I prayed and pleaded with God to turn me into something I am not.

"God, why did you make me like this? Please God just turn me into a girl, like the other normal girls who just likes boys," I pray to God.

The conflicting issue I face as a nine year old and have for the last few years is, I know I'm different from others, but I just can't comprehend why. I listen to the sermons in Church on how sinful homosexuals are, and how they have lost their way from God. These messages cast troubling emotions that I can't comprehend. Why am I so sinful?

Even at nine years old I knew I was a girl who liked girls. I can't stop those feelings and emotions. So I lied awake praying and pleading for God to turn me into a girl like the Church wanted me to be, also what God wanted me to be. My soul cries in pain because I'm told I'm sinful for having these thoughts. I can't shut them off, but I know if I pray, God will take that sin away, or at least that's what I'm taught. At nine, this was a constant conflict of who I am.

I also lied awake praying to God to let me be able to experience being pregnant and having babies. I wanted to know what it was like to have a baby when I would be older. There is a part of me that knew I wasn't able to experience it because of who I am. I might never be a mom. Why would God bless me with a child for being this sinful? I would have to be with a man for that to be possible. I know it takes a Mommy and Daddy to have a baby. I will not be blessed with children by God because in God's eyes I am sinful for liking girls. So I pray to God to turn me into a girl who is not sinful and likes boys.

Now I'm a 15 going 16 year old girl who has gone through or still is going through puberty who likes girls. My secret has torn me into isolation. It has sent me to some dark places. I still go to Church but my resistance to want to go is beginning to cast doubt on those beliefs I have been raised with. My parents said as long as I'm living under their roof I will be going to Church. I feel like I can't understand why I dislike gay people so much but I am one of them. It does explain why I dislike myself too. I'm supposed to dislike something that doesn't fit into this society. How can I be strong willed and get myself through this? I create secrets in isolation, and those layers of secrets are hard to uncover because my mind also creates secrets to protect myself. My mind is a great defensive system in the Universe.

The happiness Zali brings to my heart, mind and soul is like a raging waterfall. It's powerful enough to shed light on my darkness I have been in for years that I have built with worry and conflict of what my family will think of me if they find out my secret. It's already August and school begins soon. What would my classmates or her classmates think if they found out about us kissing and liking each other? Do I dare ask her to be my girlfriend? Maybe Zali doesn't want that and is it okay with her and I to be a summer fling? It would break my heart if summer is the only time we spend together. My secret only causes more conflict if people find out. It feels so right to be with Zali, but it constantly conflicts with my core beliefs that I have been taught in my family. I feel like screaming to the Universe to take this pain away.

I decided it will be fun to go for a bike ride after work. Zali went home to get cleaned up and returned with her bike to go exploring some cornfields. My baby sister Aurora, who is seven years younger than me, decides she wants to come along too. It is fine by me and Zali; then it might look more like friends going for a bike ride than a couple. I guess I'll take any way to keep Zali a secret. I would love to shout from the rooftops my feelings for Zali but I can not risk it.

It's another beautiful night but we must peddle fast to get our bike ride in before nightfall. Our ride takes us to one of our fields closer to the lake. There is a path through the cornfield that brings us to the back two fields. After a heavy rain the path still has a few mud puddles. I dare Zali to walk through the mud puddle. Aurora shouts with delight for Zali to walk through the mud puddle. I could see the reservation on Zali's face but with a smile on my face I tell Zali it will be fine.

A few steps in, she gets stuck in the mud. Aurora and I giggle because we both have experienced getting stuck in the mud on the farm. I remember a time when we still had our cows in the pasture. All the snow was melting with the spring rains, the pasture right off the concrete where the feed bunk was became a complete sink whole of mud. The cows would be almost up to their bellies in mud. The mud was like super intense suction, the mud hole would keep your boats stuck there. Of course, it happened to me. I was trying to herd the cows in and I tried to go through this giant mud pond. Both my feet got stuck and I tried pulling them out but my foot came out of my boat. I was trying to keep my balance and put my foot back into my boat, I lost my balance, fell arms first deep into the mud. I was now covered in mud from head to toe. My arms were stuck and I tried pulling myself up but I only sank lower. Eventually after calling for my Dad, he came and pulled me out.

I reach for Zali's hand to help her out of the mud, she loses her balance. I put my hand over my mouth to try to cover my smile and laughter but it is no use, I can't hold back. She is able to help herself up, and wipe the mud from her hands on her shirt. Aurora and I are still giggling at the sight of Zali covered in mud. Without any hesitation she hugs me with her wet muddy clothes. Zali is all smiles and laughter knowing she got the better of me because now I am also covered in mud. Aurora is laughing hysterically. I wipe the mud off my shirt, look at my hand and smudge it on Zali's face. She returns the gesture by rubbing mud on my face. At that moment we both agreed for a truce, with our smiling faces.

The three of us run through the corn rows laughing, shouting and hiding from each other. The corn is taller than our own heights so hiding is easy. I want to take a risk even with Aurora nearby. I am able to sneak up on Zali and give her a startling scream. She turns to me and I say "Hi."

I smile and give her a quick kiss on the lips, then run off again. The running and hiding in the corn continues for a few moments longer.

While I am running between the rows, I come to the open path. I look one way to see if Aurora or Zali are on the path, then look the other way. I become frozen by the sight I see. Standing in the path is a dark shadowy figure. The best way to describe it is something similar to the grim reaper. The sky begins to fill with dark gray clouds. A storm is rolling in fast. I continue to stare at this ominous figure. I call out for Aurora and Zali. No response. I call again, this time louder. Again no response. Fear has completely taken over me. I have never seen this figure before and I know it is there for me. I continue to call for them both but no response. The winds begin to rattle the corn stacks. What should I do?

"Zali, please come here, I need your help," I called out.

My hair is blowing all over my face as I continue to stare. There is no movement from this dark figure. When I say dark, it is like a slimmering pitch black, I know that seems impossible but this is what stands staring back at me. Is it waiting for me to run? Movement finally comes as it raises its arm and points at me. Then I notice all the corn starts to wither and die. I look around and the entire cornfield is gone in seconds. There is no sign of Zali and Aurora.

The figure continues to point at me as flashes of lightning fill the sky. Thunder fills the air too. Fear is consuming me and I'm all alone. Cold rain begins to fall, but I notice something is not right. I know the sun was setting just a few minutes ago. It seems brighter than before, but all these dark storm clouds only add to the confusion.

"What do you want?" I shout as the rain starts to pour.

My hair is soaked in a matter of seconds. My clothes are next as the mud that is on my face and clothes begins to wash away leaving small streams of muddy water running and descending on my face. The figure only points at me; then I see some movement from the figure in the heavy pouring rain. A faint sound of a clock is in unison with this dark figure moving its finger back and forth. The sound becomes louder and louder which starts to pierce my ears. I try covering my ears with my hands.

"Please stop," I cry out. "What do you want from me?"

The figure begins to walk towards me while the rain is coming down in sheets. Lighting and rumbles of thunder fill the sky.

"Tic Toc, Tic Toc goes the clock dear Amara!" A voice calls out from the dark figure who is moving closer to me

"No, no, no, no, no, no!" I shout out.

I begin to run in the opposite direction shouting out for Aurora and Zali. Tears begin to fall from my eyes but I can't tell if it's just rain drops. As I run, a field of wheat grows instantly around me. I pause in awe at what just has happened. The field of wheat is swaying back and forth in the gusty wind. The rain has stopped but the sky is still a dark gray. I look around for the dark figure, it is gone, but where am I? I turn to look in another direction, and a glass wall appears in front of me. The glass wall stretches as far as the eye can see and as high as the sky. What I see is a reflection of myself. I am breathing heavily because of the panic that has taken over me. I try to go multiple directions, but each time the glass wall is in front of me. I'm trapped by this wall with myself staring back at me.

I let out a raging scream so loud hoping someone will hear me, or maybe to shatter the glass wall. I walk up to it and touch the glass. My hand touches my reflecting hand. I am struck with sadness and begin to cry. What has happened? I glance up at myself in the mirror to see off in the distance Zali and Aurora in the cornfield. I turn to look behind me and there is nothing but miles of golden wheat fields. I look back at myself in the glass and see them again. I begin to pound on the glass, and shout for them. It's no use if they can't hear me or see me. My sadness begins to turn into anger. I will not be trapped here. I will be free of this place.

"You will not keep me here!" I shout.

I wipe the tears from my face and begin to step back only to stare at myself. The motion is the same. It's like she is almost taunting me. My eyes glance to the ground to look for any object to break the glass. Being a farmer, I know there are always rocks in the fields. I continue to back up until I spot a rock on the ground. I have to dig it out of the ground before I can use it. Finally, after struggling to use only my hands, I free the rock. I am no longer sad but raging with anger for whoever sent me to this place. I will not stay here anymore. I can not stay here. I stare back at my reflection, but now she is covered in blood holding a beating heart.

"What the hell is happening," I mutter.

I clench my fist on the rock and scream louder than I have ever screamed before, then I launch the rock at the glass wall. It is like time has slowed down waiting to see if the rock will shatter the glass. My eyes glance at my reflection, she is now on her knees crying, but I'm standing; and it's dark on her side. The impact of the rock shatters the glass as the glass spider webs across the entire wall. Piece by piece the glass falls to the ground. A slow blink of my eyes, and when my eyelids lift, I catch Zali's eyes in my gaze and she pauses. The next thing I know we were back running through the cornfield.

Chapter 6

Today brings a new adventure with Zali. Our summer has mainly consisted of us hanging out at the farm, with a trip to the movies. Neither one of us has stepped foot into each other's homes, but today is going to be different. She has invited me to go to her grandparents' home. They have a beach house along Lake Michigan. Zali has been telling me they have a jet ski, kayaks and how fun it will be to enjoy these two things, since I have never been jet skiing or kayaking. I have snowmobiled plenty of times so how much different can it be?

I am nervous because I'm meeting her family. It might not be so nerve racking if there isn't the romantic interest between us. We haven't talked about our relationship since our first kiss or the many kisses after. Is this a summer fling, or are we committed to being girlfriend and girlfriend? I know going to her grandparents house I will have to hold myself from expressing any emotions toward her.

After finishing chores in the morning I showered after lunch, and got ready for her to pick me up. I was debating if I wanted to put two French braids in for my classic look, or just wear my hair down. I chose to wear my hair down today since we will be in the water, and it's just easier to work with wet hair when it's down. I grab my hair ties, brush, towel and royal blue bikini. She has never seen me in a swimsuit nor have I seen her in one. One last look in the mirror before I go to make sure I look okay for her. I have never worried about making myself look good for someone before. With dark blue jean shorts on with a yellow tank top and a quick straightening of my hair. I sprint down the stairs as she is waiting for me in the driveway.

I hop into her car and give her a smile. It seems like she is expecting a kiss because she leans in for one.

"Someone might see us so now is not a good time," I tell her.

This becomes our first test in this romantic relationship that is developing. We haven't gone many places in her car. The only other time was to the movies when the seeds of emotions and feelings were planted for her. As soon as we were out of the driveway, I took her hand and held it tightly with mine. Zali glances over at me, and we both smile at each other. I pull my glasses down to get a better look at her as she drives to her grandparents home by the shores of Lake Michigan.

I tell her how beautiful she looks with her glasses, red tank top and black capris. She has two little rows of braids in her brown hair that went into two open pony tails with the rest of her hair down. Even though I couldn't kiss her on her beautiful lips, it is great to be holding her hand for a few moments. I know I am not going to be able to show much affection for her while with her grandparents around. We will need to act just as girlfriends hanging out. I have bottled up my emotions and feelings for many years, what is the harm of one more time?

Her grandparents' home is not far from where I live. A mere ten minutes, so a short car ride. Zali gave me some details of what her grandparents were like, in the car. When we arrive at the beach house I introduce myself to her grandparents while Zali shows me around the property. It is lovely. I especially love the loft overlooking the lake. After some talking with her grandparents we decided to change into our swimsuits to go jet skiing and kayaking. She went upstairs to change and

I went into the bathroom to change. My thoughts were a collection of mismatched ideas. As I slipped on my bikini, I thought about my actions so far with her grandparents. I tried my best to avoid too much eye contact with Zali to not give any flirting vibes. I kept a good physical distance between us. I have been really great at hiding my secret my whole life but of course, this was a new concept and uncharted territory for me. I didn't want to slip up because protecting myself and secrets is the most important thing right now. I take a deep breath in as I finish tying my top on. I adjust my breasts in my swimsuit and meet Zali outside.

I enjoy her fingers and hands rubbing sunscreen on my back. I knew this is the only physical touching we will have between us today. It is a short lived moment of her gentle hands rubbing my back.

Zali whispers to me while she is putting sunscreen on my back, "you are looking super cute and hot in that bathing suit."

I whisper back to her, "so do you. I love that black bikini on you."

The day is filled with laughter and fun. I have more physical contact with her than I realized I would. I was able to wrap my arms around her as well as she did to me when we took turns driving the jet ski. Screams of enjoyment were let out by both of us as the roar of the engine and the crashing of the waves seemed so symbiotic. I didn't think I had ever imagined this summer I would have fallen for someone; and they also reciprocate the same emotions, especially someone who has dated only boys before.

There is calmness being in the kayak and seeing the blue horizon on the lake. The beauty of the waves crashing on the shore and on the crest of the lake. The sound of the paddle dipping into the water by pushing through is a releasing feeling of calmness I have never felt before. I stop in the water just to take in the moment because I live in darkness and isolation; but here with Zali there is no darkness or isolation, just the beauty of nature.

Her grandparents invited me to stay for dinner, which I was delighted by the very kind gesture. I call my parents and they say it is fine but I need to be home by 10 pm because I have to work in the morning and Church. I could only imagine the conflicting emotions that will transpire after today. Zali's grandparents grilled brats and burgers for dinner. It was delightful because what Midwesterners don't love is a good brat and burger off the grill.

That evening we decided to lay on the beach and wait for the moon to rise. Tonight is going to be a full moon. For the most part I have been able to contain myself from her to not let on to her grandparents, that I am interested in their granddaughter. I do worry that I might have slipped up at some point today but for the most part it looked like two friends having fun.

We keep our distance while it is still light enough to be seen from the house. My friend, the darkness will soon protect us, and I will be able to hold her hand. As the shadows of darkness blankets us, we slowly begin to flirt with our fingers. We are still worried we might be being watched. The moon rises as a crimson ball that transforms into a beautiful orange color. It casts its light across the lake as if it is creating a light bridge for us to run across to another world to be free and together. No worries what other people think of our relationship. Telling us how sinful we are. As the moon continues to rise over the horizon of the lake, its brightness grows. The crashing of the waves are so peaceful. I am loving this moment with Zali. Our hands interlock and we turn to each other. Her radiant smile fills my heart with love as we gaze into each other's eyes. The moonlight brightens her beautiful green eyes. My guard is let down and I can't contain myself anymore.

"I like you." I whisper to her.

"I like you too." she whispers back.

"I like you more than just a friend, Zali." I replied back.

"I do too," she says.

It is a great feeling to hear her say she likes me more than just a friend. I finally feel loved by someone. Of course, I'm loved by my parents and the rest of my family; but not someone I have a crush on who grew like my garden into beautiful emotions toward her. My happiness is content in this moment under the full moon holding her hand with our eyes interlocked.

Chapter 7

My life consists of numbers. My mind is always calculating numerical concepts in my head. Math is my best subject in school, but my favorite is social studies. Numbers have an importance in my life that come through visions or prophecy; however, you want to look at it. It's hard to comprehend why this happens, but it does. Some events correspond with these numbers that pop in my head. I also rely on numbers in my garden by calculating when seeds should be planted in time for a seed to grow. The plant needs to produce fruit before the first frost comes, and the end of the growing season. Perhaps someone would think I would be into astrology, zodiac signs, or even horoscopes with my fascination with numbers. I find them fascinating, nevertheless not my primary interest. Numbers are just meaningful to me, plus in a weird way provides comfort. I have calculated out how long it takes to feed the cows, including to prepare each mix to an exact science down to the minute.

Time can be funny that way in which it might be possible I am obsessing about time. Scientists say at some point time will end which means everything has a beginning and ending. What if there is more to it than that? What if I can't fully grasp the concept of time. My mind is a powerful thing; still, maybe time is like shackles on my mind. If I don't fixate on time then maybe my mind will be able to do so much more.

When I sleep the concept of time is gone from my mind yet not entirely. My unconscious is freed from the constraints of time. If I get 7-8 hours of sleep it feels like it moves by so quickly. When I wake up with the feeling of, I just went to sleep and now I'm waking up. Even in dreams, the concept of time doesn't make sense. While dreaming I feel the dream is in real time as well as lasting sometimes hours. In reality it's all happening in seconds or a few short minutes. Time is different in our unconscious mind. The unconscious seems to know how to navigate through time differently than my conscious mind. Secrets lie within my unconscious in addition to that's where truths and desires are held.

Secrets are hidden throughout time. Things are forgotten and some things are remembered. Some secrets are known while others are kept hidden. My secrets are hidden in time for a purpose; in spite of that, those numbers that appear foreshadowing of what secrets time will reveal are something to particularly pay attention to.

I now stand on the precipice of time in a decision that could change the course of my time stream. The choices I have to make will affect me forever. Every action I take has a rippling effect on time creating new infinite time streams. This choice only adds to my time here on Earth. When making a decision, time either speeds up or slows down. How is it possible that time becomes different, even though time is constant? It's my perception of time that is different in each moment I am in. When life began, billions of years have passed but humans don't recognize how much time has gone by. Human lives are short in this Universe in comparison to the existence of the Universe. Notwithstanding, humans need to take every opportunity they get because time for their lives seems to slow, but it is racing by.

Secrets of time exist with the Church I attend too. I have been taught God created the Universe in seven days. Only now do I see the contradiction with this concept because God knows my entire life before my parents are even born. The contradiction I have begun to question is how is it possible the Universe is billions of years old, but it was all created in just seven 24 hour days? My Church states that the Universe is only about 10,000 years old. If God can transcend time then why can't one day in God's terms be a billion years. One of my bible school teachers told me a story of what eternity is like, and how to measure the time of eternity.

They said, imagine a giant stone that is 100 feet wide, 100 feet high, and 100 feet long; then a single bird comes just once a year to sharpen its beak. Once that stone is finally gone that is considered just one day in eternity. That story has stuck with me. It is also a narrative of the message that someone would rather spend eternity in heaven than hell.

Time is a strange concept. I can continue to live in the shadows of isolation forever; just wandering in my darkness, alone, despaired, sinful, and lost in time. I can wait until time takes me to the darkness of the Universe, or I take a risk that will ripple through time forever. Remember numbers are important in my life plus help give meaning to my life. I may not understand them all the time, if ever; all the same I can't deny they have impacted my life. The number 22 is just one of the many numbers that holds importance in my life. My secret is now out of Pandora's box, which Zali now has the box in her possession.

I have grown to trust her with my secret these past several weeks. We have both expressed our feelings for each other and now the choice of what to do with that has risen. The time I have spent with her has been incredible. Zali has given me hope for life even if it contradicts my religious beliefs, and also causes micro-aggression inward. I can not let time continue to pass by without taking a chance by kissing her, and she embraced me by kissing me back. I risked everything by telling her how I felt about her only to discover she felt the same. These are not three strikes and I'm out; but three great hits, if I use a baseball analogy. I want to go for the cycle, I only need a homerun. It's a hard one to get but I can't wait anymore.

August 22 is fast approaching, which means the number 22 has importance. For about a week I have been sharing this secret with Zali about the importance of numbers in my life. My Pandora's box that she now holds only opens even more. I am dropping hints to her about something big that might happen on the 22nd. I have this secret that she is dying of anticipation to know. Time begins to race on a decision I have to make, while her concept of time must be running way slower for the wait of August 22. As the date approaches I drop more hints of what might happen. Part of me is hoping Zali would beat me to it because I really want her to ask me out. Nevertheless, I have been the one taking risks which is strange since Zali has dated boys along with that's the role she is accustomed to being asked out. I am in uncharted territory, besides I stand on the precipice of time. Do I jump into the unknown, or continue to stand on the precipice of time?

Two days away from the 22nd, and she is now dropping subtle hints that she thinks I will ask her out. If she thinks that then why doesn't she just ask me out? It would be so beautiful and of course, I would say yes to her. I guess it's the teenager way of defining a relationship.

Does she want a girlfriend? She likes me yet I still have doubts that she will say yes if I ask her to be my girlfriend. Zali might be struggling with this new identity because of her upbringing, still she makes me happy. There is no better time now to take the chance with her.

August 21 has arrived and once again it's another night we are working together. She tells me she is super excited about tomorrow, and can't wait to hang out on the 22nd. Her excitement gives me confidence that with all the hints I have dropped, she will say yes to being my girlfriend. Secrets sometimes have a mind of their own. Keeping our secret hidden at work with my Dad around, my siblings, or even the other co-workers which include her high school friends (one of them is dating my brother). It's a struggle to contain our flirting, yet we find ways. I even find ways to sneak in a kiss in the hayloft while Zali throws straw down. I climb up on the other side of the hayloft to throw bales of hay down for the cows. I climb the stack of bales and crawl across the top, then climb down to her. Sometimes I scare her which makes the adrenaline pumping, plus the kiss more passionate.

After work my brother's girlfriend Miranda, Zali, and myself stay to talk for a while before Markus comes out asking when Miranda is going home so they could hang out. I guess it creates a nice buffer to show girl time with the three of us. I have grown closer as friends with Miranda while working with her, in addition to hanging out with Zali. Once she leaves, Zali and I are alone. She smiles and takes my hand.

Zali asks, "since tomorrow is such an important day for you, possibly for us, we should do something special."

I ask, "what were you thinking?"

"Maybe I could make you dinner at the Lake house," Zali divulges to me.

Zali is just beaming with excitement for tomorrow. She is all smiles which makes her beauty more radiant.

"That would be so fun," I reply.

Time in the Universe sometimes doesn't allow those numbers to be significant when I want to use those numbers to be significant.

Sometimes time is written differently than what I might want. It's now or never standing on this hill of risk. I don't know what is down at the bottom of this hill. I can continue to stand on this precipice of time in the dark, alternatively take a risk in time, called a leap of faith.

While holding her hand I grab Zali's other hand, and she smiles at me. Most likely anticipating I will kiss her yet in a shocking surprise I speak words I didn't think I would have ever said in my life because of my secret.

"Zali, will you be my girlfriend," I utter out with nervousness.

Zali has a surprised look on her face, nevertheless in this shocking surprise her face lights up while the sun comes from behind the clouds to brighten the day.

"YES! Yes, I will be your girlfriend," Zali responds.

I smile at her response and we kiss to seal the deal. Time is a funny thing. Sometimes things happen at the most unexpected time in your life. Standing on the precipice of time I have jumped off this cliff, and have landed on the happiest feeling I have ever felt. I might feel like I jumped into a cool spring, maybe a mountain of feathers. All I know is I couldn't be happier that I have a girlfriend! My secret grows with a new process of thoughts coming with this, even so I can shout it from the rooftops. I have found someone, and she is my girlfriend.

Chapter 8

Flashback moment...

The summer is winding down quickly and the high school fall sports seasons are starting. As a freshman I played volleyball; however, I am debating if I want to take volleyball again. Earlier this summer during driver's education a few of my friends wanted me to run the two mile to prove I ran the time I did in gym class to end the school year for our fitness test. It was a hot summer day, so I didn't have the best clothing or shoes to run in, besides I ran anyway.

After that day I started to go for short runs as I found enjoyment in running. It is my way of disconnecting from reality for a little bit. Running started to become a way to clear my head. The only other thing I had to clear my head was my imagination.

Running definitely fits my way of life that I am choosing. The isolation that I seek to stay hidden comes from being alone in my garden, playing in my imagination, and now running. It is rather peaceful to go on runs by myself. I am beginning to enjoy running so I decided to go out for the cross country team. The environment seems more relaxed with less girl drama than volleyball. I am excited for this new opportunity. My thoughts are maybe I don't have to be alone in this, maybe running can bring me closer to people.

I have friends, yet I like to keep to myself. I hang out with my friends on occasion; so I guess my parents were a little taken back by the friendship I developed with Zali. I hope if I play this cautiously while hiding my secret, my parents will think Zali is becoming my new best friend, and not a romantic interest. Finding ways to create hidden boundaries without fully withdrawing is key. Being in a sport will occupy my time from Zali. I would love to spend more time with her, except everything needs to be strategically mapped out so I can stay hidden. My parents are not ready nor could they handle me telling them my secret. They both are against same sex marriages. A same sex relationship with Zali will make them say I couldn't hang out with her; furthermore, my Dad fires her. I can't let that happen. I hide within this new isolation that is part of a team. It also keeps me away from Zali to create just enough distance to protect my secret and now hers.

I do worry about school starting and where this relationship will go. Will Zali ask me to be her girlfriend or maybe I'll build up that courage. We are both still gaging this relationship, nevertheless she told me she loved me. We haven't even talked about making this official, yet she said she loves me. I'm not sure if I can express those emotional feelings back yet. Those feelings will open me up to being exposed with my secret being found out. Every step I take my unconscious mind is mapping out several steps ahead to protect myself. It might not be in a healthy way but my mind is trying to protect me. I will join the cross country team for protection and a barrier between us. This will give a way to be isolated as well as to be a part of something.

It will not be easy to keep my secret because I have never felt this way about someone before. My secrets have evolved into their own sense of being. That is a hard concept to understand, besides they seem to take on a life of their own.

I balance my secret with my friends, along with being a teenager I have developed crushes on a few of my friends. It's a weird sensation because one day they are your friend, and the next day the light hits their face just right creating a magnetic attraction. I begin to blush when they talk to me. I play with my hair more when I am around them. These are all things I know I have done with Zali.

The hardest thing is having a crush on a girl while being in sports with them, or the same gym class. Is this a normal struggle for same sex orientation people to worry about seeing your crush change in front of you? I'm sure the boys locker room is the same as the girls locker room. There is no issue changing in front of the same sex/gender. In spite of that, when adding in the element of attraction to the same sex, I have more reservations of changing in front of them. I guess that would be why going to Zali's grandma's house at the beach we could easily change in the same room because no one would question us for doing so because we are two girls. If this was a boy and girl relationship no one would allow us to change together unless we were married. I guess that's part of the secret, it evolves into something of a mystery. This becomes the secrets within the secrets, but this story is about the well kept secrets.

The morning of my first cross country practice has arrived. I am nervous to be a part of a new team, just the same as most of them I know, well maybe just my classmates. The only person I really hung out with all summer has been Zali, so I see this as a fresh start. I hope to find some clarity while I run. There is also a lot to process at this moment. We haven't really talked about our relationship, or the fact she said I love you. I kind of have avoided her for the past few days as a protection to myself and her. If I let her in any more what will that mean for me?

I continue to finish braiding my hair in my double French braid look. It's my go to look especially when I run. I grab my bright pink sports bra to slip it on. I have black spandex running shorts and a bright pink tank top shirt. I love my bright colors.

This is my time to be away from it all while running as a pack of girls on our four mile run today. My mind drifts in and out of conversations with the other girls. Most of the conversations are about the summer and boyfriends. I don't have much to say besides working most of the summer. I try to keep my words to a minimum because I do have a relationship that is undefined as well as forbidden in our community and society.

I am taken back by one of the seniors asking me a question.

"Amara, do you have a boyfriend," asks a senior girl.

"No," I responded.

I have to play this just right and keep my secret hidden. In the past when I was asked this question I lied. I don't like lying yet it's the only way. I get tense and become a little defensive when I get asked about boys. Boys have asked me to dance at school dances which I have said no and yes to make sure I create this secret that doesn't exist. The illusion of me having interest in boys is just another way to protect myself.

A classmate named Arjun in middle school who liked me, in addition to I danced with him at a dance. I knew I created this illusion that I liked him. The difficulty of keeping up this illusion came to light when he tried to kiss me when a group of us were hanging out. I pushed him away because I would never take this secret illusion of me liking boys to that level. Besides, the person I wanted to kiss was sitting across from me while we all hung out. I actually turned to her for comfort from the situation in which Arjun tried to kiss me.

These emotions I juggle will tear me up inside but I really am not aware of this emotional damage I'm doing to myself. There are little bursts of anger here and there, still I don't even recognize what is causing this. The secrets and layers that keep building are slowly weighing on my consciousness.

As the week nears the end of the first week of cross country practice, I have some clarity about Zali. The 22nd is approaching and I have decided I can't keep living in this world without someone I care about. I want her to be my girlfriend. We have had a few days apart, plus with the late summer nights are now cut shorter because I have practice in the morning. When I run I think about her, including one of the practices we ran past my farm, where she was working. I so wanted to take a little side detour to give her a kiss. I found myself staring at her while she carried the milk pails to feed the calves. I don't know if she saw me or not, but from a distance she looked cute in those overalls, gray t-shirt, and her hair in a ponytail. I don't need her to be all cute with makeup on to be beautiful, she is beautiful just the way she is...

Only two days removed from her saying yes to being my girlfriend, and I had my first cross country meet. I wanted her to be there, in spite of that she had plans for us after. She is making a celebration dinner for the two of us. I am excited for tonight, yet nervous for the race.

For my first race ever I thought I ran pretty good. I ended up being the 6th fastest girl on the team. It is good enough to earn a varsity spot for our next race. The girls all wanted to go out after some team bonding, I had to decline. I didn't know if I should lie to my teammates as to why I couldn't hang out or just tell them. I decided to tell a lie with some truth. I told them I am hanging out with Zali tonight. I mentioned she works on our farm. We had been hanging out a few times this summer. I state we had already made plans for tonight. My teammates mention that usually if the meet didn't get done too late we all hang out, and get food after we get back to the school. I'll keep that in mind for the next meet.

The evening is perfect with Zali, because we have her grandparents' house to ourselves. Her grandparents didn't have a care in the world that two girls were hanging out to make dinner together. I hold her close while she makes dinner. She even starts the make out session while we enjoy a campfire. We are able to snuggle while holding hands on the hammock watching the stars. The night sky is like my home because it casts its shadow over me just to protect my secret. My mind is at peace listening to the waves crash ashore. Zali lightly touches my face like she is brushing my face as if my face is a paint canvas. I am too lost in this moment with her right now to worry about my other problems. I can't even think because she leans in with her soft lips to press them against mine to give me a passionate kiss. We end our night with no one else around as she lays on top kissing me. We kiss the night away under a star lite night as the shoreline is eroded by the crashing waves.

Chapter 9

Rain pours down from the sky as the ground dampens. Dry ground begins to disappear as water droplets soak the ground. It is merely a minute of heavy rain that the ground becomes fully saturated. The transformation from dry to wet is complete. In this context, dry to wet or wet to dry can be a slow transition or quick. As a farmer my family needs the rain to transform the ground to provide life to the crops so they can also transform. Does anyone really take the time to watch this beautiful transformation? I think I take it for granted. My family prays for rain, to then thank God for the rain, but they don't see the beauty of the change taking place. They just see rain. Life is more than just the black and white that is in front of everyone.

The ground is cracked in many places; however, the rain is the healing process for this transformation. The ground calls out for help but no one hears it.[7] The cracks begin to slowly appear but most aren't noticeable. The summer heat is harsh on the soil as it drains the moisture from the ground. There is nothing that can stop this process. The ground has to take this beating day after day in the summer heat. There are different types of soils all around the world. Some can handle the harsh summer heat and don't show cracks as fast. These soils have a strong defense, and can handle long dry spells without the transformation of the rain. Other soils are not as strong and they crack more easily in the summer heat. Why is it the farmer can support the

---

[7] Glossary of Symbols & Motifs

hurt soil by providing support through irrigation; however, that same farmer can't support someone who is different, in addition to hurting with mental health in their own family. Those mental health cracks are on the inside, along with needing support of irrigation to heal her cracks too.

Transformation is all around humans, nevertheless people don't pay close attention to all the subtle transformations. I have to be strong but my foundation has all these micro cracks that no one pays attention to. My family tries to irrigate me with love and support, except it's not the right rain. I need to fix these cracks in me. The affirming love, religious support, and care does not heal my cracks either. This is something my family, or myself cannot pray to God to send rain to heal these cracks in me. My family merely will only turn on the sprinkler to try to fix my cracks by simply dampening the surface.

As I stand in the pouring rain with my hair down, I am drenched by the rain. I can feel the cool rain run down my face. I can sense the water droplets falling from the tips of my hair. It's a cool refreshing rain that gives me some temporary relief. The rain is claiming as I listen to the rain patter off the tin barn roof. Every inch of me is now a part of this transformation the soil is going through; however, nothing happens to me. Even though I am soaked by the pouring rain it's like the rain doesn't even touch me. I stay dry because my crack[8] runs deep like they are canyons. There will be no transformation for me today because this is my standoff with the rain. I live in my imaginary world facing my demons.

----

[8] Glossary of Symbols & Motifs

Secrets within my imagination are layered that cannot be peeled back like any fruit. The layers are hidden so well by many doors that one needs help to navigate; nonetheless, there is no road map to help navigate my imaginary world of secrets. I find isolation in this world transformative. It's not like the rain with how it transforms the dry soil to wet. In a context I can be someone different, plus at the same time accepted by anyone and everyone. I can imagine different worlds and Universes that I can travel to. My demons also live in these other worlds that I travel to and face the demons in. Is it possible my unconscious thoughts are manifested in my imagination? Could it be this is the only way I know how to process what is going on in my life?

I hold in my hand my weapon of choice, a sword. It's a wooden sword; for all that, I imagine it is a real metal sword. The rain droplets run down the blade as the blade points to the ground. My left hand squeezes the handle as I feel the rain tickle my fingers. My breathing is light, yet deep. I need to stay calm as I stare my demons down.

Lightning flashes in the distance as the air rumbles with thunder. The air is literally electric tonight. This storm brings transformation in all facets. The bridge between the sky to the land is only created for merely less than a second; just the same, it creates colorful beauty that is incredibly destructive. How can something so beautiful be so destructive? Add in the thunder which is the sound humans fear as children. Humans fear what they can't see, as those things are incredibly different. Nature brings people wonders like none other. The secrets that are hidden within nature only someone can imagine.

The rain is falling at a steady rate now. I am alone in this world. I am different, still nature seems to accept me even though others will view me contradicting nature. I don't fit in with nature because I want to be with my same species. People say it is not natural, and I need to change. Little do they know I can't change.

My world exists outside their world. My pain comes with me. This is what I am beginning to notice. My hurt and my anger is funneling in through some opening. Where is the gateway that the hurt along with anger is creeping in? This world and identity I have created is my sanctuary, moreover now it seems to be falling apart. I have no one to help to carry the burden. The pressure of hiding is cracking me just like the soil cracks when it dries in the summer heat. I am having a hard time understanding my life now. I have found happiness with Zali, except it also has brought more pain and hurt. I struggle in addition to losing the will to fight my demons. Please someone else take this burden of mine. I am trapped by my demons. They march from a far, across the hayfields and through the corn. They are coming to get me. The rain pours down while the sky rumbles. It's the battle cry of this fight.

My stance is ready as I grip my sword tight and raise it in a defensive stance. My armor glimmers with every flash of lightning. The elements of silver and gold cover my body for protection. The gold plated chest and breast plate with silver lining. My golden boats are lined with silver straps that climb to my knees. Rain drips from the pointed ends of my madi silver gold lined skirt. My arms are covered in sleeves of gold with an intricate silver design that looks like vines of flowery leaves. The shoulders are protected by the extension of the breast plate, covering the edge of my shoulder with a metal rounded pad. These transform from gold to silver at the end points of the shoulders. Lastly, is my head. There are many ways to protect my head, except this design is unique as it protects my eyes. My eyes are a shield as this is the mystery of my armor to protect the gateway to my soul. If one cannot see my eyes then I can not let them in.

The rain streams down my armor and my hair is weighed down by the rian. I wonder will my armor protect me this time? Can I face these demons alone anymore? Even though I have someone in my life that loves me as a girl and I love her as a girl, I still feel alone. My demons will only take her from me too. I will not let that happen. They will not carry her off into the darkness where she could be lost forever. I face these demons alone as they begin to charge. Brace yourself Amara, as I close my eyes and take a deep breath in to try to calm my nerves. This is my stand against them. I am cracked, yet I must press on. Zali will never understand my pain that I can't fully be myself around her and others. I actually might be trapped in this world even though previously I could willingly come and go. It's time to go. I might be a little more prepared to face this dark ominous figure that holds Zali in its arms. Not today will you take her from me. This fight will hurt like hell, and probably crack me more than I can even imagine.

Chapter 10

The battle rages on as my demons come from all angles. The fields are fully saturated creating a muddy terrain. The transformation is complete. This time is different facing my demons; nevertheless, are they actually demons, well no, but yes. Each one has its own representation that I am dealing with in life, even so I probably am not actually dealing with it. I just create creatures to face that are causing harm to me and the world.

Lightning dances from cloud to cloud as if it's an audience watching this battle. The thunder presents the roaring of the crowd. I yield my sword in battle, and strike to defend against my demons. A giant flash of lightning strikes the ground, igniting the ground in flames. Now the battlefield is filled with fire. The heavy rain seems like it can not stop this raging fire from spreading. How can something so beautiful as lightning crackling in the sky also be so destructive and harmful? Am I also like this lightning?

From afar people observe I am a beautiful teenage girl; all the same, if you get too close, and begin to understand me I become destructive. I stay hidden in the clouds just like the lightning dancing from cloud to cloud fitting in the element everyone wants to see it as. I too want to strike the ground to be seen and to be heard as thunder. My voice is shadowed by the thunder because sound doesn't travel as fast as light, there is a delay. My voice cries out in the clouds, besides it is so delayed that people have moved on. It might be possible that my thundering voice is still traveling to catch up to my dancing light in the clouds.

Today my lightning bolt has struck the ground. I rage hot just like the field of fire. My demons are able to scoop up the fire and hurtle fire balls at me. I am hit with fiery blasts from the front. I try to withstand these blasts the best I can. My gold and silver armor is my protection.[9] What does this armor represent as well as the color? Colors are linked to emotions. Gold is a warm color that is cheerful or enlightening. Gold brings illumination, love, compassion, courage, passion, magic, and wisdom. Silver provides energy of the ebb and flow of the tides. Sliver is fluid, emotional, sensitive, and mysterious. It can be soothing, calming and purifying. This color is a protection of negativity, reflecting any bad energy back to keep me safe. I feel the color silver helps cleanse my soul in my imagination by helping me confront my demons. It provides strength for the future. The combination of gold and silver in my armor gives me a sense of triumph, nothing will defeat me no matter how hard things are.

In my imagination I can be something different as well as empowering. My life consists of fighting the mold of society to be the perfect little girl who sits in the pew at Church on Sunday listening constantly. I have to be a girl who wants to be pursued by a man so I can make this man whole again. I feel like the Church makes me feel, as a teenage girl, less of a person.

Women will never be in the same status as men; in addition, it seems the Church also paints the picture, without a man in your life a woman can never truly be Godly enough. As a young teenage girl I'm supposed to grow up to serve God, plus my man so he can be a better person. I'm supposed to conceive his children; of course, you need a male and female

---

[9] Glossary of Symbols & Motifs

to procreate. The message I receive sitting in Church is, I must follow God and a man. This has always conflicted me for years since I knew I was different. I put on a show at Church, for the community, and my family. This toll is one of the many fiery blasts that now has knocked me to the ground.

Anger represents this fire, it has to be. What am I so angry about? The illusions I have to create in society to keep my secrets hidden. I let out a scream as I pushed myself up off the muddy ground. I have to keep fighting. I pick up my sword to defend myself as one of my demons is right on top of me, ready to attack.

I have opened my secret to Zali, only to now create a secret of her own. I am happy with her, except it's still just an illusion. I still have to be hidden with her. The illusion that is created is just friendship that the world needs from me and her. We can't be known as more than just friends; otherwise, these demons I am facing now will find a gateway out of this world and confront me and Zali.

I block an attack from my demons with my sword and spin with a heel kick. Is it enough to take out this demon? Of course not. It only stuns it. I'm mentally exhausted from several years of hiding; nevertheless, now it's taking even more of a strain on my mental health. The more I fall for Zali, the more I have to hide and can't be myself. I lash out with anger because I can't fully be me. Time spent with her only gives me temporary relief, but I need this heavy rain to transform me.

How can it be that I'm happy while sad at the same time when I am with Zali? If my life is a game of hide and seek, I would be winning because no one has found me yet. I guess Zali has found me, or perhaps she has joined me in my hidden place. This is not a place that I want anyone to join me in because it's miserable in this hiding spot. The company is welcoming, besides it seems as though it is at an impasse in this world.

Is it possible the clouds are weeping in this world because I can't be who I want to be as well as telling people? My family and Church will say God is weeping because of my sin, and I lost my way from God. This seems contradicting on my part. Fire rages on while continuing to be hurled at me. Each one of the fiery blasts that hits me stings and hurts, but my armor provides some protection.

People don't know the hurt someone is actually going through mentally because the physical body doesn't look damaged unless there is self harm, even when people don't notice. I have never caused self harm, still plenty of mental harm. When the floodgates do open with people sharing what is bothering them, mental health is not perceived well. For me my mental health is being taxed; in spite of that, this is also bigger than just mental health.

My demons have captured all the fire and are ready to hurl it at me in an attempt to destroy me. I draw my second sword and brace for impact. I will defend myself until the end. This is not just for me anymore, I have also taken the burden of Zali's secret too. I have to be strong, I only get to live once so I might as well make the best of it. I will not die with this burden. I am strong! Maybe someday I will find a life to live in peace. I don't want to live a life of regret. I want to remember the good too. I grip both my swords tight and cross them in front of me to create the best shield possible. I brace my stance in the mud. Be strong Amara you will make it, if not for me, then for future generations.

"AAAAAHHHHHHHH!!!!!!" I let out a siren scream.

The fire blast is intense and pushes my feet through the mud, for all that I'm holding strong. I scream to give myself as much strength as I can. Tears begin to fall from my eyes as they let out their own rain storm. The blast subsides, and I'm exhausted as I drop to my knees in the mud. My hands are weak, what's more I can no longer hold on to my swords as they fall out of my hands. As the heavens pour out their tears, I weep my own rain storm while kneeling in the mud. I do notice my gold and silver armor is not damaged, except I am hurt.

A hand is placed on my shoulder. I am startled as I gasp for a breath. I turn my head to see who or what might be placing their hand on me. To my surprise it's my first true love in my imagination, Kelly. She is smiling at me.

"Hey beautiful. I missed you. Let me help you up," Kelly speaks with a soft comforting tone.

My tears of sorrow turn to joy. Since I have to hide in reality, in this world I don't have to. In this world I fell in love with Kelly as she fell in love with me too. It still is a forbidden love because she is a princess and heir to her family's empire. Until that day comes, she can be with anyone, she is with me.

"It will be okay," Kelly insists, as she wipes the tears from my face.

She reaches for my hands and helps me up.

"I will always be here for you Amara. You have a very special person waiting for you, so let's take care of these demons and get you back to her," declares Kelly.

Kelly picks up both my swords and hands them to me. She gives me a smile and turns to brace for battle. This is far from over. I only get one life, so I might as well live a life I will remember. It might be hurtful at times; nonetheless, I am strong, moreover will press on through this storm. The light will come sooner than I might expect.

Chapter 11

The summer clock has ticked down to the final hours of summer vacation. The days have gone from getting longer to now getting shorter. The Universe has changed in our present time but the night sky is always filled with the wonders of the past. Change is always happening all around us. Most people have a hard time with change. The fear of the unknown shakes people's control of their current environment. Look into the heavens of the Universe with the vastness of it, what do you see? Stars have the same appearance to us each night. Sure as the seasons pass the horizon of stars changes; all the same, it's a slow gradual change that humans can get used to. Each night it seems like no change is taking place, yet once again secrets exist all across the Universe. These non noticeable changes of the night sky are the greatest changes that have taken place light years away. All the light we see of the stars is from the past. Change has already taken place. No one judges or hates this change. The sky still looks beautiful as each star twinkles in its own unique way.

This summer has been full with changes. To the average eye it might look like two girls became friends while their friendship grew into what possibly looks like best friends. The Universe knows how to hide things from people. Growing up in a religious family I would call it an act of God. It's God's plan, and God is revealing it for me. Even if God and the Universe are one of the same, everything is hidden from us. As the seasons pass the stars align differently in the sky. The Universe is changing so fast it is perceived as a slow change. I have changed this summer, except I stay hidden like the Universe hides its past. Zali has changed, even so she has also stayed hidden. The changes she has gone through are far greater than mine. She is like a beautiful spiral galaxy thousands if not millions of light years away; furthermore, I am seeing her light for the first time. I feel like I'm a close star to the Milky Way galaxy that its light didn't have to travel so far. I stay hidden to the naked eye, besides if you look deep enough you will see my true light.

This is the beauty of the Universe. Our two lights have finally reached each other's galaxy and we begin to change. My past slowly begins to shine each night with each night of observation she is able to see the beauty, and not the flaws of this new light. I'm not this simpleton farm girl who loves to have her hair in two French braids; there is more to this 15 year year old girl.

Maybe the better comparison is that Zali wants to explore the dark side of the moon. We only see one side of the moon while the dark side is always hidden. Like I said, the Universe is full of hidden secrets. I have known my true light for a long time, I have just been waiting for someone to look up into the night sky to see my light. The self discovery of this new light must be a wow moment, or perhaps disbelief that you have discovered this new light in the sky. Zali's past is filled with the same wonders that everyone else sees; however, the rapid change of Zali's Universe over the summer, no one has taken notice. She has now joined me on the dark side of the moon where no one can see us. The Universe over the summer has become our shadow of protection. Our fiery passion ignites when our lips locked for a kiss as if we were meteors burning up in the atmosphere. We create sparks between us like a meteor shower raining down on the Earth.

I wonder on this last night of summer vacation if anyone will notice our Universe change that has taken place over the summer. I worry we might not be able to stay hidden, along with someone who will discover our new light. Sometimes new discoveries turn out, while others do not. If we are discovered, my fear is it will not go so well for us, almost like scientists realizing the Earth isn't flat, or the sun actually doesn't revolve around the Earth. Change can be a good thing, but it needs to be slow like the night sky changing with the seasons.

The day is passing from morning chores to cross country practice to the final hours of summer vacation. It's September 3rd, we have been dating for thirteen days. It's not that long but for me having my first girlfriend, well I guess the same goes for Zali having her first girlfriend too, it's a long time. I want to do something different the night before school begins. Zali had to work tonight which was fine for the reason that I didn't get home from cross country practice until 6:30 pm. To keep it casual as friends I said we should celebrate the last night of summer by getting ice cream, which makes everyone happy. It's one of my favorite things to eat.

Zali went home to shower before she came back to pick me up. I quickly shower to get ready too. We have a short time before we need to be home, since tomorrow is the first day of school. It's a warm muggy night so I slip on my yellow dress with sunflowers. It's a spaghetti strap dress so it will be nice and cool. I keep my hair down for the night. I grab my purse and sandals, then head out the door for Zali's car.

My Mom shouts, "Be home by 9:30 pm since it's a school night."

"Okay Mom I will," I replied back.

The illusion is set once again that two friends want to enjoy one last summer treat. Ice cream is the treat, once again it's just an illusion. What my treat is going to be is, I want to kiss Zali by the lighthouse. Of course, it will be risky because other people will be around. For some reason I just want to take this risk just in case we are discovered at school. I know this kiss will be packed full of excitement and adrenaline almost like our first kiss.

I hop into the car as I wave to my Mom looking from the window. Behavior is everything to keep up the illusion. Zali has on a red tank top and jean shorts. She looks cute with her still wet combed hair.

"Wow you look amazing Amara. If I would have known to get a little more fancy then I would have worn something better," Zali flirty states.

"Thank you! You look cute too. Anything you wear, you look beautiful in," I reply in a flirtatious manner.

We are now out of sight of the farm so I take Zali's hand, give it a kiss to hold it the rest of the way. I know I need to enjoy this final moment because with school starting our schedules will get crazy, besides it will be hard to spend time together without people picking up on anything that we are more than friends.

I wanted to get ice cream at the ice cream parlor by the lake so we could then head over to the lighthouse after. Instead of sitting we take a little walk to enjoy the sunset. The clouds are lighting up with pinks, oranges and purples. Similar to the summer nights talking while sitting on the bales of hay. I ask her about navigating school, and if she has any concerns. She knows that she is a senior while me being a sophomore that our schedules are not the same. Our lunch times are opposite, so we might pass each other in the halls. We might even exchange a few words during our passing periods. She doesn't seem to worry about keeping this relationship hidden.

Zali worries about missing me. Being so close all day too only seeing each other by passing each other in the halls is like a comet passing the Earth. The comet is only visible for a brief moment. I have cross country until the end of October; of course, my weekends are filled with Saturday morning meets or work. Zali's schedule will be filling up soon with the musical and band. We know we will find time, besides the positive is our busy schedules will keep us hidden. It might make it easier to slip up on account of once we have a moment together our guard will be let down too much, and we will be exposed to the rest of the Universe. Even though I have expressed my concerns and fears to her, I'm still anxious about hiding this relationship.

Part of the mystery of our relationship is keeping distance between us. There is a gravitational pull toward one another, yet we both know we need to resist this pull in public. The second our hands interlock all eyes will be on us. Maybe no one will say anything to us; nevertheless, I know I feel the micro aggressions of society. This is new for Zali. She thought she was a cis straight teenage girl. I don't want to let her get hurt by society due to me. There is mutual understanding that we both have to resist the gravitational pull to each other in public.

The lake is relatively calm tonight, with little small waves crashing ashore. It's a peaceful sound which brings joy to me as I smile at Zali while walking the pier. I give her a shoulder bump as we walk. She smiles and bumps me back. She and I know this is the best we can do in public is walk close to each other. The night sky fades into darkness in the lake horizon. A few stars twinkle through passing clouds. Most of the people are minding their own business. People are all in their own little worlds separate from one another. Sometimes it's hard to notice what others are doing because people are worried everyone is paying attention to them.

The waves crash up against the rock breaker, creating a peaceful sound. The darkness that is my friend, will once again protect us. We finally reach the lighthouse while being far enough away from the shore there is a cool breeze and less light from city lights. Zali and I circle around to the back side of the lighthouse where visibility is blind. I peek back to see if others are coming, there are still I might have a chance to get a quick kiss in. There are two other people on the same side of the lighthouse we are on now, so my chance will have to wait. The lake horizon is dark but there is an aura of city lights from the harbor. There are a few boats out in the water that give a guiding light for those looking outward.

The two people that were standing near us started heading back around the lighthouse. Now is my chance to give her a passionate kiss in the romantic setting. This is how I want my summer to end. I just want this one beautiful moment with her. I have traveled lightyears to find her and now our galaxies are intertwined. I take her right hand with my left hand. My heart skips a beat feeling her soft fingers between mine. Zali turns her head to look at me, within the darkness I can see she is smiling. Before she has a chance to brush her hair behind her ear, I pull her towards me. I place my right arm and hand around her waist and pin her against the lighthouse. Zali lets out a little scream of excitement. My heart is racing with adrenaline, and my breathing is heavy as I lock eyes with her. Please Universe just protect me for just for a minute so I can kiss her. Please cast your shadow over us to protect us.

I know I am at odds with society, but please let me have this. I lean in slowly to build the anticipation. I can feel her breathing heavily as if I have taken her breath away. Our lips lock and I can feel both our bodies unleash the tension in all our muscles as the sensation of relaxation fills our bodies. It's not our first kiss, yet it sure feels like it. The kiss deepens as Zali squeezes my hand tighter. I feel her try to pull me closer with her left arm as if we weren't close enough.

The tips of our galaxies have collided; what's more, it's the most amazing thing. I just want to continue to kiss her here behind the lighthouse, all the same the Universe of darkness has always helped protect me so it sent me a warning sign. A boat in the distance sounds its horn as a way to warn us people are coming. As I pull back from her lips I utter words I thought would never come out of my mouth this summer. I figured I wouldn't tell any other girl this until I was long gone from this county or even state.

"I love you Zali," I whisper

"I love you too Amara," Zali whispers back.

She gives me one more kiss before people come around the corner as we space apart. Our galaxies collided together, now we separate as if we are lightyears apart again. I want to hold her close to finish the night off heading into school. It tears me apart. I can't even hold her hand walking back to the car for the fear of what people might think of two girls holding hands. I managed to get the most wonderful kiss of the summer before school starts. It was the perfect way to end the summer. To start summer I didn't know I would fall in love at 15. She is perfect and I love her.

Chapter 12

The summer of green begins to peel back from the plants. Leaves become less green each passing day to reveal their true colors. Each season trees, flowers and many more plants bloom to fill the bare nature with color once again. Winter months bring dark barren colors, and it seems lifeless in the world. It might seem that nature goes on pause in cold wintery months, except life in plants lies below the surface. The only way plants can stand tall to reach their fullest potential, which is reaching for the sun, is to create a strong base hidden from the world.

When digging a hole and someone encounters the roots it becomes a nuisance and inconvenience. Does the root know it will be cut to keep digging? There is no beauty in the roots or at least humans don't realize. What keeps people grounded in their roots is their core beliefs, values, norms, and morals. Without these what do they become? If someone or possibly oneself challenges these roots what happens to the surface image? Does it crack us on the surface? Do scars form inside us or underground like a root?

Once the hole is covered back up, do we know if that root sprouts new roots off the severed root, or is it scarred for life? Plants need the roots to create life on the surface and to grow. People see the different colors of the seasons as the plants transform. For a tree the transformation is unique from new growth, like a baby being born in the spring, to a colorful adult in the fall. That's just one transformation as the tree limbs, branches, trunks grow and expand too. Even the roots grow deeper to help it find water to provide life and protection against the weather.

Sometimes plant roots are exposed at the surface. Maybe we trip over them, or perhaps we cover them with colorful mulch. Roots are the diversity of each plant. No two roots are the same as they find a path underground. My roots are grounded with Christianity seeds. I guess my plant didn't come up like the rest of the plants in my family.

There are invasive species of plants from all across the world. Some of these invasive species are harmful to the environment while others blend into the environment. Their roots interlock as they grow amongst the native species. This invasive species might go undetected for quite some time. Some invasive species are rather destructive, while some are not. All plants are trying to survive to grow in the direction of the sun. Some plants like to have their space to grow while others grow well around other plants to use them as protection. Their roots twist and turn around each other making an underground chain of roots so the trees or plants don't tumble down to the Earth.

What am I then growing in a community of Christian faith? I feel like I am an invasive species, except I have not been detected yet. There might be more like me, well now Zali is too; in spite of that, even if I am an invasive species I blend in well with the rest. My roots stay hidden for a reason. Sure the Christian values are in me but it conflicts with my own self will. It's almost like pouring weed killer on me to get rid of me or possibly if someone just removes this one root of homosexuality, then I will be a better plant, possibly not an invasive one.

There are so many different people in the world. Humans are the same species; just the same, they treat each other differently. Sure some plants don't get along with others and won't grow. Some plants can't handle the cold, like succulents. Succulents do well in warm/hot dry climates. People are like plants, they need the right environment to grow. Human's true colors sometimes come out at the right season, while for others the true colors aren't as beautiful as they thought. Those true colors actually are harmful to the environment.

There are times when roots get exposed on the surface including the one no one notices, not even ourselves. When those roots are exposed on the surface with self realization that is when an individual tries to cover them up. Perhaps it's a form of embracement, they don't want to be judged by others; however, they could be physical or even emotional scars. They will try various ways to try to cover those roots back up. It's possible no one will question it too deeply, even so it can create anxiety.

I feel like I was planted in the wrong flower box, or I'm getting the wrong support to grow as myself. I keep getting sprinkled with Christianity water hoping I will grow, besides it almost feels toxic and burns me on contact because of my attraction to girls. I want the water and I need the water to keep growing; not with standing, no one realizes it's not helping and it's harmful. My roots may not be growing the best too but my outward appearance seems stunted.

I said this before, maybe I'm an invasive species. Would it be better for me to speak up and confess what my Church and family believes is the sin of homosexuality? Would it help if they knew? No, I can't have those thoughts. Look how my family and others in my community actually treat others who are different, what I mean by different is the color of someone's skin, their culture, beliefs, and sexual orientation. The community says negative and hateful things at family gatherings or at the coffee shop.

If I tell my family, or if they find out about Zali and my secret, they would outcast me and Zali. They would rip me out of the garden like a weed. Maybe they would try to replant me in a different pot to see if that will change me into a different plant; nonetheless, I'm not this plant they want me to be. Why can't they see I am a unique plant that wants to grow into a beautiful flower, tree, bush, or whatever. Just let me grow to accept this is who I am. I'm not trying to harm anyone, can't you see I'm hiding as a small plant in this garden waiting for them to see I am no different than anyone else. I'm still a person, yet I will be treated differently by virtue of their eyes. I'm a weed, or an invasive species in their Christian world.

September 11, 2001 will always be an emotional day filled with anger, sadness, fear, confusion and hate. I will always remember where I was, shop class, then I found out what happened in second period English. Walking through the halls between classes there was an eerie quietness in the school. I can go into details of the events, but I'm not going to. For those that don't know, terrorists crashed two planes into the World Trade Center in New York City. One crashed into the Pentagon in Washington D.C., and the last plane crashed in a field in Pennsylvania. The aftermath of September 11th is heartbreaking; furthermore, only gives more confusion to my own self.

The message from the media, community, and family was not to trust anyone that looked Middle Eastern. Before September 11, 2001 no one had a major issue with Middle Eastern people in their communities, now people are thinking twice about who they can trust. I guess the same happened with German immigrants during WWI and II. History tends to repeat itself in some format.

The terrorist organization only thought Western American culture was an invasive species, therefore needed to be removed. This same terrorist organization only exposed themselves as an invasive species. The hatred towards something different begins. I can hear conversations in my family that Muslims are trying to destroy our Christian communities. Is that what they really think? What would they think of me if they found out I was a homosexual. They would look at me differently, like they now do about Middle Eastern people. They would talk badly about me behind my back. Would they call me evil like they call the terrorists, or even other Arab Americans because they think they are trying to destroy Christianity?

Every plant is trying to live and reach for the sun, people are no different. Sure human beliefs are very contradictory following people can't see the similarities of their own species. Human roots don't grow very well in certain soils, what I mean by soils is cultures. Human root beliefs want to grow well in other cultures and vice versa is true, hence the terrorist attack, this is known as ethnocentrism.

Zali and I didn't really talk on September 11, but by the end of the day I wanted to see her. I didn't need to talk, I just saw her too give her a hug making sure she was okay and myself. I know deep in my subconscious this will only make me want to hide more. The illusions will surface so I am seen as a plant that is supposed to be in this garden. I look at my beautiful sunflower when Zali arrives, and I can tell she is a little damaged. Will she see that I am too? Tears are shed between us in view of the fact it's been an emotional day. We know others are still alive, unlike thousands who died today. I don't know what it is, but something is coming, or is going to happen as if today isn't enough. Tic Toc, Tic Toc, my emotional anxiety only builds.

Chapter 13

How can I weather the storm I face? My inner conflict only grows each day I am alive. I don't even know what is really going on with reality anymore. My days are consumed by school, cross country, work, and when I get a chance, Zali. Maybe no one is actually putting pressure on me; for all that, I feel intense pressure to conform to what society wants me to be and not focusing on what I want to be. I need to be loving and caring for this boy, along with waiting for him to one day grow up, and propose to me. I'm supposed to give myself to this man to make him whole again. Only in marriage is a man whole with a woman. What does that mean for me? Am I not whole even if I'm with a man. It's so confusing, the messages I keep hearing from the Church. I am not a heterosexual girl who fits in the society of the Christian Church.

Pressure has been building for quite some time to fit in as a "normal girl." What is normal? That is really hard to define. What's normal for me might be abnormal behavior for someone else. I guess I am not normal in any sense, which makes it hard to continue to fit in. Being a sophomore girl in a small Christian town I need to start creating the image everyone else wants; even though, at the same time, I continue to hide my secret.

The pressure has brought me to a volcanic world. I am a defender and protector. Even though I'm trying to defend and protect the ones that will not accept me for who I am. My parents would throw me into the volcanic pits to destroy the sin I carry. Here I am fighting more fire demons in this volcanic world.

My armor is strong and protects me; nevertheless, in this world the atmospheric pressure is greater than Earth's. My gold and silver armor seems to not be adjusting to this new pressure, something is definitely wrong. I slowly begin to step with caution as the ground I walk on is unstable. There are rivers of lava everywhere as these fire demons lurch below the rivers of lava, ready to attack at any moment. They are almost like alligators stalking their prey in the water waiting for the animal to get close enough to attack.

The movements I take must be calculated out to not draw attention to myself. My head aches from the pressure of this world as well as the intense heat blocking my ability to think clearly. The sky is filled with toxic clouds that rain sulfuric acid which only causes more damage. The danger is everywhere; furthermore, it seems like I have no choice, but to navigate through this world. Why did I come here? What is the purpose of me coming here?

Navigation in life has been assiduous. My emotions seem almost fake at times. It's incredibly difficult not being authentic myself. People want me to continue to be something I really don't want to be. I don't know how much more I can take from this. Putting on a happy face for everyone.

The lava is starting to pour out of me. Maybe I might be even drowning in these rivers of lava. I am struggling with every aspect of life. I have a wonderful, beautiful girlfriend who makes me happy only temporarily. If I could have her over like my brother can with his girlfriend, that would shift my environmental mood. My uncle is getting married and because everyone assumes I'm not dating a "boy" that I don't get a plus one. My brother gets to bring his girlfriend, yet I don't get to share this day with my girlfriend. I would love to get all dressed up with Zali and dance the night away. I want to be able to slow dance with her. I want to be able to feel her dress with my hands as we slow dance, and give her a kiss while we dance. Everything my brother gets to do I will not. I am stuck pretending to be a straight girl, including making myself girly as possible so a boy might notice me just to make everyone else happy, only to protect my secret.

The darkness has been my friend for so many years but now that darkness seems to become less friendly each day. The emotional weight is causing pressure that is beginning to crack my armor. My armor is the only thing that can keep me going. I begin to realize my armor has even become a little heavier. What can I do to protect myself anymore? Navigating through this treacherous volcanic world seems to be impossible. My mind is clouded with the pressure I am in. I want to scream out my pain; in spite of that, I must stay quiet to not alert the lava demons.

I feel like I'm lost in this world. Am I going in circles of confusion? I'm not confused of who I am, but more confused of life and how to navigate it. I see everyone is able to be themselves, yet I can't. Ugh! I'm just stuck in this continuous battle with myself and society. I can only let out a piercing scream at this moment. I can't take it anymore. The demons awaken by my scream. I let out another scream while this time fire blasts from my mouth and hands. Am I on fire? It's an angry rage. Can I fight fire with fire? The lava demons move quicker than the rivers of lava. Another battle I now must face.

My happiness may be expressed with finally having a girlfriend, except I still need to keep up the illusion that I'm a straight girl because I live in a Christian home and community. The pressure of illusion has created isolation at times. It might be unintentional, but I do it anyway.

What emotions can I feel, express or fake ones to make everyone else look at me as if they are real?

There has been more outpouring of fire from me in the form of anger lately. I am hoping that being in cross country would help to protect me and Zali from people finding out, except the opposite of that has happened. No, it's not that anyone found out about us; just the same, I possibly have created a wedge between Zali and me. My way of protecting myself has been so far an independent journey. I have no idea how to navigate protecting two people, so I do the best thing my mind knows how to do, withdraw from Zali.

We have been together for a month now, still I have gone into a spell of not talking to her, partly because of school, cross country, and the farm. It's hard to throw a secret girlfriend into the mix. I have also made some really good friends on the cross country team so I have been spending more time with them after meets. It's possible I am unintentionally avoiding Zali to keep up this illusion of being a straight girl in a Christian community. This continues to bring me emotional distress, which has brought me to this volcanic world.

It's a Thursday night cross country meet and we are eight days away from homecoming. It's a steady rain and the cross country course is going to be a sloppy mess. I have my usual double French braids in my hair for my race. It's a cool September 27th, and of course us girls brought multiple blankets to stay warm while we wait for our races. There are four races total; jv boys and girls followed by varsity boys and girls.

The varsity girls are last so I wait the longest. Our cross country team is small, along with very close bonding as a team. I guess that's what makes it so great. A few of the girls on my team have asked me if I like one particular boy on the team, since they assume I'm single. Well there is someone, his name is Ted and he is a junior on the varsity team. We have become pretty good friends this season. Don't get me wrong, I have made friends with girls too. Maybe it's the fact that Ted's family is also farmers so we have common ground.

When I am asked if I have a crush on Ted or if I like him. I once again have to lie to my teammates or other friends. It just creates another layer in my unconscious mind. What will those layers amount to, only time will reveal what they are doing to my psyche. My navigation on the Ted question is always the same, we are just friends. Well everyone else thinks that's a lie, moreover they think I actually like him. Only if they knew the truth. That's the point of keeping up this illusion, it causes confusion for others too.

The rain patters on our team tent as it trickles off the sides to drip to the ground. Ted and I are huddling in the tent next to each other with a few other teammates trying to stay warm with our blankets. Ted and I are having our usual farm conversations as well as talking about random stuff. I know that he likes me because when you are on a small team, it's easy to find out these things. Maybe that is why I'm not surprised during our conversation. Ted asks if I'm going to the homecoming dance with anyone. I told him I think a few of the girls on the team were planning on going. I ask him if he is planning on going.

"I would like to go," says Ted

"What do you mean you would like? Do you have to work," I responded with laughter.

"No, I don't have to work. I was hoping...," Ted mutters with hesitation.

"You were hoping what," I ask inquisitively.

"Will you go to the homecoming dance with me Amara," blurts out a response from Ted.

I am shocked and taken back by his question and my mind starts to race at lightning speed on the best answer. If I say yes to quickly he might think I like him, and this will mean more to him than me. Also Zali and I haven't talked about homecoming, well we also haven't been talking much, plus that is mainly my fault.

"Hey Amara lets go cheer on the jv girls," shouts Amber.

"Okay," I called back.

Saved from answering the question. I throw off the blankets to get up to meet up with Amber.

"Ted, we'll talk later," I turn to respond.

"Oh okay," Ted utters back.

I can tell that's not the response he wants right now but being eight days from homecoming I need to think this one out. What would Zali say if I told her I was asked to homecoming by Ted?

"Ted asked me to the homecoming dance." I tell Amber as we walk together under her umbrella to watch the jv girls.

"Oh that's exciting!" Amber says with a smile with excitement in her voice.

I think Amber thinks I like Ted, except that is the illusion I guess I have been creating this cross country season.

"What did you say to him," Amber pokes me with a question.

"I didn't give him an answer because you called me over." I answer.

"Well, he can wait. It's not like he is going anywhere. Everyone knows he likes you," Amber ignites back.

I try to change the subject as the race has begun. I cheer for my teammates; nevertheless, my mind wanders to the situation with Ted. Those thoughts roll through my head during warm ups. How do I navigate this? I don't mind going as friends, all the same I know he likes me, yet he doesn't know I'm not into boys. I feel like I'm playing with his emotions if I go with him. Also, if I say no I might hurt his feelings. I guess I better just make it clear we are just going as friends.

I didn't get a chance to talk to him after the cross country meet so I will have to wait a day. I'm glad I had a chance to sleep on it, and after practice the next day I talked with Ted.

"Hey, sorry I didn't respond to your question about the homecoming dance. The meet got in the way," I give a quirky response.

"No, totally we both had races to prepare for," Ted proclaims with a nervous tone.

"Well, I'll go with you as friends to the homecoming dance," I stated. I wanted to make sure I threw the friend's word in there.

"Awesome! Great! Cool! Ya," Ted remarks.

I can tell the friend's words bothered him a little. I'm sure he is feeling the same emotions that I had about Zali this summer. I'm playing this cat and mouse game with emotions, still he's probably at least happy he can go with me. Now that is set, how do I tell Zali? She is coming over to practice for the powder puff game next week for homecoming. My emotional weight has only grown. The pressure to keep this illusion up only cracks my armor some more. My happiness seems to be burning away when I thought this whole time I was happier. I guess that is an illusion too. Can I even tell what is real and not real anymore?

Here I am with my gold and silver armor showing cracks that I didn't realize while I fight these lava demons with my two swords. I fight and scream as I cut down these demons the best I can, besides they can just grow back their limbs. In the middle of my fighting I notice the demons are cooling and hardening into rock. I glance up in the sky and it appears ash is falling from the sky. With each flake that touches the hot surface, I hear the sound of sizzle as water quickly evaporates into steam. The lava has cooled at a rapid pace as the atmosphere has changed. It's not as hot as it once was. What is happening? This isn't ash that is falling, its snow; but how is that even possible? This world has changed from a volcanic world to an ice world in mere seconds. It's cold, dark, lifeless; except for me.

Chapter 14

I tip toe down this fine line between reality and alternate worlds. These two worlds seem blended more than I can even realize. Is it possible I'm blinded by my scaring emotions I have been carrying? How can a 15 year old girl really know who they are? Maybe someone will just say it's a phase, that I like girls. It's just hormones on overdrive so you are not thinking clearly. Why is it I keep getting tormented in my dreams? Are my dreams real too? What I think is reality is just a dream? No matter what, I'm stuck in a nightmare. Every action I do or perform in my life creates anxiety because I don't want anyone to find out my secret. I thought having a girlfriend would be better, except I feel like I am struggling even more. I thought maybe I could be more of myself with Zali, nonetheless the anxiety is always high. We could be in the driveway together while my mind is worrying what if we are being watched? What if my brother finds out when he brings his girlfriend back to the house? Instead of living in the moment I am worried more than ever.

I wander this world more alone than ever, but not really. Humans are all never alone in this world. It's the perception they create that they are alone. Human minds put on blinders so they don't see all the people around them. It feels like people are emotionless zombies just walking this world. Conversations exist, yet they feel like whispers in the wind.

I wander in this world in vast open fields. Tall grass waves back and forth as the leaves of the grass tickle my legs. I walk alone in the filtered rays of sun in the gray skies. My hair is wispy in my face as I stare off into the distance horizon. I feel like I'm stuck in a trance staring at basically nothing. Is it possible I can feel nothing; in spite of that, at the same time I feel so much mixed emotions? How can I possibly continue with myself because hiding has created an anxious monster that I can not see. This monster is faster than light itself. I can't fight this anxiety, as it has been created by so many micro aggressions of anxiety that have been scattered throughout time. These micro anxiety strikes at every moment. Maybe it's like a swarm of bees, yet invisible. It makes me weak, plus unmotivated to continue with myself.

I stand in my room wrapped in my towel with my hair also wrapped in a towel. I stare into the mirror that hangs on my door trying to figure who I have become, or what has become of me. I need to get ready for the homecoming dance. I'm going with the cross country group, except Ted is my date. Last night was a rough night since Zali found out that I was going to the dance with Ted. I mentioned to her I was planning on going with my cross country friends, I just didn't want to mention Ted. I wish it was easier in this current time, and community to just go with Zali.

We could easily go as friends, still it's difficult that Zali and I wouldn't be able to slow dance together. Sure there are always girls dancing with girls and boys do it too, it's a joke to have fun. I fear our body language would give people the indication there is something more than just friendship. This is where this anxiety comes from, I am constantly conscious about my actions to make sure I am seen as this straight girl. I know I am different, what's more I wish I could shout this from the rooftops that I like girls and I'm proud of it. No, I'm stuck with constant anxiety worrying people will find out about me. I have to be something I am not for people. I would rather just go to the dance with my girlfriends from the team. Why did I say yes to Ted? I like him as a friend, but now I'm playing with his emotions. Isn't society forcing me to play with my emotions too in the view of the fact being a lesbian is not accepted, especially in my community.

I find myself drifting out of this reality for a moment as I struggle to control my breathing. I wipe tears away from my eyes as I begin to cry. I don't think I can do this; I tell my reflection in the mirror. I can't be this person who can keep up this illusion anymore. My mental health can not continue like this. No one knows the struggle I go through on a minute to minute, hour to hour, or even daily basis. I feel like I'm on edge or walking on thin ice. I don't know when the ice will break, what's more I will fall in and drown.

Zali doesn't even know the constant struggle I go through. She says she understands why I'm going with Ted, even so I don't think she will ever truly understand. She is still trying to figure out her new sexuality. She has dated boys before me, too now has to hide this new identity. At least it has been established in the community that she likes boys. Everyone thinks we are just best friends. I have not had a boyfriend so there might be more of an expectation I should be interested in boys and have a boyfriend soon. This is just too much pressure for me to handle. I wipe more tears from my eyes as I can't contain myself anymore. I try to take a deep breath while fanning my face with my hands. I glance at my clock to realize more time has passed than I realized. I need to get going. Deep breath in.

The homecoming dance is a semi formal dance which makes it fun to get dressed up in cute dresses. I have a red spaghetti strap dress with silver sparkles on it, I guess you could call it silver glitter. I do simple curls in my hair and apply make up. I go with a silver eyeliner with a pink rose eyeshadow. When I'm finally ready my Mom is ready to take me to

Amber's house for pictures. It must be a Mom thing because all the mom's are there saying how cute and handsome everyone looks. I hear several comments about how cute of a couple Ted and I make. My Mom tells me Ted is a nice boy and says it with glee, almost like she would love to see Ted and I as a couple.

Amber pulls me aside to tell me, "Claire told me, she heard from Mika, that Ted told him, Ted is planning on asking you to be his girlfriend. Isn't that exciting?"

Amber takes both my hands with excitement as she does a jumping dance. She is way too excited about this. Of course, I'm taken by surprise because this only adds to the pressure of hiding myself. I don't want to hurt Ted's feelings. I also don't want to lose Ted as a friend. Oh God this will make things awkward between us when I turn him down. I find myself going along with the excitement, yet playing it off like I didn't know he liked me more than a friend.

"Come on Amara, it's totally obvious you both like each other by the way you flirt with each other," Amber states.

Once again I play it off as if I didn't know people were catching on to Ted and I. This is not how I wanted the night to go. I am having an anxiety attack in my head. All I can think of is Zali at that moment. Amber is talking and I'm just nodding my head with a smile. Oh God, what have I done? The illusion I have been trying to keep up is overcoming me like a raging thunderstorm that pops up out of nowhere in the summer. I can't avoid Ted, moreover the best thing I can do is to never be alone with him. I can avoid him asking me out.

"OMG! What if Ted kisses you tonight? I'm super excited for you and I can't wait to hear all about what happens. Amara, promise me, you will tell me all the deets," Amber gleefully proclaims.

"Of course Amber," I reply with my enormous fake smile.

"Let's get back to the group," Amber states.

"I just need to run to the bathroom real quick,"I retort.

"Okay," replies Amber as she gives me a few excited claps.

I have been to Amber's house several times so I know where the bathroom is. As I walk down the hall to the bathroom, I find myself having a harder time breathing. I lock the bathroom door and stare at the mirror. I am in panic mode, my anxiety is through the roof. I grab tissues as I'm an emotional wreck. Tears begin to form in my eyes as I quickly wipe them before it affects my makeup. As I lean over the sink I close my eyes trying to escape this world. I am now living in a nightmare. I don't want to be here anymore. I can't keep living like this.

A cold chill comes over me as goosebumps form on my body. I have found a way to escape this world just for a moment. I find myself back in that grassy field. The wind is blowing but instead of a warm breeze it's a cold wind, almost like winter is setting in. I'm still in my red dress for homecoming while standing in this grassy field. I stare off into the distance because I notice I'm not alone. The figure looks familiar as it walks toward me. I wrap my arms around myself while I begin to rub my arms to try to get warm. It's so cold I notice my breath float away from my body. I take another glance over at this person coming towards me, and I notice it's my gold and silver armor. I'm starstruck at what I'm seeing. How is this possible?

Knock, knock, knock. "Amara, it's Mom. I'm heading out," my Mom calls out.

"Okay Mom. I'm coming to say goodbye," I utter back while wiping the tears from my eyes.

I flush the toilet and wash my hands to make it seem like I actually went to the bathroom. I say goodbye to my Mom. She tells me to have fun, then gives me a hug and kiss goodbye. The nice thing about going as a group is that I don't feel like I have to be in the same car as Ted when we head to dinner.

After dinner is over we head to the dance at the high school. I hope that by some chance Zali would have changed her mind to come to the dance but my hopes never come true as the night passes. My anxiety never wanes about Ted on the account of I am consciously making an effort to not be alone with Ted. Amber keeps coming back with information that Ted wants to slow dance with me. Well I can handle that as long as Amber is next to me, and I made sure I told her that. She says of course she will. I now have at least some out.

Eventually towards the end of the dance Ted asks me if I want to dance to the slow song playing. I cordially say yes, as he takes my hand to lead me to the dance floor. I gesture to Amber, while the other cross country girls smile with a thumbs up sign. Oh shit! Damn you Amber, I'm thinking, she set me up. She is not going to come to the dance floor to give me support. My anxiety begins to take over as I slowly begin to panic. I wish Amber never would have told me Ted was going to ask me out. Ted wraps his arms around my waist as if we were already a couple. I am not comfortable at this moment, nevertheless the illusion must be kept up. My friends are watching from a distance. I have no choice but to let him keep his arms wrapped around me. Oh God, we are way too close to each other. I place my arms on his shoulders, as I feel so awkward. I wish this was Zali I was dancing with right now and not Ted.

We engage in small talk at first about the dance. He tells me how pretty I look, and out of common courtesy I do the same for him. As we dance, which seems like a lifetime, how long is this song I wonder? I feel like all the eyes of the school are on me. They are watching me to see if I will slip up. It just feels like so much pressure.

I continue to glance over at my friends mouthing things at them.

I hear them call out "Ya Ted and Amara!"

Ugh, those A-holes I'm thinking. I feel my face turn red as I'm probably blushing. We continue to have small talk while the song continues. I try to create some space between us while we sway back and forth; just the same, it seems like he is trying to bring me closer to him. Finally the slow song ends, yet another comes on.

"Do you want to dance one more time," Ted asks.

I hesitate to respond to Ted's question before he begins talking again.

"I really enjoy hanging out with you. I mean, hanging out at practice and at meets." Ted tells me.

"It is a lot of fun hanging out with you too. We have so much we can talk about. That's what makes our friendship so great." I needed to throw the friendship word in there to possibly deter him.

"Our friendship is great," he replies.

"Well I..." Ted pauses.

I get this pit in my stomach that he is about to ask me out. Please Ted don't do it. Don't put this pressure on me. This illusion I have, no one has an idea about, only becomes intense to hide. The pressure to say yes, just to protect my secret intensifies. Why am I even thinking of saying yes. Zali would be heartbroken. I would be trapped in a relationship I want no part of. I have no physical attraction to him. Heck I'm way more attracted to my cross country friends in their dresses than I am to Ted in navy blue button down shirt with silver tie. Can I just scream now? What am I going to do?

"What I'm trying to say is. What I need to say....," Ted stutters over his words.

"Ted, just tell me what is on your mind. You seem nervous about something. I'm your friend, you can talk to me," I calmly, yet sternly reply.

I can't help myself from being a nice person anymore, damn me!

"Well..."

"OMG Ted, What is it already," I snip in response.

Maybe getting snippy with him will deter him or not.

"I like you more than a friend and I am wondering if you would be my girlfriend," Ted blurts out.

Oh shit! Time feels like it is standing still. I feel like everyone in the room is staring at me. My secret is on the line. I have a chance to bury my secret deeper to add protection to myself, however what about Zali? What about me? How much will this hurt Zali? How much will it hurt me? It would end our relationship. I would have the shield of Ted to protect my secret, not with standing I don't think I can bear these kinds of emotions. Hiding myself has been incredibly hard, still now I have to hide with fake emotions to Ted, my friends, and family. I feel like this thin ice I am on will crack even more if not break me. I have no idea what words will come out of my mouth. I do need to respond.

"I'm sorry Ted, I like you as a friend and nothing more. I'm so sorry," I state as I pull my arms away from him. "I'm so sorry Ted. I have to leave."

I don't even give him a chance to say anything as I v-line it out of the gym. I don't even look back at my friends to see their reaction. Tears begin to roll down my face as I hurry past people. I'm heartbroken at myself that I felt like I led a friend on, which I just broke his heart. I never wanted to hurt anyone as I try to protect myself. I find myself taking my heels off, and I start running the best I can barefoot in the parking lot in a dress. I don't even feel the pain on my feet, I just run. I am overwhelmed with emotions as tears are pouring from my body. I hurt in so many ways. I hate myself for doing this to Ted. I hate myself for being a jerk to Zali. I especially hate myself for being so different. I hate that I'm different which makes my life difficult, including that I have to hide. I did not choose to be like this. Why would I sign up for this life?

I run and cry not knowing where I will end up this late in the evening. My run stops outside of Zali's home. Surprisingly the lights are still on. Someone is awake. I am breathing heavily and trying to catch my breath from running. I'm sure my feet hurt from running barefoot, but I didn't notice. I find myself stepping towards Zali's door. I have no idea if she is awake, or the one that is home. I just need someone right now. I knocked several times. I know it's late and whoever is inside is thinking who the hell is at the door at this time of night. I knock again as I wipe the tears away from my face. I hear the door unlock, the door pulls open and there she is the one I need the most right now. I can tell Zali is shocked to see me, yet before she can say anything I wrap my arms around her for a hug.

Chapter 15

The sun brightens the sky on this late August morning of 1990. It's the first day of school, but not for me, my brother Markus is starting the 1st grade today. I'm four and half while my baby sister Zoey just turned one. My other sister Aurora won't be born for another two and half years. Why is this day considered one of my core memories of my young life? We had just moved to the farm house that summer. We previously lived in the town a few blocks from the schools. My parents bought the farm in 1988, except the house was not part of the sale. Once the house went up for sale in 1990 my parents jumped at it. It only made sense to have a farm, and live in the house on the same property. When we lived in town we were only a mile away from the farm, except it was inconvenient for Dad to travel there and back especially when he got home at night. There would be nights when a cow was giving birth, what's more after he tucked my brother and me in bed, he would go back to check on the cow. Now living in the farm house, checking on cows is just a walk out to the barn.

This is the first time my brother gets to ride the bus. My Mom is holding Zoey and I'm standing next to Markus while we all wait for the bus. When the bus arrives it's an older lady who is probably my grandmother's age. She smiles to tell us to come on board. My brother is excited, and hops on the bus. My Mom calls out just one this year. She will go next year. The bus driver asks how old I am, and I tell her I'm four. She tells me she can't wait until next year to see me ride the bus.

As I waved to the bus driving away with my brother, I felt sad Markus was gone for the whole day. Last year he was only gone for half the day to kindergarten. We were still able to play together. The sadness surrounded me and I sought comfort in my Mother. She told me it would be okay. I had Zoey to play with but she was one and only started to walk. I wanted to play with someone closer to my age. I played with my Mom when I could when she wasn't busy with Zoey. I decided to do the next best thing living on a farm, it was time to explore.

We had only been at the farm house since June. Markus and I had done some exploring together, besides now it was just me. At times I would spend time with my Dad in the barn while he did chores. My Dad would give me tractor rides when he went to haul manure. Those were fun times. Dad would stick me in the seat almost similar to a shopping cart with my legs dangling in the back of the tractor. Dad would gently rest his back on mine so I would be sandwiched tight so as not to fall off. The rides on the tractor felt so freeing, No one cared about the safety of the child because heck we were safe. In today's context they wouldn't make open cab tractors like they used to because of safety reasons. It was great sitting there, and feeling Dad's warm body heat on cool fall days. I loved watching the tires rotate quickly on the road. I was mesmerized by the tire tracks as it rotated by. It was a great way to spend time with my Dad too. Just like my Grandpa Ed taught me so much about gardening, my Dad taught me many things about tractors and the farm. I could have spent that time in the house with Zoey and Mom, except I didn't while Markus was gone to school. It was my time to spend with my Dad.

I learned quickly how to play by myself once my brother was attending school full time. As I stated, I could have played with Zoey, still for some reason I found peace and solace in being by myself. Maybe it was my way of coping with not having Markus around to play with.

We were the closest we ever were when he wasn't in school full time. For boys and girls life begins to take separate directions based on gender roles right around time children start attending school. Children are extremely adaptive when they have to be. All changes are difficult, nevertheless children will find a way to adapt especially in the safe environment of their own home. I was still getting used to this new home; however, there was so much I could explore by myself. Children's imaginations are used on a daily basis when they are playing by themselves or with others. Kids create their own fun with their imagination, and I believe that's part of their innocence. They can create a world of their own. That's actually what I started to do.

I'm sure other children had imaginary friends, besides that's where my imagination started. I created my imaginary friend who I played within my now isolated world. I filled this world with people, why would I fill this new world with people is the question. Was it to not feel alone because in reality I felt alone since my brother left, perhaps. I became so comfortable in my new world that once Makus returned from his school days, I started to play less with him. I would rather be alone. As I continued to proceed in my childhood, I still chose the path of isolation rather than playing with Zoey or Markus.

I would get annoyed and angry when I was playing in my alone time with someone bothering me. I wanted no one to be part of it. I perhaps, also didn't want anyone to understand it either. When my youngest sister Aurora was old enough to play, I tried to bring her into my world because I saw some similarities in her. Of course, not to the extent of myself, not with standing she loved to explore her imagination too. She definitely had more of a creative side than Zoey. I guess Aurora and I connected better, while Zoey and Markus had a better connection too. We became pairs in a house of four siblings.

My cognitive development only enhanced my creativity in this imaginative world I had created. It became my daily life after school, if I wasn't doing farm chores of course. Was my imagination becoming my obsession? It wasn't consuming every aspect of my life, still it was a big part of it. This imagination translated to playing sports in the driveway, including playing in the backyard by myself too. Even look at my gardening, it's all about isolation, to be by myself.

The ultimate question is when did my imagination develop into an unconscious coping mechanism? Was it when puberty started when my body really started to change? I have no control over the physical changes that are happening to my body. My chest hurts as it continues to grow breasts. I bleed out every month which is also painful. My imagination is something I have control over. I had become so hidden in this imagination that hiding my sexuality at an early age was the thing I learned how to do. I created the walls of protection. From the pictures I drew of my friend Emery in kindergarten where I said to my Mom, I'm going to marry Emery, who was my first crush. I began to learn that these emotions weren't accepted, so I had to hide them. Continuing to navigate locker rooms, friendships, dances, body changes are all compounded in some way in my unconscious. My imagination was a way to control things I had no control of.

As teenagers humans might not feel like they have control of anything. There are so many life changes happening that humans are cognitively aware of. Maybe that explains the difference between a young child and a teenager. Teenagers can see more physical changes, they are a little more in tune with their minds and bodies; however, the control is not there. Humans seek out anything to control so they can overcome that anxiety that might be building. Control can come in many forms. It could be drugs, alcohol, anorexia, bulimia, cleaning or anything as long as the person has full control. What happens when that control gets disrupted?

My imagination is my way of controlling a reality I wanted, except it has been disrupted. New challenges I have been faced with seem to be disrupting my imagination. The pressure of my life is starting to get to me. I seem to be compounding everything in my life into my imagination. The floodgates have been opened and the struggle has started. My emotions have morphed into something I don't even recognize. I'm losing control of this world, plus I don't know what to do anymore.

Depression begins to slowly fill to replace the slipping of control. It's a slow and unnoticeable process. There are signs of depression; in spite of that, at first glance human minds find ways to protect themselves so no one can pick up on their depression. Humans start to wear masks as a line of defense so no one can see their depression. Behaviors also begin to change. Either someone will notice to talk to you about the behavioral changes; or they will go unnoticed until one says they are depressed. For me, I have learned to hide everything so well, in addition to constructing it into something new in my imagination. I didn't even catch on. I was in a depressive state of consciousness and unconsciousness.

The events that have unfolded for homecoming cracked all levels of consciousness; the ID, EGO, SUPEREGO were all in full swing. In that split second decision when Ted asked me out, the control I thought I had was gone. I stand in that split second, now it turns into minutes in my mind. I'm back in this world that is a volcanic world, now having gone through a major ice age. It's like I had been transported to this new cold, icy and snowy world. I face a decision, what do I say? I open my eyes and I'm faced with a new demon. My control is gone and my ID takes over, fear and desire are pulling in all directions. In this one split second I really have nothing left, still my ID and my unconscious mind on overdrive. My demon stares at me in Amber's bathroom mirror. My demon has followed me to the dance, which is reflected on the window, watching my every move. There is no escaping it.

There is no control and for this one moment that might bring me a little peace, Zali has invited me to stay for the night. Do I say no and run away? What am I running from besides myself? There is nowhere to hide from this demon. It will find me. Tonight for a few hours I have found a sanctuary. Zali becomes my fire to warm me up, just for a few hours. I have lost all control of my life; for all that, for this moment my desires shadow my fears and hide me once more. The bed covers add another layer of protection to hide me and her from the world. We slip into our own world to explore. It's new for the both of us. I want to explore her world and I want her to explore mine. This new exploration brings temporary joy, yet when I open my eyes when the sun rises I will feel a cold inch closer to me, and be staring at my demon self.

Chapter 16

The seasons have changed from summer to fall. The sports seasons are changing from fall to winter. My cross country season is ending on a cool frosty morning at the state cross country meet. Our girls team made it to state. It is an awesome experience and accomplishment for our team. The memories of staying overnight in the hotel with our conversations with our team bonding. We didn't win state or take runner up, however the enjoyment as a team to be there was incredible.

I went out for cross country this year to try something new. I found running as a way to isolate myself, yet still be a part of something. I made friends and memories. We laughed, we cried, even so we had fun. I have created a new identity for myself. What exactly is this identity and why do people have so many identities?

Humans create identities without even knowing or people are willingly creating them. It's an image humans create for themselves. Do humans want to keep up with the Joneses? It can start with their homes. People buy expensive cars, RV's, boats, or even homes to create an identity of "I'm successful."

Maybe it's not identity; maybe, it is an illusion as humans are seeking. Are illusions and identity similar or different? Identities are given to them the second they are born. People have no choice in them. The world sees them and says I give you the identity of a boy if the doctor sees a penis and a girl if the doctor sees a vulva. Their first identity is created. The whole environment that a person is born into creates the identity of male and female. Their development is formed around this identity too. The second identity people get when they enter into this world is their name. Babies have no choice in the matter because their parents choose the name. As babies take the first few breaths they have been given two identities. These identities will shape our lives. Are these identities labels? Are labels different from identities or are they the same?

There is another identity that is given to us when we enter this world and that is the color of our skin. Parents don't give you a name because you appear to be white, black, olive, brown or any other skin color; oh but society does. Humans are labeled or given an identity by their skin color and the biological sex at birth. Add in the name and there is your trifecta of identities or labels. I've barely had a chance to adjust to the new world I am now a part of, yet I'm labeled with these identities. My life will now take shape based on two of the identities I have been given, while the other was genetically given to me.

I have grown into my own identity of my orientation of who I am attracted to. This is just another form of our many identities. For some this identity doesn't form to the "norm" of what society wants. There is language now that I understand being 15, I am a lesbian. When I was younger I just thought liking girls was normal, but apparently I was wrong. I realize my sexual identity did not fit into my community along with the society I live in. I began to hide my identity in ways I didn't even know I was doing.

People hide their true selves from other people by virtue of they have been taught and raised to think a certain way. Teenagers are always trying to find their identity and place in society. What group of friends can I fit into? Parents can struggle with this identity crisis teenagers face.

Teenagers want independence to be themselves, yet are constantly worried about what others think of them. Teenagers believe the whole world is focused on every aspect of their life. If every teenager is going through the same thought process then in reality no one is focused on them.

Teens join sports teams or groups for the reason of their interest; however, it does create an identity of who they are. Sometimes people do things they don't want to continue to do; maybe, it's continuing to play basketball to please parents and friends. This identity is masking their inner desires. People's inner desires are in a constant battle with their environment they are raised in.

I have hidden many aspects of my true self from the world. Most of my friends know nothing about my imagination, only thanks to after middle school I stopped sharing. It's a complex thing, and it is a part of my identity. My imagination is my escape from my reality where I fully can be me. I have a completely different identity in my imagination than I do in reality.

I am a strong leader that helps my team of friends to defend the world and Universe. Everyone turns to me for guidance to know what to do. In reality no one seems to listen to my ideas since they tend to be not out of box thinking. My identity in reality vs imagination has taken a 180 degree flip. I have created an identity of being an introvert in reality, however it seems in my imagination I'm an extrovert. I try to avoid conflict in reality, while trying to resolve it in my imagination. I might even create conflict in my imagination, while facing it. This is why I have stayed hidden for so long. Telling my secret will only create conflict; furthermore, I know I'm not strong enough in reality to face it.

I avoid my girlfriend for several days or over a week. Maybe I'm afraid of any conflict with my identity with her, or avoiding her because I can't be fully myself around her. I hide in my imagination to be an extrovert, and something I'm not in reality. I don't really know how to be myself in reality anymore. Summertime is easy to relax, besides adding all the extra stressors, and I hide myself in my only identity that feels right. Liking girls doesn't seem right in view of the fact that I am in constant conflict with my Church and family beliefs. I withdraw from reality because I have nowhere else to turn to. Society doesn't want to listen to me when I cry out for help. If I told them I want to share a burden that has been with me for nearly ten years, they all would turn me away. I don't have a trusted adult to even talk to. I don't trust my counselor at school to say anything to because talking about sexuality especially to a counselor would just feel wrong.

This new identity of being someone's girlfriend is all new to me. I can't be fully me with Zali and I don't understand why that is. I can't fully open my heart to her thanks to getting too close, it will hurt too much. Why will it hurt, as a consequence people will find out about my secret. My parents, her parents, friends at school; it will all just create issues. Instead of opening up to her, I withdrew from Zali. It's not nice or loving of any kind, in spite of that it's all I know as I have been alone for so long. Being an introvert I guess does that to you. I can become cold to people and even to myself. It's hard not being able to express one of my major identities to the world. I feel like I have to walk on eggshells each day of my identity. I have to make sure no one knows that I like girls.

I see Zali in the halls at school, which we sometimes talk about, except when I am in these funks I can barely make eye contact. I'm sure Zali is wondering why I am withdrawing from her. Zali hasn't done anything wrong, it's me who is the issue. The weight of this burden I feel of my sexual orientation has taken a toll on me. I'm tired of being something I'm not. Will she wake up one day to realize, no girls are not for me anymore. Then I am left alone to hide in a world I created; of course, this new world I created in my imagination sometimes isn't the safest place to be. There are dangers all around, plus they come with a price. That price weighs on someone for a long time. All I know is I stand in my imagination withdrawn from Zali and the rest of the world. No one knows what I am struggling with as the new dangers that await. I am here with my cracked gold and silver armor, while standing in the cold with snow flurries falling. Standing and staring at me is my next challenge. Maybe withdrawing isn't the best choice. This identity will be tested in a way I never imagined would happen.

Chapter 17

The November skies have lost the beauty of the fall colors. The days are shorter than the nights and the coolness can be felt each morning and in the evening. There are a few warm days that pop up here and there, all the same, overall the days are getting cooler. Long summer nights are fun, yet there is something also nice about long dark nights, except this particular day is not one of them. This morning brought the first snowflakes of the year which are always wonderful, it means change is coming. Change is sometimes good, nevertheless sometimes it's really hard for others. Today is a change I didn't expect to happen, including I don't know how to manage myself going forward.

The early part of November is filled with withdrawing from Zali, yet she is also busy with the school theater production. I went to her performance on Saturday night and she looked cute in her costume she had on for the play. While watching her perform on stage, jealousy took over me. It is a strange feeling I had about myself and her. Am I jealous of the costume she is wearing because I viewed it as a symbolic aspect to be something different? Maybe it is jealousy because she had a kissing scene on stage with a boy. I know it means nothing because actors and actresses do it all the time. I wish it was me on stage kissing her.

It would be like the world would see the two of us kissing, what's more we would be free. For that split second moment we would be free. The world would just see us acting, still the kiss would be real for us. Maybe it isn't jealousy at all, maybe it is remorse for withdrawing from her. Everyone else is spending time with her except me. My secret goes deeper than the love we have for each other. I don't remember at what point of the play it was, but a cold chill came over me. I started to see red droplets fall to the stage floor, I was lost in a trance. My imagination world slowly is casting an eclipse on reality. I was cold, as I could feel tears begin to run down my face. During a light change, this trance ended with the image that has been following for a few months. On stage stood that dark shadow figure that resembles the reaper.

I bought Zali flowers for the show performance. Zali also didn't know that I was coming. This is going to be one of the few times we saw each other in the past few weeks. She hasn't been working much on the farm with the play since it's showtime, but that will change once the play is over. I was busy with cross country, yet now that has ended I have some time to see her, however now my time is filled with work. Zali has offered me rides home; nonetheless, I have found a routine of running in cross country that I now run after school to stay in shape. It's also a nice way to isolate myself from the rest of the world. I guess I really have withdrawn more than I thought I have. When I am not working I just get lost in my imagination. This world is my escape from whatever is going on with me.

Most people have pictures of friends around their room. I try to hide any pictures of Zali and me due to the fear my sisters might catch on to my Mom or one of my friends. Since homecoming my friend Amber and I haven't seen eye to eye on things. I overheard her talking about me one day with some other friends.

I heard her say something like, "Amara ruined a perfectly good thing with Ted. She has never even kissed a boy yet. I just wish she would have hooked up with Ted. She won't tell me why she ran away on homecoming. Something is definitely up with her."

I now worry Amber is on to me. What will Amber think of me if she finds out I'm a lesbian? Would she tell everyone or not? Oh my God, I just can't deal with my secret being found out. I know I will feel so ashamed of myself. I would feel like a failure to my family, plus the community for letting this sin take over. I fear the wrath of my parents yelling at me. What would my parents do if they found out? They would send me to counseling to see if they can treat this illness. This is just too much for me to handle.

I feel like the walls of the world are closing in on me. My only escape is into my imagination. No one cares if I am a lesbian there. I also have my secret love interest in my imagination. Her name is Kelly and she is not from this Universe. She lives in a different Universe. In my imagination she is my first relationship before Zali. Kelly is also a young princess who has her life all planned out by her royal family. Kelly has taken a liking to me thanks to I'm different from what is planned for her.

Kelly found me and actually saved my life. She came out of nowhere launching arrows from her bow killing the monsters that were attacking me. I fell for her right there and then. She is a warrior, heck a princess warrior who is defiant of her family. She fled her Universe and stumbled on to my world. We became very close over the time we spent fighting together; in spite of that eventually she did have to leave.

Time runs differently in her Universe, so she needed to get back. Before she left she gave me a mind key to enter her Universe and kingdom. The mind key is planted in the unconscious mind so no one will ever know what the key is. It is kept secret from your conscious mind until it is needed to be used. When things are bad I will escape to her world to see her, to be with her. She is the first girl I believed I kissed, but only in my imagination. I previously stated time is different in Kelly's Universe and it passes faster than ours. For every year that passes on Earth it's almost three years in her Universe.

No one in my imagination cares that we were in love. No one questions it, besides it feels normal. When I need her to lift my spirits because I am struggling with a new demon I am facing, she would always find a way to do so. I had a hard time when she had to go back to her Universe. She managed to slip out to come see me as I would do the same for her. As time went on it became harder to see her. Almost two years had passed since we had seen each other but it was almost six years for her. I decided to visit her during this time of withdrawing in my own reality. I wanted to see her and ask for help with the new danger I am facing.

Rejection is a hard line to encounter when it stares you in the face. To my surprise Kelly ascended to the throne during the time we were apart. Kelly is married and has a daughter. She is now a Mother and a wife but also the Queen. At the age of 21 now her whole life has changed. Kelly is in her own war as her planet is under attack from an invading force. There is no way for her to leave. We were able to have a private moment together, except it was short lived. I knew time went faster, but now seeing it with my own eyes is hard to believe how fast it actually moves in Kelly's Universe. I am now younger than her. Kelly's hand touches my cheek gently as we speak. Before she left she gave me one last kiss. The thing that hurt the most is she was married to a man. It is the kingdom's rule to produce an heir so it would make sense, it still hurts.

Maybe that's how Zali felt at homecoming, including now I felt seeing her on stage kissing a boy. The possible rejection. I didn't want it to be awkward between us because I worried someone would catch on to the tension between us. When I saw her after the show I knew I would need to act like a friend excited for her show. All these emotional hidings I have to go through are unbearable. My world is crumbling on me, as well as I don't know how to stop it.

When I see Zali, I show her excitement for her performance and present her with the flowers while we exchange hugs.

I hear her whisper in our warm embrace. "I miss you."

I say nothing in reply, only strike up a conversation about her performance. There are so many people around I am worried someone will catch on to my body language towards her. I would love to go back to her place and admire her in her costume and make out. The people around all want to congratulate her, so there is no time to really chat. I do put in a remark of maybe we could hang out after she is done here, except she said she has the cast party tonight.

I say goodbye as others greet her. I did this to myself by withdrawing from her. I leave the school to wait for my Mom to come pick me up. While waiting, snow begins to fall from the sky. I could feel the change coming in the air. The constant hiding of my secret is getting to me. Zali had no idea, actually no one had a clue. The pressure to be someone you're not is always on my unconscious mind. Tic Toc, time is running out and I don't know how quickly it is going to run out. As I stand here in the cold with snow slowly falling from the sky, I hear a familiar voice ask me if I am okay. This voice is what has kept me going until this day. On this day the cold has overtaken my imagination. The snow is falling as I feel the cold snowflakes land on my face and begin to melt. I blink and time feels like it stands still for a moment. I am at the edge of time on this particular day.

"Tic Toc, Tic Toc," says the reaper.

Chapter 18

I wander around in mental drunkenness as my feet stagger side to side. My mind is clouded with heavy gray fog, which is perhaps, causing my mental drunkenness. I have undone my braids in my hair as it has become wavy from being braided. It rests on my shoulders and back with a few pieces of hair blowing in the wind. My eyes are glassy, causing my vision to blur at times. This also might be contributing to my staggering walk.

I feel completely empty inside, yet I can feel the crushing force of the world squeezing me like a vice grip. I feel hopeless, pointless, emotionless, and tired. Chains are wrapped around my ankles, wrists, and my shoulders as I stagger and drag the burdens I have carried for the past several years. Even in this mental drunkenness I can hear the weight grinned across the surface of the ground. I have been pierced by over a thousand tiny needles from all my sins. I've been told I have been living this secret life. I can hear screams of hate from people. My mind is so fogged with my glossy eyes; and my head turns to see who is saying it, yet I have no idea.

I want to cry, except the tears have been drained from my body by my community's heat of hatred toward my indifference and sin. I am no longer allowed to show or express my emotions to the world. The tears have been replaced by sand from the desert. It's painful to cry out sand from my eyes so I no longer cry. I believe I have hit my end. My body is weak and can no longer drag these burdens of chains. I fall and crush my knees to the ground. My eyes glaze over with a gray lens as the last of my sight disappears. Blindness is all encompassing.

I laid awake most nights between the ages seven to nine wondering and praying to God to change me into something else. Maybe it would be better if I wasn't a girl? Maybe if I was a plant or some kind of animal I wouldn't be stuck with this feeling of being different. Some nights I would wonder what it would be like to have a baby. I knew even at the age seven or eight I was different from other girls, but I didn't understand why. I knew girls had babies, but a part of me knew I wouldn't ever be having kids.

I would pray, imagine or wonder what it would be like to have a baby in my tummy. I would pray to God just to experience it just once. Then the praying changed to a few months of being pregnant. That probably will never happen either. I would continue to pray, almost trying to bargain with God for just a few minutes to have a baby in my tummy. In these three years of this ongoing process, my prayers never got answered. God never turned me into an older woman with a baby in her tummy. It is never going to happen. How does a seven to nine year old even comprehend this, she doesn't. The sorrow of knowing I would never carry my own child in my tummy, has weighed on me ever since.

When I learned that girls get pregnant from boys, all those years of praying seemed to be a waste of time, or those prayers were shattered into a million pieces. I now know that being a lesbian I am never going to get pregnant. I would never know the experience of having a baby in my tummy. I guess I have been grieving that for years, but not fully understanding what my unconscious was grieving.

I fear I will never be able to marry who I want because society is not accepting of my sexual orientation. That means I will never be able to wear a beautiful wedding dress, or have my Dad walk me down the aisle. Even if I were to marry another girl, my parents would not take part in this sinful act. I will not have a Father to give me away to the girl of my dreams. It is an incredibly sad feeling. It also means no Mother daughter bonding time looking at and trying on wedding dresses. More thoughts and emotions to grieve. Of course, I don't think I have ever grieved any of these thoughts being so young. I didn't know how to process them so they just got buried deep into my unconscious mind.

"Are you okay," calls out a familiar voice.

I have tears in my eyes as I try to quickly wipe them away as I take a breath in. I don't even turn to the familiar voice yet before the voice calls out my name.

"Amara, are you okay," the concerned voice calls again.

This time I turned to see my friend who transferred to another school this year. Her curly blonde hair with a smile excited to see me.

"Adelaide, what are you doing here," I question back.

"Well, to see some friends in the play. I didn't expect to see you here," Adelaide answers.

"I didn't know you were even coming into town," I responded.

It's not like Adelaide was traveling from far away. She transferred to a school 20 minutes away. Adelaide is the girl I tried to kiss at the roller skating rink. She is the only other person that knows I like girls; however, out of respect for me we have never talked about my sexual orientation. Our relationship is a unique one, since we seem to come together as friends at the moment when we need each other the most. It's like we have a sixth sense for each other. During middle school we were a little closer while we were in seventh grade together. We became a little more distant after that year, yet always watched out for each other, and had each other's backs. We would always go our separate ways with our own friendships. Our bond is just different, I guess that is the respect we developed for each other.

Adelaide has always been grateful I befriended her when she moved to our town. Maybe that is part of the reason she has kept my secret to her heart. Our freshmen year our distances grew even more, except it wasn't like we wouldn't talk; it's just hanging out wasn't in the cards. Adelaide made new friends in high school who she fit in better with, still when she was having boyfriend problems I was there for her as our friendship picked up right where we left it. It is like no time passed between us.

The Universe knows to pull us back together at the right moments to be there for each other. I can't hold myself back as tears start pouring down my face.

"Amara, what is wrong," asks Adelaide.

Adelaide gives me a hug in the cold snow filled sky. A warm hug feels great, as she squeezes me tight. I don't even know what to tell her. I can't even understand what is going on myself.

"Okay girl we need one of those girl nights, because you can't be alone tonight," Adelaide states.

Saturday night girl night would be fun, but would my Mom allow it. Adelaide's family wouldn't care, still Adelaide has a way with my mom. Just then my Mom pulls up to pick me up. Before I can say anything to my mom, Adelaide pops her head through the car window, when my Mom is saying hi to Adelaide.

The next thing I know Adelaide turns to me with a smile saying "we are all good for tonight. I'll be right back."

I found out later that night she played the Church card on my mom. As long as they come to Church then they can stay overnight on a Saturday. Of course, she probably sweet talked her way to convince my Mom to stay the night.

Adelaide came running back saying, "My Dad said it is okay!"

Maybe this is what I needed more than anything else in the world. As much as I would love to be with my girlfriend right now, a part of me that has withdrawn from Zali is fine with this distance. Maybe it's my way of having a defense mechanism to not let anyone else catch on to our relationship.

Adelaide and I set up our girl night in the basement. There is a couch and a few love seats so it's a cozy spot to hang out. It's not like we can hang out in my room since I still share it with my sister. We made some popcorn and milk shakes. Nothing is better than some form of ice cream to try and cheer yourself up. At first we do some catching up about school, including what is going on with our families. Why is there distance between our friendship, nevertheless we seem so close when we are together. Adelaide has this energy about her that I have never seen in any one else. It doesn't seem like anything can get her down; just the same, she has needed my support at times, but tonight I need her for support. This night is what gets me to the moment I am currenting facing.

For some reason in our laughter and storytelling I just break down into tears. The flood gates open in my mind. In my imagination there are no more emotional tears. Remember they are dried up and have been replaced with desert sand. Adelaide doesn't skip a beat to take my hand, and pulls me in for a hug and snuggle on the couch. I have never had a chance to open up to anyone before because I have kept it all bottled up for so long. I can tell Zali certain things, except I have reservations in what I tell her.

My sadness and tears change, maybe morph into anger. Anger of all that has happened. No one has ever listened to these words before. I have only told Zali the surface of my past. Zali is only new to this new orientation of hers. It's only been four months for her. For me, it has been my life. I can't fully be myself around Zali because she doesn't fully understand what mental toll this is on me.

I unload the burdens onto Adelaide; she doesn't say anything. She just listens to me speak while I lay my head on her lap. Adelaide gently runs her fingers through my hair like a Mother would do to keep their child calm when they aren't feeling well. How can she be so calm while my emotions turn to anger? I am angry at the world for not accepting me for being different. I am angry at God for not allowing people to accept different people. I am angry with God for making me like this and being stuck with this burden. Why do I have to suffer alone? I am angry that I can't be myself while others walk freely to be who they want. I have to watch them all from my glass cage.

As I pour my emotions out to Adelaide I feel like I'm walking through my own river of tears. I have a black dress on as I mourn myself. The water passes around my legs and at that point the water hits my legs it ripples up to get around my legs. My hair is dripping wet as it flows long on my body. I step through my river of tears, but I have no idea where to go. I am lost. I share the struggles I have with Zali. This is the first time I am able to tell someone about Zali. That has been a weight on me like none other I have experienced. It's hard to hide someone who you love. I have to keep those emotions close to me to not be vulnerable. I want to share my emotions about what I'm going through, yet I haven't had a chance. Now I find my emotions pouring out in anger. Do I have the right to be angry with everything; when I mean everything, I mean everything from the breath I take, to the steps I walk. I am different but this burden has become too much. I have never been able to fully be myself with anyone. There might be a few subtle moments with Zali; nonetheless, I would have to be cautious so no one finds out about my secret.

When I was pouring out my emotions I must have fallen asleep as well as Adelaide. As I lift my head off her lap, I grab a few blankets to cover Adelaide up while I snuggle into my blanket and drift back to sleep.

Chapter 19

These deep dark secrets that have created the river of tears, I venture through the river in my black spaghetti strap dress. My bare feet can feel the sand and stones on the river bed. I have no idea where this river is taking me. Is this my imagination world, or is this a dream? The bottom of my dress is soaked from the water. I am shivering cold as I wrap my arms around myself. My hair continues to drip with water as if water is pouring out of my hair. Emotions pull me like a magnet to something I have no idea where. It is night time and the moon is a waning gibbous, which acts like a flashlight for me. I hear an owl hooting while crickets chirp their songs. I would get out of this river; however, I feel like I am anchored in the river as I will not be able to step out.

I reach the end of the river as it has turned into a waterfall that falls into a canyon of water below. It's a giant hole in the Earth that is fed by three rivers falling into the canyon. I feel drawn to the depths of this canyon. There is no turning back, only diving deeper into my river of emotions. How deep is this canyon? Does this lead to my death? Why do I feel compelled to dive in? What is drawing me in? I need to find out.

The wind begins to blow with intensity, almost as if nature is forcing me into the depths of this canyon.

"Tic Toc, Tic Toc," whispers float through the air.

The whispers send chills down my spine and I most certainly sense something else is here with me. Three, two, one, I jump off the cliff and fall to the canyon of water. The sound of roaring water fills the air as I fall. SPLASH! The cold water swallows me as I sink deep into the canyon. This compelling feeling drives me to swim down into the depths of this canyon. I have no idea if I can hold my breath long enough. I tread water trying to make sense of my direction and my decision. I try to look up to see anything at the top of the cliff of the canyon. I notice a figure standing at the top of the cliff. The figure is recognizable as this is the figure who is continuously following me.

"Tic Toc Amara," it calls out.

I dive under the water and swim to the bottom. This feels like I am forcing myself into a drowning state. I can't keep swimming deeper and deeper because my lungs begin to burn from lack of oxygen. I will run out of air soon. I decide in a panic to swim back to the surface to face my fate. My lungs burn with intensity as I need air desperately. I swim as fast as I can to the surface. It's so dark I don't know where the surface is anymore. My lungs are on fire and my head begins to ache, I need air. Suddenly an arm grabs my arm and pulls me out of the water. I gasp for air as I am pulled out of the water. I lie on the ground trying to catch my breath.

"Hello Amara," a voice calls out.

I look up to see who has pulled me out and is talking to me. They appear tall at first glance but not sure who this person is.

"Are you surprised to see me," the voice asks.

That voice sounds familiar. I'm still trying to catch my breath and gather my thoughts. Their arms reach down to help me up. The voice is deep and surely a man's voice. I extend my arm as they take my arm and help me up.

"It's been a while since we have seen each other. You look surprised to see me," the man states.

I finally see his face, and the shock overcomes my facial expression as I place both my hands over my mouth and nose in disbelief.

"How is this possible," I mutter.

"We need to get you dried off and warmed up. Come follow me," Darius utters.

"Wait, how are you alive," I ask.

"We need to move. Let's go, Amara," exclaims Darius.

"Wait, wait, wait a minute. Can we talk and answer my question as to how you are alive Darius," I question with confusion.

Darius takes my hand to guide me through the dense woods, except he doesn't say anything. We walk in silence until we reach a small cabin. I am so confused as to what is happening. He lights a fire and gives me dry clothes to change into. He turns away to not watch me get undressed. I pull my wet black dress off. Then I remove my bra and panties. I peak over my shoulder to make sure he is not peaking at me. I put on the dry shirt and pants then sit next to the fire to get warm

"I'm dressed, Darius," I utter.

Darius turns around and sits next to the fire too.

Darius begins speaking softly "Yes, would be an understatement to your question. I'm sure you have lots of questions. You don't have much time so let me get right to the point with you."

"Can we please start with how you are alive." I ask as I brush my wet hair behind my ears.

"I have carried the weight of your death with me for so long. That pain has not gone away. I can feel my unconsciousness thinking about you daily," I sadly state.

"I'm sure you have. I put you in a tough choice and you made the decision you did. It has caused a burden for you that is affecting you in a horrible way," replies Darius

I begin to cry again. I don't know if these are tears of joy or remorse.

"I am so sorry for killing you," I said sadly.

"I know you are. You had to do what you needed to do," affirms Darius.

"I have missed you so much. I didn't want to do it. I really didn't want to kill you," I profess remorsely.

I am sobbing with sadness. Darius pulls me in for a hug to give me comfort. As I cry on Darius's shoulder I flash back to that day. I am still trying to figure out if I am dreaming or in my imagination. The last thing I was doing before ending up in the river was talking with Adelaide. I fell asleep so I must be dreaming, or unless I am in my imagination world.

My mind drifts back to that day as I continue to cry. The latest adventure had just ended, but not in a good way. Darius sacrificed himself to save the team. The only issue was for our team to escape the evil, Darius sacrificed to let the evil possess him. It was the only choice we had. Darius knew we couldn't let this evil into our world. Darius could feel the evil slowly taking him over before he would be gone from us. He asked one of us to kill him before the evil took complete control. Once the evil consumed him we would be back to square one as the world would be in grave danger. As the leader of the team I took it upon myself to kill him. I pleaded with Darius to find a different way, nonetheless time was running out. Darius handed me his sword. I kept pleading, but he kept reassuring me this is the only way. Darius laid himself on the ground as I gripped the sword as I looked down at him. I couldn't do it. Then Darius's voice changed to a dark sinister tone.

"You can't do it can you. I am coming for all of you," the dark sinister voice called out.

"Amara, you need to kill me now. I am losing control of myself. Please don't let me die by the hands of this evil," called out Darius with teary eyes.

The turmoil I was going through was unbearable as tears filled my eyes too. The inner conflict was tearing me apart. The evil in Darius taunted me again.

"Please do it now! I can't hang on much longer," shouted Darius.

"NOOOOOO!" I screamed out as I lifted my arms up with both hands gripped around the sword.

Then I plunged it with all my force into his heart. I fell to my knees and began to sob. I heard the last breath escape Darius's body. What have I done?

I pick my head up off Darius's shoulder, wipe the tears from my face.

"Please forgive me," I ask Darius.

"It's not your fault Amara. I made my choice to save the team, and then you made the next choice for the team. This has been eating away at you. I do forgive you," contends Darius.

"I can't keep going on like this. I feel like I am at my end and can no longer lead. All the pressure is on me to make all the decisions. I don't want to make the decisions anymore. What if I have to take someone else's life, or put the team in harm's way again? I can not live with that burden again," I proclaim.

"Listen to me Amara, I don't have much time and nor do you. It's okay to be sad. I miss you and the team. Someday we all will be together, however unfortunately your end is coming. The darkness is following wherever you go. Please come to peace with these terms that you killed me out of protecting everyone else. You made a moral judgment. Yes, you have to live with this burden for the rest of your life; in spite of that, please know you did it out of love for humanity and for a friend.

Now, you are going to be faced with a decision soon as that choice will affect your life in a way you have no idea. I see the pain in this world and in your reality. You need to keep pressing on even when the pain is too unbearable for you since you are a great leader. You will set the path for others to come, yet the pain will come with it too. If you stay hidden in the shadows that pain will keep tearing you apart from the inside out. Your strength needs to be found. People will never see the world through your eyes, even so the world will one day see you," expresses Darius.

My eyes open as light filters through the basement windows. I look over to see Adelaide still asleep. I am saddened by what I had just experienced. I don't know if I can keep going. I feel my eyes water as I reflect on everything. What did Darius mean by I have a decision to make? I wipe the tears off my eyes and give a sniffle. Adelaide moves and opens her eyes.

"Are you okay," Adelaide whispers.

"No, I am not," I whisper back.

Adelaide can tell there is more that is bothering me than what I might have let on. She sits up and wraps her arm around me.

"You look like you are in so much pain. I'm sorry I will never understand what you are going through. It must be incredibly hard to hide part of you from the world. I wish I could do more for you," reciprocates Adelaide.

Adelaide kisses my forehead for comfort. How is it that a friend seems more like a Mother than my own Mother? How is it that I have a friend who shows more support than my own parents. I will have to continue to hide for the time being but this pain is real and it hurts.

Our heads leaned on each other as Adelaide whispers, "I hope I can meet your girlfriend Zali someday. She is lucky to have you."

I give a little chuckle in my sadness.

"What is so funny," she replies.

"It's just your voice saying my girlfriend, you are the first person I have ever heard those words said to me besides Zali. It means a lot. Thank you," I responded.

This night is exactly what I needed to get to this particular day. I have a choice to make. The choice stares me in the face. My pain has become unbearable. I drag these chains of guilt, sorrow, remorse for killing Darius. Sinful discomfort of myself for being different. Sad from all this pain of not being able to be me. No one really knows who I am so the choice needs to be made. Tic Toc, Tic Toc! The coldness fills the air, as the time has come to make my choice.

Chapter 20

Depression doesn't discriminate from anyone in this world, it will attach to anyone it wants. Depression doesn't care if you are male, female, transgender, non-binary, gay, bi-sexual lesbian, straight, white, black, Latino, Asian or Indigenous. It will attack with vengeance, terrorizing every physical aspect of one's body. Depression's carnage sometimes can be seen on the physical body. Blood can be shed, scars are left, or even the air we breathe can be stolen. Nothing will stop this depression from destroying so many people. Depression isn't always seen on the physical body. Emotional scars begin long before the physical ones ever appear.

I see depression as slow burning embers of a campfire. There is plenty of heat being produced by these embers. There is no visible flame, besides one may think there is no harm; or damage that can come from these embers. Truth be told the embers are the ones that can do the most damage. There is beauty while staring at the embers at the end of a summer night as the campfire is winding down. The heat that is being produced is unnoticed, it's just overshadowed by the kindling of the embers as they dance with each other.

These slow kindling embers are the depression that slowly eats away at you. The embers seem to last forever, longer than a log burning. I continue to get burned each and every day. I'm trapped in the beautiful glow of the embers, yet I am screaming out in pain as no one can hear me or wants to listen. I go about my daily life with each second, minute, and hour passing by being hurt by these burning embers. Once again I just look like a beautiful glow as no one seems to care. Does that mean I am trapped in these burning embers forever? I don't think I can survive the heat of the embers.

The emotional scarring will never be seen by anyone. It might come out in a physical form for others to see; however, even then the blinders are sometimes on people, moreover they don't notice the physical results of depression. For me I just continue to burn in hiding. I walk the halls at school while no one has an idea what I am mentally going through. Maybe a clever person would pick up on subtle behavioral changes. The brain is funny that way in projecting oneself. Why do the defenses go up when depression comes burning down our mental home? There might be major behavioral changes, except it seems more like slow and subtle changes just like those embers burning.

I hide my face from people by putting my head down and walking through the people in the halls. No, my head isn't actually down, it seems like it is. If I just go unnoticed from my last class to the next. Please just leave me alone and don't talk to me. Why is this how I am feeling when I am screaming for help in this fire pit of depression? It's the ultimate battle with oneself.

Where does depression start from? Being different? Bullying? Harassment? Not enough positive feedback? Rejection? Are all these answers correct? I would think so. Each person who has experienced depression has their own unique situation. Heck it might be from being over praised. The pressure of being the best on the sports team or straight A student. I guess the possibilities are endless.

My depression is rooted in multiple facets. I can't express my true self to the world. I have to hold back a part of me from the world. I am confused by the hateful words of my sexual orientation. I want to hate myself as a consequence of I'm taught to dislike people similar to me. There is also bullying involved too. Getting physically bullied in the halls is one thing, but it isn't as simple as getting a little shove by someone. The words are the most painful. The words cut deeper each time I hear them.

The layer that I can peel back from a bully in school is during my middle school years. This boy would make fun of me in the halls or at lunch. He knew what he could get away with so he wouldn't say much, still the words can hurt, especially building up over time. Why do teenagers need to be so mean, yet in some form people all do things or say things that hurt someone. What draws this particular boy to bully me? What have I actually done to him besides exist? Is it my reservation of myself that bothers him? One time I confronted him as to why they picked on me.

The response I got was mean words, especially the one of "you are just a dumb dyke."

No one knew that I like girls, yet to use offensive language like that is to hurt me. I tried for so long to just ignore them and be a better person. A bully wants some kind of reaction to make themselves feel better. When no reaction is given it only frustrates them. In both situations the bullying won't stop.

It was hard to find partners to work with on projects because no one wanted to pair with me. I felt lonely and rejected in those moments. I ended up working with someone else who no one wanted to work with either. The rejects had to work together. When Adelaide moved to our school in 7th grade, I felt like the new girl all the time. No one wanted to be my partner. I wanted to show some compassion for her, being new.

An ally in this might be beneficial to me. For so long Adelaide and I never talked about my sexual orientation, but to tell someone officially is a saving grace. That is what has brought me to this moment. Even though I have this ally, all these years of compounding the aspect of depression has taken its toll.

The embers of depression have been tossed into the fire at once. Now the depression feels like I am drowning. I can see everything fading as I sink to the cold depths of the ocean. There are moments when I am just about out of breath and the depression gives me a little more air. It is almost like it wants to torture me. While I slowly drown I have no one around to help me. No one wants to listen. I feel lonely, still in reality I am not. I have parents, except I can't tell them what is bothering me. I have Zali, even so I don't want to burden her with my emotions. What I did tell Zali is that this relationship is wonderful. At the same time it's causing me so much pain. It's almost worse being in the relationship because the mental consciousness of hiding is so hard. I can't talk to my friends about my struggles because they would not accept me for being different. I feel like they would reject me, then I wouldn't have any friends. There are no teachers I can turn to. No pastor, bible, or Sunday school teacher either. I feel like I have no one.

I have sunken into the depths of the cold ocean, with no air to keep me alive. My motivation is sparse plus weakens me from wanting to do anything. I do my best to hide my depression from people, just like my other secrets. Since I have this other world I can escape to, all my burdens come with me. These burdens are hidden in plain sight, all the same I can't tell the differences between each demon in my imaginary world. Even in this other world I have called home for so many years, this world has been harder to save.

This is the day I have met my match. For so long I have been victorious over demons I have faced, but not this one. The demons I am now facing are so strong and clever I can no longer be the leader in this world. What is the point of trying to keep fighting? The demons seem to only be getting stronger each time. There will be more after these, then more will come. The demons will keep coming. I will keep bringing them here. It's better they are here than in reality. What would happen to me if the demons escaped from this world? I don't want to find out, except I might be finding out soon since this day has come.

I have no tears on this day. My emotions are gone. I am not even finding peace on this day. Maybe that's because my emotions are numb. My heart and mind have gone cold to my surroundings. I have fallen to my knees as I am blinded with this numbness I am feeling. My demons are coming towards me. Tic Toc, Tic Toc! Time will fade from my sight, breath, and sound. My eyes wander around looking into the sky as snow flakes begin to fall. The footsteps of my demons approach louder and louder. I am not going to stop them from coming. This is the day they win and I lose. I hear my friend's voice screaming. The time has come as I open my eyes to see my demon standing in front of me. Snow falls between the two of us. The demon's arm is drawn back with its sword in hand. I let out my breath, and before I can finish letting all the air out of my body the demon thrust and plunges their sword right through my abdomen. I gasp and gag. As quick as the sword is thrust into me it is pulled out with great force.

A second thrust from the sword impacts my throat. Blood pours from my body. The warmth of my body has been replaced with a cold sensation I have never felt before. The light of this world begins to fade to darkness. This darkness is also new. There are no shadows in this darkness. It's like a void of nothingness and completely quiet. Maybe some peace will come or maybe not. I do know as the last fading light leaves my sight my burden is finally gone. I might not have peace, just the same, at least my burden is gone. My body has fallen to the ground in my pool of blood. My darkness that has been my friend all these years now becomes a part of this new darkness of death. The final light evaporates from my mind as I have become one with the eternal darkness.

Chapter 21

Silence! There is not a sound that I can hear. I feel like I am walking in this abyss; however, I don't hear my feet striking the ground. When things are silent there is always a white noise of something humming especially in a home. When things appear to be silent outside there seems to be some noise traveling through the air. This abyss doesn't have any noise in this silence. My footsteps don't create a sound, in spite of that I can hear myself think and talk in my mind.

When I let out a sound asking "Hello" to whatever is out there, there are no sounds admitted from my vocal cords.

The abyss has taken the sound out of everything. This is also a new kind of darkness I have never experienced before. There is not a hint of light but a strange sense I know where I am walking to even though at the same time I have no idea where I'm headed, it's a strange sensation.

I fear peace has not followed me to this abyss. I am not in heaven or hell. Am I lost in death? Death has taken me to this unknown. I want peace, yet I have not found it. I am more alone and lost than ever in death. I want this death to bring me peace even though I think something has gone horribly wrong. I want the hateful messages to be gone in the silence of death. I want the silence to take my secret away. Where is my peace in this silence? My senses have also been stripped away from me in death.

Beep, Beep, Beep! I hit my alarm that has sounded for me to wake up. The morning darkness that creeps in my new room. Finally as the older sister I get my own room. I have been asking for some time. My alarm will no longer wake up my sister in the early morning to go out for the morning milking. I turn on my lamp to provide light to get changed out of my pjs into something for work. It's a Saturday after Thanksgiving in November and Zali's birthday is three days away. I have tried to communicate more as of late, except Zali doesn't know what I just went through.

As I slip on my sports bra and shirt, I stare in the mirror to wonder who I am? What have I become? Part of me seems to be a little empty; but also I don't have to worry about being a strong person anymore. Can I be a normal teenage girl; of course, what does that even mean. Look at me, I am some kind of freak.

Change is hard for anyone to handle and process. This is a new change for me. How can I move forward without my imagination? In middle school I shared more about my imagination with some friends, still I didn't get the response I hoped for like I would in my imagination. Maybe that's part of it having something so different being presented to friends, how do they respond. I set high expectations that they will embrace me and my ideas. I get the first initial reaction when presenting myself to people shouldn't be based on what I see their first reactions are. My unconscious mind must have known that by sharing my imagination, while trying to understand people's response to my story I could gauge if they were ready for me to share that I'm a lesbian. I guess I didn't get the response I wanted when I shared my imagination with my friends, so why share that I like girls.

Society establishes what "Normal" is, in addition to anything that is outside that context people have a hard time understanding. People say I thought I knew them. I didn't know they were struggling. I didn't know they were depressed. Why didn't people know? Is it due to people knowing how to hide their true emotions so well regardless if you are a male or female. Those that are the happiest, are they content with themselves since they can be themselves? Any change disrupts the course of normal. People are surprised, shocked, taken back by this change. I guess hiding is a skill that people all learn, while some of us master it.

How do I adjust to this new change in me? Maybe I haven't adjusted to any of the changes that have happened in the past five months. I have just gone to a dark place in the past few months. I am not blaming anyone for the darkness, from being my friend; and keeping myself hidden, to now my enemy. I have not fully been able to adjust to being Zali's girlfriend. I can finally be somewhat myself with her, yet still not fully myself. We have to act as friends when we are around other people; I can't act how I want to be around her.

This new environment of being with someone has created more challenges than I had anticipated. I love that fact I actually have found someone I can share my imagination with and share my secret with; however, it has been a struggle being in this relationship with Zali. It seems like she wants to navigate this relationship like any other relationship Zali has had before with a boy. It's not the same and I feel she doesn't understand I still can't be myself. It's within arms reach to be myself around her, yet I still can't be.

As I head to work these thoughts weigh on me all morning. Have I really been able to fully be myself around anyone? Not really! Being an introvert I can only be myself with myself; of course, that is the challenge by society and family to be something else. Conflict is everywhere for me. Zali doesn't understand this, I'm sure she doesn't understand any of this. At the same time I also haven't told her any of this so how is she supposed to know or even to begin to comprehend? She has gotten me closer to being myself, nonetheless at the same time has made it worse for me. It's the constant worrying about slipping up with my secret.

I feel anger towards her as these thoughts enter and leave my consciousness all day. Zali and I are going to hang out for an early birthday celebration since her birthday is on a school night and I have to work. We haven't spent much time together this past month so I am a little nervous if she is upset with me for withdrawing from her. I haven't talked to her that much either since she hasn't worked much this past month either. There have been a few moments we have hung out after work as well as when she attended lunch after she attended Church with Adelaide present. It is hard to be around Zali sometimes. She is way more soft spoken than me, besides way more compassionate too. Zali has the ability to be like that and I am not that kind of person. As the years have passed I feel like the depression has been followed with anger towards others because they can be themselves.

The night starts off with Zali picking me up like usual. She has a smile on her face seeing me. I kindly respond with a smile, even though my mind is weighing with some deep thoughts.

"Is everything okay," she asks

"It's fine," I reply.

I really don't want to ruin her celebration night.

"I'm sorry for being so distant lately," I blurt out.

Well so much for holding back this information from her. We drive to her house because she has the house to herself again. We barely get into the house as I break down in tears. Zali embraces me with a big hug.

"What's wrong darling," she says to me.

I guess I'm going to ruin her celebration for her birthday. Tears are rolling down my face, as Zali wipes them from my eyes, then gives me a kiss on my lips. I try to compose myself so I can talk. I take a deep breath in, then let out a deep breath.

"Can we sit down and not stand in your doorway? Oh, here I almost forgot to give you your gift," I ask and I give Zali her gift as we head over to the couch.

"I will open it later," Zali utters.

Zali sets the gift to the side on the coffee table. She definitely is more concerned about me than opening her gift.

"Please open it now, I don't want my crying and messed up self to delay your birthday celebration," I responded.

"Are you sure? It seems like you really need to talk," asks Zali.

"No, I'll be fine," I responded.

I wipe more tears away from my face. Zali gets up to get tissues for me and hands me the box. She sits down next to me with one leg bent on the couch and pulls me into her arms. I reach for the gift for Zali to open. I would rather see her enjoy her birthday before I unload on her with my troubles.

"Okay, I'll open my gift from you," says Zali.

I sit up as the tears begin to dry up in my eyes. She peels back the tissue paper in the bag to find a little box. She looks at me and smiles.

"The box is so pretty," Zali says excitedly.

"Happy Birthday, I got you a box," I exclaim.

We both laugh. Zali opens the box to find a bracelet.

"Oh wow! It's beautiful, Amara. Thank you so much. I love it." Zali states as she leans in to give me a kiss.

"You are welcome. Let me help you put it on," I utter.

The bracelet is white gold with music note charms with her birthstone and other gems. Zali holds out her hand and I place it on her wrist. Zali stares at it for a moment and then pulls me in for a kiss. She pulls me on top of her as we lay on the couch. I guess my thank you is a make out session. I know the make out session is only a temporary distraction for me. There is plenty I need to share with her. I have no idea how she will respond to what I have to say, except for now it's about making her happy for her birthday celebration. If that means we make out for the night, then that is her birthday wish. I won't object to making out with my girlfriend. I have missed her touch, kisses, smell, and sincerity.

Chapter 22

Whoo! Whoo! Ribbit! Ribbit! Crickets chirping The sounds have returned to my senses as I walk in this darkness. My arms are out trying to feel anything, nonetheless my sense of touch is still gone. I don't feel anything at this moment with my emotions. I must be in nature somewhere, possibly the woods. Crack! I think that is a branch breaking by my feet or another animal. If I wasn't dead I might be fearful of what is out there; but at that element I don't feel that fear of the unknown.

"Amara! Amara, are you here," a female voice calls out.

That's my mom. What is she doing here?

If I can hear, I might be able to speak now. I try to speak in hope my Mom can hear me.

"Mom," I called out.

On the sound of speaking to my Mother my sight returns. Where am I? There is a low dense fog rolling on the ground, while there are barren trees all around. This place seems lifeless, yet how can it be if I heard animals calling out. There is an orangish and brown glow that fills the sky. The ground is a dark brown similar to actual soil with a tint of orange and black. It seems like nothing can survive in this place.

"Amara! Amara, where are you," my Mom calls out.

"Mom? Where are you," I shouted back.

I navigate through the lifeless trees and bushes that have low lying branches. Some of the branches have sharp thorns that are unavoidable. I get cut a few times as I step through the woods.

I see someone else walking towards me so I call out, "Mom is that you?"

"Hi sweety," my Mom says softly.

My Mom brushes my hair behind my ear and gives a smile.

"Mom, where are we," I ask.

"You don't know," my Mom replies.

My mom's demeanor changes.

"This is your new home Amara. This is where homosexuals go for all their sins," states Amara's Mother.

"Mom, what are you talking about," I inquired.

My mind is confused. What should I say?

"I saw you kissing that girl," professes Amara's Mother.

"What girl and what kiss," I pose.

"The girl that works on the farm," states My mom's with an upset tone.

"I don't know what you're talking about," I responded in defense of my Mom in my confusion.

"You know very well what I am talking about. Your homossexual friend that works on the farm," proclaims Amara's Mother.

My Mom steps toward me and I retreat with a step backwards.

"God does not love homosexuals, Amara. That is a sin that God has a hard time forgiving and you will be here for all eternity if you don't repent your homosexual sin," my Mom commands.

"Mom, I am scared, can we just go home? I want to go home." I state as I keep retreating from my own Mother.

"You should be ashamed of yourself. I thought we raised you better than this. How could you let the devil lead you astray into homosexuality? I am ashamed of you," professes Amara's Mother.

Tears begin to fall from my eyes. How did she find out? I want out of this place.

"It is not right for a girl to kiss another girl. It is wrong and you need help. Take my hand and I will take you home so we can go talk to the pastor," claims Amara's Mother.

"Mom, I am sorry I have no idea what you are talking about," I affirm.

How can I tell her the truth, this can't be real.

"You know what you and that girl who works for us did. Both of you need to talk to the pastor. I am disappointed that you committed such a great sin. You just need to get back on Jesus's path and your sin of being homosexual will be gone. Just pray and God will cast the devil and this sin out of you," conveys Amara's Mother.

Tears continue to run down my face, as I wipe them away. She seems so upset with me over Zali and I.

"Zali, that's her name," expresses Amara's Mom.

"Wait, what? Do you think Zali and I kissed," I inquired.

Just keep playing the denial card, that is the best I can do right now.

"Sweety you are in denial, and yes you and Zali have been kissing," denotes Amara's Mom.

Is my Mom reading my thoughts?

"Yes, I know what you are thinking. Do you think I don't know? I'm your Mother. I know what you're thinking about and what you do," discloses Amara's Mother.

"Mom, I'm sorry, it's true Zali and I kissed. I like Zali and she likes me," I confess.

"No!" My Mom shouts as she points to the ground. The ground cracks open.

"Mom, what are you doing? Please stop," I shout back.

"Homosexuals belong in Hell. I want to be in Heaven with all my children when I die. There is no place in Heaven for homosexuals. Be ashamed of this sin you have Amara. Ask for forgiveness and this sin will be gone. Dad and I will get rid of the temptation of Zali that is influenced by the devil. We don't want the little temptress having you fall into the devil's hands," declares Amara's Mom.

My Mom reaches out and touches my face. Tears pour down my face, and my Mom wipes my face of the tears.

"Amara, it's ok to cry over your shameful sin. It's the first step in the healing process of your sin. Let me pray with you that God will take this sin away," whispers Amara's Mom.

Something in the words that my Mom just said struck me in a wrong way. My sadness instantly transforms into anger toward my Mother. I pull away from her normal warm arms as they now feel cold. I look up at her and notice the sky line behind her is changing. The orange, brown and tan color is transforming to gray, white and blue.

"No mom, I will not pray with you. You have no idea how hard it is for me to always hide myself from you and Dad. I have to sneak around to be with the girl I like. I have to watch my brother being able to be with his girlfriend, yet I can't be with my girlfriend," I assert.

"Girlfriend? Excuse me," contends my Mother.

My mom's face is filled with disgust at the sound of me saying girlfriend.

"Yes mom, Zali and I are dating," I reply.

My Mom fights back her tears.

"How could you do this to me and your Father? How could you do this to God? How could you let this sin consume you," claims Amara's Mother.

The ground cracks more as the cracks widen as it lets out an orange glow. The colors in the sky seem to be battling it out for space. War is raging in the sky as a lightning bolt crashes to the ground between us.

"God is telling you right now they are unhappy with you. Repent your sins or God will cast you to Hell. Please Amara, ask for forgiveness. Please do this for me," pleads Amara's Mother.

My Mom has tears coming down her face. The lightning bolt starts a fire as the ground begins to burn. The ground begins to shake and tremble.

"God is angry with you Amara. I am begging you," pleads Amara's Mother.

I close my eyes to try to get some clarity in the moment of what is happening, I didn't expect what is going to happen with my body next.

"AAAAAAAHHHHHHHHHHHH!" I let out a piercing scream of rage and anger.

My scream shatters the sky as the war between the colors part from each other. The blending of the gray, white, blue with orange brown and tan stops. My echoing scream parts the colors into two. After my scream I look at my Mom and begin to speak. The heat from the fire warms the air, but I could now also feel a coolness creeping in.

"Mom, you have no idea how much I have prayed for this sin to be taken away. God never took it away. I have always felt ashamed to be at Church because I didn't understand why God created this sin in me, but wouldn't take it away. It's been incredibly difficult to live like this. I had no one to turn to and talk about why I felt like this. The weight and burden I felt God put on me. I always felt ashamed of Mom. I don't want to feel like this, yet I do. God won't take it away. I have liked girls my whole life, and it's been difficult to live with this pain. This pain has caused me to close up and withdraw. I have to feel ashamed of who I am on a daily basis. To hide that only makes it worse. You will never know how I truly feel," I articulate.

Snow begins to fall from the sky as the ground burns. This world is split in two and I have no direction to go.

"If you did pray to take your sin away then you are so lost, your prayer hasn't reached God. The devil has too much influence on you. If you choose to follow the Devil's path then you will never be with your family in eternity. I hope you will find your way back to God," implies Amara's Mother.

My Mom claps her hands together, as the ground underneath me opens up.

"Mom!" I call out as I fall.

"Aahhh!" I shoot up in bed panicking and breathing heavily.

"Are you okay, Amara?" Zali's voice whispers to me.

I turn to look at her, and look at my watch, 2:37am

"Oh shit I'm so late," I insist.

Zali runs her fingers on my back as I sit up in her bed.

"When did we fall asleep," I ask.

"We must have fallen asleep after we were done making out. We were going to just snuggle for a few minutes before I brought you home. I'm so sorry," replies Zali.

"It's not just your fault it's mine too." I state as I search the floor for my shirt and pants.

"Did you have a bad dream that woke you," Zali asks.

I handed Zali her clothes as I found hers. Then she hands me mine.

"I think so, but we need to go," I contend.

After gathering our things we head out to the car so she can take me home. Snow is lightly falling as the ground is slightly covered in white snow. I breathe deeply wondering what tomorrow brings.

Chapter 23

The daily life I live is surrounded by people I am jealous of. They can go about their day and be who they want, yet I can't. My friends can hold hands with their boyfriends or girlfriends in the halls of the school. Maybe jealousy is envy, perhaps it's both. I really dislike that I can't be like everyone else with the person I love and care for. I'm envious they get to hold hands at school or in public. They get to dance with the person they want to dance with.

I don't get to express my feelings to others or my parents. If I have trouble with my relationship with Zali, who can I talk to about it? I'm sure in a hetrosexual relationship they can talk to their friends and parents about their relationships. I can't even talk to my Mom about my relationship with Zali, that would end in a disaster. I want my Mother's input with things that I am struggling with. Children should be able to turn to their parents for guidance and advice; however, I can not because being a lesbian goes against everything my family believes in. I'm envious that others can have a better relationship with their parents while I hide a big part of me.

My parents, siblings, and the rest of my family think they know me so well, besides the fact they only know a part of me. How can they even be proud of me when I feel shame at this moment. The jealousy and envy of others is a powerful emotion driving the anxiety and fear of being discovered. I feel ashamed of being different so I hide myself because of the shame, it's a never ending cycle. I find a hiding spot within my hiding spots so jealousy and envy doesn't show. I worry constantly with fear that my envy and jealousy will show, while my secret will be found out.

This is a constant turmoil with my consciousness which filters into my unconscious. I have no one to process this with besides myself, which creates this loneliness feeling. Even if I brought this up to anyone, about these concepts, I would fear someone would catch on to my secret. Fear follows me like a shadow does on a sunny day, or a moon light lighting up the night sky. It is everywhere I go the fear follows me. I am constantly on edge but no one can even see the cracks this fear has caused. I don't want anyone to find out my secret because of what they might think of me. The shame also drives that fear of shadows to follow me wherever I go.

December brings the talks with friends about Christmas as well as the winter formal after winter break. Girls are talking about going shopping for dresses over break with their moms. Regardless if they have a date or not, they will be attending the dance. It's fun to get dressed up and hang out with friends. How much fun will I be able to have if I can't dance with my girlfriend. It would be great to have a slow dance with Zali in our formal dresses. To see each other's hair done, going out to dinner before the dance. What enjoyment can I really have?

The jealousy and envy of my friends being able to dance with their significant others while I hide in fear is a compelling emotion that weighs on my consciousness. If Zali and I end up going to the dance together, I fear someone will catch me looking at her all night. Every body language I express I will fear I will be seen and my secret will be revealed. What if we went together, how would the pictures go? Will I be able to contain myself because I want to wrap my arms around her and have fun pictures of the two of us. The issue I face is fear. I know I would withdraw into myself at that moment. I wouldn't have fun because I would be living in fear with every moment, and in every movement I make my body language expression towards Zali. I fear someone would pick up on it. The worst thing is my Mom or Dad would pick up on it. I don't think I could face them.

What if I came out to them at snowball by holding hands with Zali. Could I do it? It's hard to say, all I know is they wouldn't let me leave the house and go to the dance. Could I even look them in the eye or face and say I am a lesbian to my parents? I don't even know if I could be comfortable enough to be in the same room with them once they know I'm a lesbian. The shame would be too overpowering for me to handle. All the pent up emotions of hiding might boil over. Would I scream out in anger at them or cry in front of them?

If I am forced into the situation to come out to my parents I believe I will feel like less of a person. The shame that I have grown inside me would make me feel socially awkward too. I will feel like withdrawing into myself because I don't want to face the shame. The shame feels terrible. I just want to cry a river, and let that river carry me away. I hide to bury the shame. No one knows about my secret; I take that back, Zali knows and Adelaide. It's not enough to be free of this shame. Maybe more friends would be more supportive, except I just can't face my parents. The shame is too powerful, so I lock it up in its own box and seal it shut. I just don't want to face my shame. It's not healthy, just the same right now I have no other options.

Adelaide and I don't even talk about my sexual orientation. Should that drive me to tell others? Maybe they won't be so accepting. Who can I really trust with this struggle? I still haven't had the chance to tell Zali of my emotional baggage I am carrying right now. Will she even understand? Before she met me she was a straight heterosexual girl. She only has experienced liking girls for a short time. Does she feel the same burden as I do?

The pressure of hiding these emotions is definitely taking a toll on me. Have I missed out on opportunities with my friends because I have feared every aspect of myself? Why can't there be someone to talk to, and share what I am going through. My difference of liking girls in this community does not make me feel any better. Shame follows me wherever I go. Looking in the mirror each morning, talking with my mom, seeing an actress I think is cute on T.V, or a movie

Zali and I have been together for a little more than three months. No one knows except Adelaide and she isn't around enough to share this experience with her. The jealousy and envy sets in, knowing others can share their significant other with friends and family, yet I can't even put up pictures of Zali in my locker, or in my room out of fear someone will figure out my secret. I will forever stay trapped in this secret.

Chapter 24

Tis the season to be jolly. As the Christmas season approaches, a well deserved break from school is needed. I spend most of my break working on the farm anyway. Some of my friends are taking trips away for the holidays which I would love to just get away for once, but the farm ties us down. The holidays also seem so rushed in our family. We try to cram all of our events for family gatherings in two days. Christmas eve is with my parents; then Christmas day is packed with chores, Church, grandparents, evening chores, and lastly other grandparents. It's not a relaxing day. Rushing from one event then to the next with never really enjoying the moment and relaxing.

My brother will probably also be splitting time with his girlfriend Miranda and her family. I can't even have my girlfriend come without outing myself, besides then my parents would forbid it. Zali has a family so she wouldn't even be allowed to come either probably for the same reason. We don't invite friends over, just significant others.

There have been plenty of things that have transpired over the past month. My emotions have been all over the place. The holidays have always been hard these past few years since puberty started and I really started noticing other girls. I knew that I would not be able to bring a girl to family functions like my brother could.

Driving is also on the back of my mind. A little more freedom to come in less than two months. I already have a car, but I have to wait for my birthday to come to get my license. Then I can drive to Zali's instead of her driving me around. I will be able to hang with other friends if I choose.

Our winter formal is also approaching near the end of January; in addition, Amber wants to go dress browsing before her and her Mom go shopping for real. Amber has her license already so she is picking me up. Her and I have been a little distant since homecoming; of course, it didn't help that I am also going through several things in my own relationship and personal life. I hope this is a way to repair our friendship.

I just remember how excited she was about knowing Ted was going to ask me to the homecoming dance then she found out Ted was going to ask me out. Her excitement only increased for me with both those accounts. She has had a few different boyfriends in high school so being a good friend, she only wanted me to be happy with someone like she was. We have been friends since elementary school, I have never had a relationship; of course, she didn't know the reason for that.

Her new boyfriend's name is Andre and he attends a different school. The little I know is he is athletic and plays three sports. They met at a cross country meet in early October and she started dating shortly after that. I am getting filled in a little more tonight by the details of their relationship. The afternoon is more about catching up and looking at dresses for our formal. Our conversations are casual to start before she asks the burning question that has caused us to stop talking, Ted.

"What happened between you and Ted," Amber asks me as we look at a collection of dresses.

"I don't know." I replied.

This is going to be hard to explain without outing myself. I'm walking on eggshells here. I turn my head so Amber can't pick up on facial expressions.

"What do you mean, you don't know? You were the one that left the dance floor and the dance," Amber brings forward.

"I just didn't want to ruin a friendship, but I guess I still ruined that friendship. We haven't spoken besides a few words in passing in the halls," I profess.

"I thought you liked him? What happened? You aren't going to find many guys like Ted," Amber insists.

I'm trapped in this moment to answer hard questions and I don't even know how to tell her the truth. My breathing starts to panic as I fear my secret is in trouble. My friend should know that I like girls, besides no one will understand or accept me. I will be turned away and rejected. If Amber knows how long it will take before it gets to my brother, someone at Church, and then my parents.

"I only liked him as a friend," I assert back.

"Well it didn't seem like that during cross country. You two were so close. There is no way you just liked him as a friend. You two were flirting all the time," Amber discloses.

"Ted and I were only friends and I thought it was fine if two friends went as friends to the dance," I denote.

My heart is pounding and I can feel my defenses rising. The fear creeps in behind all the dresses on the manikins. I see it and feel it. The shame for liking girls in this community has walked in the store doors and stares at me. It has found me again. Why can't I get away from this feeling?

"Ted is just confused about what happened. If you want to be friends, why haven't you talked to him since the dance," asks Amber.

I hear the footsteps of guilt walking towards me. I am surrounded by emotions that have been a burden for me.

"We were just friends and that's all I ever wanted. I wasn't interested in dating him," I asserted back at Amber.

I snap and give a snarky tone to her. Amber is a little taken back by the change in tone of my voice. My body is filled with a cold chill after my response. I glance at the entrance of the store to see if someone just walked in. It would explain the sudden chill in the air. No one has entered the store but I still feel the chill on my body.

"Sorry about that. It just seems no one wants to listen to me when I say I wasn't interested in him and I just wanted to be good friends," I affirm.

"It was the first boy you have ever had any interest in. I was hoping you would finally have a boyfriend," implies Amber.

"Boys are so immature at this age so why would I want to date one," I responded.

That was the best defensible response I could come up with.

"I would agree they are immature, but Ted seems like he is mature enough," Amber proposes.

"I just don't want to date anyone right now," I exclaim.

"No judgment, but at some point you gotta test the water to find out what you like and don't like," offers Amber.

"Like you going from one guy to the next," I insist.

"Hey, now," responds Amber.

" What? Andre is like your third boyfriend this year," I commented back.

"Hey, this girl just wants to try out different boys," states Amber.

It's something we share a laugh over. We finish our dress browsing by trying on a few different dresses. Besides the almost panic attack, the afternoon turned out pretty good. When Amber dropped me off, she gave me a hug to tell me we need to hang out more. I agreed with her. Amber asked if on Friday I wanted to come with her to Andre's home basketball game. I said I'll ask my parents and let her know.

I waved to her as she pulled away in the driveway. The cold winter air cuts through my coat and scratches my face. My hair blows across my face as I brush my hair out of my face. I look up into the night sky, and I see a few openings in the clouds to see a star. The thought of who I am as well as who I have become drifts through my mind. I breathe in the cold winter air while closing my eyes. I need a moment to collect myself before I enter the house. I exhale and open my eyes.

"BOO!" Shouts Kumari.

I am startled at the flash of an enemy from my imagination standing in front of me. I shutter looking around as I turn to walk into the house. Before I enter I hear a call out of a familiar voice.

"Amara, Help!"

Chapter 25

I lay awake the past few nights with the voice continuing to call out for "Help." I toss and turn as I know what the calling is, besides that part of me is dead. I can never go back, I'm dead. No one comes back from the dead, well except Jesus apparently. I am definitely not Jesus. I have been lost in this world and the world I am dead to. Then again I have been lost in emotional purgatory, well maybe it's emotionless purgatory. I don't even know who I am. These past few nights since Amber dropped me off I have laid awake wondering who am I? There is a part of me missing, also a part that will never be seen by the world. Those two parts are more similar than the part of me that my parents, siblings, family, friends, or anyone else actually sees. No one will ever know who I actually am, if I don't even know who I am.

Zali will never truly understand me, or know who I am. Even though I have shared my imagination with her she will never fully understand me. If I don't understand myself then I will never let anyone else in to be close enough to truly understand me. My friends don't know me as well as they think they truly know me. If they truly knew me they would know the torment it is to be a girl who likes girls in a very Christian community and household.

I stare out my window on this cold earlier morning. It's Thursday December 20th at 2:48 am, and I watch the snow fall outside. Just two days left until winter break, but I have unfinished business that is calling me. Someone needs my help, even so I can't go back. There is pain everywhere I go, I just want to escape, yet I can't. Can someone die a second time when they are already dead? That's an interesting question that pops in my head.

The calling for help pierces through my brain like the ringing of bells outside of stores. Those Christmas bells bring hope for so many people as well as joy, not this voice. The weight of the Universe awaits me once again. I can see it out my window in each snowflake that falls. The Universe is all around, scattered into millions if not billions of snowflakes. Time floats differently for each snowflake, just like each person here on Earth.

I change out of my pajamas and braid my hair. I have no idea what exactly I am doing at 3 am and why I am heading out into the cold. Even if I wanted to do chores, that's not for another two hours. I sneaked quietly down the stairs to head down to the basement to put warm clothes on. I make sure I open doors as quietly as possible as well as shut them as quietly as possible. I enter into the cold morning as snowflakes land on my face. The cold air cuts my face as I lift my ski mask over my nose. The snow crunches with each step I take. Maybe I didn't think this one through, my footsteps will be seen by my Dad when he goes to the barn in the morning. I guess that's the least of my concerns.

The wind swirls around snow that is on the ground. There has been a few inches of snow already on the ground for a few weeks. December has been cold so no snow has melted. I head over to our little shed that I have stored all my wooden weapons I have made. What is compelling me to come back to my weapons? It seems like forever ago I have touched any of my weapons. I grab my sword and close the door to start walking behind the barn to my normal spot where I would play by myself in my imagination. My eyes water from the bitter cold as snow has now stopped. A few clouds have cleared the way in the northern sky to give way to several twinkling stars. Is that a feeling of calmness I begin to feel? Even though the cold pierces my face and eats away at my fingers and toes; nevertheless, being in the early morning cold I feel the warmth. I know what needs to be done. The calling of help needs to be answered.

"What is it you want from me in the Universe," I called out.

"What is it you want from me, God?" I call out again.

"Listen to my cries Universe. My pain and hurt, it's all right here for you to look at and take." I shout and raise up my arms with my sword in my right hand.

"Is anyone listening to me!?!? Anyone?" I cry out.

I close my eyes for a second as the calmness seems to be fading from me as the cold becomes overpowering.

"We hear you Amara, and we are coming to save you!"

"GASP!" I suck in air as the air fills my lungs once more.

I'm breathing.

"GASP!" I take another breath of air and open my eyes.

How can this be? How am I alive? Why am I alive again? I close my eyes to drift away just like before. I remember this exact moment from before. This is when I died. Is this why the question popped into my head is it possible for someone to die again once they are already dead? I know what's coming, but how is this possible? I know there is a monstrous beast about ready to gouge me with its sword. I am reliving the moment I went suicidal. Why am I back here? This time I am not alone in my mind. The dark and dreariness I was in is not here. It's being blocked by something. I can feel it inside me. What is this feeling that has replaced all the other pain I have felt? It's not happiness. I am not happy I'm alive. I'm mad at whoever did this to me. Even though I was not in a great place in my death, I would rather be there than here.

My heart aches as I feel the cold pierce through my heart with tiny needles. In that exact moment my eyes open with rage rushing in like water falling over Niagara Falls. My hands rise up and clamp down on the sword that is a mere centimeter from piercing me a second time. I stare at the beast with my rage filled eyes, still clamping together in the palm of my hands their sword. I rise off my knees to my feet to let out a literal bone chilling scream that freezes the monster sold. I twist my hands as I shatter their sword. I don't even realize what is happening at that moment. As I turn to walk away from the frozen beast, armor forms around my body. This isn't my silver and gold armor I am accustomed to, this is new armor. It's a shiny blue and metallic color. It shimmers with different shades of blue, as I stare for a second at the transformation that is happening. Never have I had new armor in my imagination. What am I now? I am no longer the same person I used to be.

"Amara you're alive," Aisha calls out.

"It actually worked to bring you back," Jamir states.

"The odds were against us to travel back in time, but we did it. We saved you," Aisha remarks.

They saved me. Those words filled my brain and circulated through every fiber of my body. They didn't save me from anything. I was dead and gone. I didn't need to be saved from death. Why didn't they just let me die? I didn't want to be back. I don't want the pressure of leading the team again. I don't want the weight of the world on my shoulders. All I can feel is anger at the gesture they just did. I see the tears of joy they have in their eyes; for all that, I'm not happy, I'm angry at them. I am angry at all of this.

"Why would you bring me back? You should have left me dead," I shout at them.

The joy and sadness to have me back is wiped away by my angry tone into confusion.

"We thought you would be happy to be alive? No one wants to die, Amara," Aisha expresses.

Their tone indicates the confusion is why I'm not happy to be alive.

"You were dead and you are the strongest of all of us. You bring the best out of us. We need you. The world needs you. This Universe needs you," divulges Jamir.

"I am mad at you for bringing me back. You have no idea what I actually want," I vocalize.

The transformation of my new armor completes as a helmet shields my face. I hear another beast call out to me, that it doesn't matter if I have new armor or not, there is no stopping them.

I call back with my back turned to the beast, "You have never met the Frost Princess have you?"

I turn to the beast and two ice spears lunch, one from each shoulder, right at the beast destroying it into thousands of ice pieces. I turn back to Aisha and Jamir to walk right past them. I guess the question no longer is who am I. I am now the Frost Princess! What does that mean going forward, I have no idea. I just know the pain and hurt is frozen in me for the time being.

Chapter 26

I need to escape from these two worlds that are now colliding. What has become as I sit on top of a mountain overlooking the landscape. The air is thin and brisk. Tears fall from my eyes as I stare upon the landscape that seems to not be touched by the human hand. I'm alive, except I don't want to be. This is a new feeling of loneliness I'm not sure of. I am just lost in my own self. I admire the mountains, valley and skyline. Is this peace, and if it is why do I feel so lonely? Why can't I just be? I try to constantly be something I'm not, along with I'm tired of it. I wipe the cold tears from my face and breathe in while shutting my eyes trying to take it all in before the pain begins all over again.

I'll go back to reality putting on my armor again, in spite of the fact that this is not the same armor I'm used to. I can feel a burning anger at the world. I hate hiding from everyone. Outside this world I now must put another layer on to mask my identity even more. I am not in balance in any world I live in. Do I have a world I can actually call home? I place my helmet back on and run and jump into the unknown.

It's New Years Eve and Adelaide has invited me and Zali over for a New Years Eve party with a sleep over. Of course, I have to work the next morning thanks to all the non-family workers on the farm getting to have the day off, but not me. At least I can stay out past midnight and spend time with my friends for the party. I know Zali and I are not going to be the only people there. Adelaide has invited some of her friends from her school too.

I feel like a new person since being brought back, even though not in a good way. I have a badass attitude, well that's what it feels like. Does that mean my personality also changed with this new attitude? I feel like I just don't care anymore. I'm tired of all this hiding, nonetheless isn't this just more hiding with a different attitude?

As I change my normal look in how I go out, I spend time curling my hair and styling it really cute. My Mom asks why I am getting all fancy. I tell her because it's New Years Eve and we all want to get fancy to bring in the new year. Only if my Mom knew my secret, then what would she really think? She asks who is going to be there. I mentioned it is an all girls sleepover so it definitely eases her mind that no boys will be there. What would it matter since I work in the morning? If she knew I liked girls she probably wouldn't let me go. I still can't let her know, it would be heavy religion talk and most likely with the youth pastor present.

Zali picks me up to head over to Adelaide's house.

"Wow you look so pretty," Zali tells me when I get into her car.

"Thank you! Not bad yourself," I responded.

"I'm so looking forward to the three of us just hanging out together," declares Zali.

"Oh, Adelaide didn't tell you she also is inviting some of her friends from her school," I profess.

Zali reaches for my hand to hold it like normal. My mind flashes to the mountaintop being alone and angry. I question why must we live like this? I grab back and squeeze her hand. We look at each other and smile. Her smile is sincere, even though mine feels forced. Inside I'm not happy.

"At least we have a twenty minute drive to be alone together," states Zali.

"Yeah," I replied.

I went cold the rest of the drive. Questions run through my head of what will become of the night. Adelaide knows about us, but not her friends. More hiding, ugh I can't stand this. We arrive at Adelaide's home and Adelaide introduces us to her friends.

"This is Skylar, Nika, and Jade," announces Adelaide.

We all exchange names and make small talk before grabbing snacks and heading to the basement. To be honest it's nice to be around people that aren't from small town USA. Can I relax tonight, maybe? I also find it odd that my girlfriend and my first real crush are together tonight.

The evening is turning out rather fun to be around Adelaide and her friends. I can tell my mind is at ease and I'm relaxing with the conversations. There are two hours until midnight and how will I sneak a kiss on Zali is my main thought. I have been such a jerk to her for the reason that I'm dealing with so much. I want to tell her what is going on, even though I still don't think she understands what it's like to hide your secret from the world. She has been in relationships before with boys which sometimes I think she thinks it's okay to continue to act like it's a heterosexual relationship. Well it's not and that's what is so frustrating.

"Who wants to play Truth and Dare Jenga," exclaims Jade.

"Oooh exciting," replies Skylar.

"I'm totally in," Adelaide agrees.

"I have never played Truth or Dare Jenga before. Sounds like fun. I'm in. Zali? Nika? Are you in," I ask.

"Sure why not." Zali states.

"Okay," Nika states.

The twist to Truth and Dare Jenga is to complete the truth block and Dare block once you remove the piece you chose. Some of the questions make us laugh. It definitely is a fun way to relax to end the year. Hanging with a few people I know and new friends to make.

"Amara, it's your turn," exclaims Skylar.

"What are you going to go for," asks Zali.

"Whatever is the easiest to go for," I reply.

"She is going for a dare," shouts Nika

I remove a dare piece and read it to myself first. I am shocked and horrified at what it says. My secret will be out if I do this dare. I flash back to that breath I took when I came back from the dead. Anger fills my mind with the world and everyone in this room. Why me?

"Come on, read it, Amara," states Jade

"Ya, what does it say," asks Adelaide .

Then I realized at that moment, I didn't care. One of the girls in the room is my girlfriend. Another knows about me and Zali. The other three just think it's a game.

"It says, kiss the person next to you," I announce.

Skylar and Nika let out a scream of excitement.

"OMG," exclaims Jade, who is sitting next to me. "This is so dope."

Zali's face almost looks worried for me.

Adelaide is shocked, but responds with "who's it going to be? Zali or Jade?"

I know if there is any hesitation it might raise questions.

"Hmm? I think Zali needs a kiss," I insist

This works out to my advantage. The other three girls think it a game as they won't think anything of it. I actually get to kiss my girlfriend in front of people. I guess this dare worked out for me.

"Get ready Zali," Adelaide exclaims.

"Don't worry Zali, I'm a good kisser," I say with a flirtishness tone.

Wow there is that new attitude. Instead of just leaning in for a quick kiss I found myself standing up and stepping over Zali and sitting on her lap.

"Hello," I said.

"Hi," Zali replies with a smile and her face as red as a tomato.

I grab her shirt and pull her in for a deep passionate kiss. I am not going to hold myself back with this opportunity. I can hear the other girls scream with excitement. I don't think I have ever kissed Zali like that before. After a few seconds I release my lips from hers and stand back up and touch my lips with my fingers to make a sizzle sound.

"Wow! Amara, that was so hot," Jade states.

"That was some kiss Amara," replies Skylar.

"Well it said kiss the person next to you, so I didn't want to disappoint," I remarked back.

Zali lets out a chuckle, "Well you didn't disappoint. You are a good kisser."

Zali gives me a smile as I give her a smirk back.

"Amara, you go all out for dares," states Adelaide.

It felt great being able to kiss a girl in front of other people, and being my girlfriend too. My mind flashes back to the mountaintop in that peaceful view of the sun shining on the valley with the mountaintops all around. It felt freeing. I didn't feel like I was in isolation anymore. For this one night now I could kiss Zali or any girl if I got that piece. No one would ever know I like girls. Even if it's for a split second, I can finally feel free. I feel empowered by what I did. I want to do it again. Maybe I won't have to sneak a kiss later at midnight, I'll just do it.

We continue the game with several more interesting pieces before we start taking pieces that we had already taken out. This time Adelaide pulled out the piece that said kiss the person next to you.

"Dam girl! Who's it going to be? Skylar or Zali," asks Nika.

Adelaide would never kiss Zali because she knows. The other three have no idea so it's just a game.

Adelaide turns to Zali and says "I think I will kiss you, Zali. Amara seemed to enjoy your kiss so I'm interested to see how you kiss."

"It's a dare you can't back out," replies Jade.

I want to turn away but I can't. I can see the fear, and almost shame that this is happening to Zali. I realize, Zali might finally realize what I have gone through my whole life. Zali is hesitant because I'm here. It's not that Zali wants people to find out her new secret of liking girls, but it's something entirely different. Zali's eyes glance over at me and are saying I'm sorry. I find my eyes telling her it's okay. Wait what? It's okay, a split second ago I'm upset that Adelaide chose Zali.

Adelaide leans in for a kiss while Zali hesitates. That's when Aleladie took action and also grabbed her by the shirt and gave her a deep passionate kiss too. We all let out a scream of excitement for the kiss. I'm surprised at how I feel about Adelaide and Zali kissing. Adelaide was the first girl I wanted to kiss and now Zali got to kiss her, well Adelaide kissed her.

"I think Adelaide and Amara know something about kissing Zali. I might have to get a kiss at midnight from you," Skylar says jokingly.

I am surprisingly fine with what transpired with Adelaide and Zali. I still feel free and I am hoping Zali also is feeling the same. We could finally be free around other people without judgment. A part of me thinks Adelaide did that intentionally for me. She knows I have struggled with this secret. I think Adelaide realizes Zali didn't fully understand the struggles I go through being a lesbian. Adelaide put the spotlight on Zali and took it off me. Sure I was upset at first, yet her intentions I believe were genuine.

By the time we wrapped up Truth and Dare Jenga before midnight; Zali was kissed by me three other times, by Adelaide twice more and Skylar once. I even got two kisses with Jade. It has been a night of freedom from the chains and burdens I have been carrying. I have never felt so alive since the first time Zali and I kissed when we went coon hunting. Tomorrow I have to go back to be hidden, however for at least another hour before I leave I can be free.

I just don't care and maybe that is the attitude I need for the new year. Of course, the consequences of my family finding out are too risky, but I have a taste of freedom to be me. As we clean up our Jenga game and get our New Year's hats on, I notice Zali seems a little off by the game. Is this how she felt with me for the last few months? I have been distant from her, and not sharing what has been going on with me.

"Hey go talk to her," Adelaide tells me.

"I should, but what do I say? You kissed her," I whisper back.

"Well, more than once, but who's counting," Adelaide states while giving me a shoulder bump.

"Ya, what was up with that anyway," I inquired.

"It was to give you a chance to be you. My friends don't care if you like girls or have a girlfriend. If you want to kiss her at midnight, you should totally kiss your girlfriend," Adelaide divulges.

"Thanks," I reply while giving Adelaide a shoulder bump back.

I walk over to where Zali is sitting to talk with her. I reflect on what Adelaide just said. I look around the basement to look at the other girls. They are watching the clock for midnight. Less than five minutes until the new year. An idea pops into my head. This might be my only day to be free so I want to make the best of it.

"Hey beautiful, how are you," I asked Zali.

"I'm sorry about tonight. I was just playing the game. Then you kissed Jade twice. Do you even want to be with me? You have barely talked to me these past few months. I don't even know what is going on with you. I need to know, do you want to be with me," Zali asks.

"One minute until midnight," Nika shouts.

I'm a little taken back by Zali's response but it's a fair response. It's a question that I need to answer. I flash back to the mountaintop. It's no longer a peaceful view. Dark clouds begin rolling in. Tears are rolling down my face as they turn into ice on my cheeks. I let out an icy scream of anger and pain. Being alone is hard, even though being with someone that you love. I have to hide from everyone else and bring shame on who I am. I will never be truly free to be myself. I had this brief moment of what freedom feels like. I felt normal with friends. I felt like I didn't have to hide. No judgment. Now Zali asks me this question: if I want to be with her, I want to say yes, except at the same time I want to say no. I have clearly caused more pain to her than I realized.

It is impossible for the two of us to be truly happy in our community and families. She could do better along with being happier if she didn't have to hide with me. I have lived in isolation for my entire life until she entered my life. She brought me joy and happiness, in spite of that I have to do it in secret. The secret that conflicts with my religion every time I hold her hand, kiss her, or snuggle next to her. I have felt guilty and shameful for being like this. The burden of sin that has been ingrained in me by my family and Church. I hate it so much. I don't want to listen to my family telling me I'm sinful while having to go to counseling to "fix" me.

If you truly love someone you let them go so they don't have to suffer too. I have made Zali suffer in my own suffering.

"Well can you please answer me Amara," Zali whispers to me.

"Ten, nine, eight, seven, six, five, four, three, two, one," the other girls count down.

Pause the Universe for a second. Decisions ripple through time and across time streams. I want to ask her out again and make an announcement to this group of friends so a total of four people in this Universe know that I am different from others. What time stream does that create? Then there is saying no and walking away. It is almost like that will destroy several time streams.

The room goes dark as it's me looking at me, a very defensive me. It makes me wonder why I was brought back as the Frost Princess. Ice fills the walls as the room goes cold. Snow falls from the ceiling as I glance at my Frost Princess self. She stares with a cold hearted stare. She is armored up and ready to defend. The basement floor is now covered in snow. I continue to stare at myself. Suddenly she pulls out a pocket watch. She holds it up above her head and moves her wrist back and forth. With each movement I hear a loud Tic Toc, Tic Toc. I cover my ears as the vibration rings through the room to pierce my ears. The ticking continues until she drops the pocket watch into the snow. I am shot back to the basement, seeing Zali staring up at me waiting for a response.

On Zero,"Happy New Year!" Everyone shouts.

"No, I can't do this anymore," I reply.

Chapter 27

"No, I can't do this anymore," I responded to Zali.

It's not the response I figured would come out of my mouth, but it's the best response my defensive mind can come up with. I have mixed feelings about this, which I'm torn with emotions pulling me in opposite directions. It has been incredibly hard hiding the secret, even now living with my secret relationship has taken a toll on me. The pressure has broken me too. I can not keep living this double secret. I know how to live in isolation to protect my secret, nonetheless this added relationship is breaking me.

Zali looks up at me with tears rolling down her face. Do we try to talk about this here and now and cause a scene? Everyone else is celebrating while our relationship just ended. Why am I not sad about this? My emotions have gone cold. My mind reflects back to staring at myself as the Frost Princess, I'm cold, emotionless, and angry.

"Zali and Amara, come on, it's the new year," Jade exclaims while she places her hand on my shoulder to get my attention.

Jade looks down and realizes Zali is crying.

"Zali, are you okay," asks Jade.

"I'm fine," Zali responds by giving a sniffle and wiping tears away from her face.

At that moment Zali stands up, and pushes past us as she heads upstairs.

"What's wrong with Zali," Jade asks me.

The mood of the New Year's celebration has changed because of me. How do I respond to Jade's question? Do I lie and say I don't know? Do I reveal my secret and tell her essentially we just broke up? My defensive mind is screaming to keep my mouth shut to lie to Jade. It's the best way to protect myself. My night of freedom is gone as no one knows what I am experiencing, or for that matter what Zali is going through.

"Hey I'll go check on her," Adelaide chimes in as she walks past us.

Skylar and Nika come over by me and Jade to see what is happening.

"What's going on with Zali," Skylar asks.

"Zali was crying and then got up to go upstairs," replies Jade.

"I just noticed she was by herself so I came over by her to bring her to the celebration," I rescinded back.

"Did she say anything to you," Jade asks.

Now how do I respond to that question? We just finished playing truth and dare. I could say the truth, in addition to more questions will arise. Do I dare try to cover my tracks to say she didn't say anything?

"She said something like, I can't keep doing this," I replied.

What the hell brain, why did you lie and say what I responded to Zali. Oh shit, what have I done?

"What does that even mean," Nika asks.

"You don't think it means, you know what," Skylar states.

I knew what she was referencing, suicide.

"I don't think so, Skylar. Must be something else," I declare.

Just then Zali came down the stairs to tell me she needed to bring me home to make sure I didn't miss curfew. We say our goodbyes.

When I hugged Adelaide goodbye, she whispered in my ear, "She is worried that you are breaking up with her. Be gentle with her."

Adelaide is a strong character. At first I'm mad at her for kissing Zali; but then my thoughts changed to understanding that she was making Zali feel what I have had to experience my whole life, and Zali for only like six months. This is a tough situation to process. Why does it have to be so hard to have a relationship? Why does it have to be taboo for being a lesbian?

We step out into the darkness of the cold of the new year. Zali is an emotional wreck, yet I feel calm at this moment. I don't even understand my own emotions right now. This car ride is going to be quiet and awkward. Most times I go quiet in the car ride anyway, just the same my mind is focused on the words I muttered "I can't keep doing this." What can't I keep doing? Being in the relationship? Hiding the relationship? Hiding myself from the world? These are the questions that roll through my head as we drive in silence back to my house.

When we pull into the driveway, Zali breaks down and starts to cry. I guess an instinct reaction when you see someone hurting you try and comfort them. I reach for her hand and hold it. She turns to me in tears. All I see is hurt and pain. This is what this secret does to you, it destroys you. I'm sure Zali has experienced hurt and pain from a break up before, except only from boys. How much different is the hurt and pain between a boy or girlfriend breaking up? Is there any difference? I wouldn't know on either side of that, I only know the pain of rejection and hiding. If I ask her, will I get the honest truth of what she is actually feeling? Defense mechanisms take over in the time of pain. I am the prime example of defense mechanisms right now. Since coming back to my imagination, I have become more defensive and angry.

"I hurt everyday. I'm in pain everyday and have been for a while. We have never really talked about how hard it is to be a girlfriend with a girl. It's almost harder than hiding my secret without a girlfriend. I have to worry about so much more, so no one ever catches on to me. That is why I can't keep doing this. I have treated you like crap these past few months. I have gone cold and unresponsive to you. It's all about protecting myself. Everyone knows you as a heterosexual girl; however, this is what is expected of me, but that's not who I am. That pain is tearing a hole in me. Why should I keep bringing you through this horrible lifestyle? I don't want you to also have to continue to feel the same pain I do. You can go back to not having to hide, but I will always be hidden from the world. It's not fair to you," I proclaim.

"You are so much more than any other boy I have dated. Even though I have to stay hidden I would choose to be hidden with you than going back to dating boys. You are so worth the hide," responds Zali.

"It's not fair to you. If I wouldn't have hung out this summer with you, you wouldn't have to hide. I have to hide, you don't get it, Zali," I declare.

Tears fill my eyes as my voice raises out of all the frustrations I have been experiencing for years. Zali reaches for my other hand to try to comfort me. She pulls me in to put her forehead to my forehead.

"I know darling," Zali tells me.

"But you don't," I imply.

I pull away from her in more frustration.

"Okay, maybe I don't know what you're feeling, but why don't you talk to me then," pleads Zali.

"Because I can't," I shout.

Zali is taken back by the change in my tone.

"Do you know how much my family hates, dislikes, or whatever it is of gay people they don't like? My family hates gay people so much that I hate myself. I hate myself for being gay," I shout.

I begin to cry uncontrollably.

"They don't hate you. I don't hate you. I love you," whispers Zali.

I turn to her in my teary self when she says she loves me. How can someone love a sinful person like me?

"No one can love a gay girl. A lesbian girl. A homosexual," I snip back.

"That's not true. I love you for you. You are kind, compassionate, cute, caring, funny. How can someone not love you," affirms Zali.

I don't even know how to respond to her words. It conflicts with everything I was raised by. Heck I conflict with my family beliefs.

"How can you ever understand my situation? You seem to fall in the category of bi-sexual. You can just go back to liking boys or choose another girl. You can choose to hide or walk amongst everyone else. Whatever is easier for you, you might do it," I assert.

"You can't say that about me. I chose you. The girl that is in my car right now," responds Zali.

"Then tell me, have you ever worried about your secret coming out? Have you ever had to walk through the halls and think oh she looks cute, yet worry about too much eye contact and someone will find out. Did you ever have to worry about someone finding out that you want to send a valentine's day flower to your crush, which is a girl and people finding out," I shout in frustration.

"Well not like that," mutters Zali.

"That's what I thought," I snarl back.

"I haven't been in the best relationships myself. They cheated on me and didn't treat me well. You treat me way better than any other boy has ever," expresses Zali.

Listening to her talk to me doesn't help because she has no idea what it actually feels to be different from everyone else. Zali's time of reference of being "different" is just a few months. For me it's my 15 years of life.

"Sometimes I think you see this just as another normal relationship for you without worrying about the consequences of what would happen if anyone found out about us. The community would make our lives miserable. My Church would, well I have no idea, probably Church counseling. My family would disown me; or worse, send me to a Church camp. I live in fear everyday that someone will find out about our secrets. Do you live in fear," I state in frustration.

Zali pauses as if she is thinking about what I just said. Maybe she hasn't thought about it. I have no idea.

"I can't keep doing this because each day it gets more and more risky that my secret will be exposed. I had a moment of freedom tonight to kiss you in front of people, that was it. I get one little moment, even though I have to go back into hiding. So ya, I can't keep hurting you and having you a part of my pain. You can be free, except I can't; so we have to be done," I articulate.

I wipe away tears from my face while I glance at Zali as she begins to tear up.

"Are we really done," Zali asks.

"Yes! It's for the best," I responded.

We both start sobbing in the car. What else am I supposed to do? There is no one who truly understands what I am going through.

"I have to go. I have to work in the morning," I utter.

I open the car door and exit the car and close it behind me. I can't even look at her anymore. The curse that God has placed on me won't even let me have someone special in my life. I try to wipe the tears the best I can before I walk into the house. What if my Mom sees me crying, I can't explain why I'm crying.

This is not the pain I expected for tonight or to enter the new year. I take a deep breath in and wipe the tears from my eyes and face, then let out an exhale. I grab the door to open it but my mind drifts off. I can feel myself standing in that beautiful valley again, in spite of that this time I am screaming in a rage. Ice is shooting from all directions of my body as I have frozen the beautiful valley.

After my scream, I breathe heavily as if I have drained my energy to zero. Where do I go from here? I drop to my knees into the icy snow. I pick the snow up in my hands and stare at it. The snow is cold and fluffy.

It's like a powder or dust in my hand. I bring it up to my mouth and blow it off my hand.

I stare in a trance of the snowflakes falling back to the ground. The world seems different seeing the snowflakes fall as individual flakes to form one whole snow blanket on the ground.

"You know you are not alone," a voice calls out.

My trance is broken by the voice. I stare past the last snowflake falling to the ground. Standing is a mystery woman in a white ice blue snowflake dress. What I mean by that is it sparkles in the moonlight of the night just like when you catch the reflecting snow on the ground, it shines different colors. It's a beautiful long sleeved dress that has a long arm train and long train on the bottom. It shines, glimmers, and sparkles.

I stand up from kneeling on the ground and respond with only this, "Who are you?"

Chapter 28

"Who are you," I call out

"I am Amara. I am you," She calls back to me.

"How can you be me," I question.

"Would you like to find out," older Amara inquires.

"I don't think that's a wise idea." I proclaim as I get defensive and draw a sword.

"You don't need that. Just put it away," remarks older Amara.

She starts walking towards me as the snow crunches beneath her feet.

"I'm sorry but, I don't even know who you are, and where you came from," I insist.

"You know I always thought that the Frost Princess armor was so beautiful, even though I always preferred the silver and gold more," expresses older Amara.

"That doesn't prove anything," I contest.

I get defensive in my stance being ready for any surprises she will bring. She reaches out to touch my armored face.

"You are in pain right now because you just broke up with Zali," exclaims older Amara.

Hearing those words uttered from her mouth lowers my defenses as I soften to be vulnerable and receptive. I lower my guard and sword.

"You are hurt by the pain the world brings you. You retreat into yourself with that pain. I can feel that pain all over again. I remember that day, I think nothing will change. I will always be alone," confesses older Amara.

My helmet retracts so she can see the pain on my face. I notice tears in her eyes too. How is it possible that she is me? As my defenses soften as she pulls me in for a hug. She embraces me with her arms as tears fall to the ground. The sky opens up with millions of unique snowflakes falling on us.

"You think it's bad now and I thought the same thing when I was here in this same spot many years ago," explains older Amara.

"Wait, what?" I mutter as I pull back from her embrace to look at her.

"What do you mean you were here before," I inquired.

"I need to show you something. Things about this world you don't understand, furthermore may not understand for quite some time," replies older Amara.

"I really don't understand. If you are me, then you are from the future," I contest.

"Come, we must go." She grabs my right arm with her left hand to pull me through a portal she opens with her other hand. We enter into this different plane in the Universe I have never seen before to only come out on the other side of the portal. Billions of voices are scrambled into an audience of voices like we are at an entertainment event of some kind.

We entered a bedroom with a baby crib. There is a picture on the wall of her, or really of me holding a baby. I hear a soft breathing coming from the crib.

I glance over at her and whisper, "is this your child?"

She whispers back, "That is my baby girl, or should I say our baby girl."

"I'm confused as to why you're showing me this. I'm not going to have children," I remark.

"I remember thinking that too, still the Universe has a way of surprising you," states older Amara.

"How old is she," I ask.

"She is five months old, and it has been a blessing like no other. This is a love like no other you will experience," older Amara expresses.

"But why is this important? I only broke up with Zali," I inquired.

"To give you hope where you think all hope is lost in humanity to accept you for who you are. Come I want to show you something else," denotes older Amara.

We walk through the portal again, yet this time we don't leave. There are millions, maybe billions more possibilities of portals to go through with a touch of her finger. My mind is overtaken with memories of another life.

"This is a world, like many that are out there, that you are different in too," explains older Amara.

Older Amara spins with her hands raised in the air, gesturing to all the possible parallel worlds.

"There are different people all over the world and in the Universe. We are just one of many who can be different," explains older Amara.

Older Amara points, "in this parallel world you struggle with your gender identity and want to be a boy. You still like girls but want to be a boy."

She taps my mind again and a new memory takes over.

"In this world you are a boy and like boys," older Amara articulates.

Another tap on my mind and she continues this where I see multiple worlds of myself either as a girl or a boy. I want to be a boy but born as a girl. Born as a girl and wanting to be a boy that likes boys, then liking girls; followed by liking both boys and girls. The possibilities are endless.

"Okay, I get it. My mind can't take it any more. How is this supposed to help me," I question.

"It doesn't matter what Universe you are from, you will always face the fact you are different just like others out there," professes old Amara.

"This doesn't fix anything about what I face now," I state.

"You are correct, but things will change. You have a chance to continue to go down the dark path you are heading down, or change the direction you want to go. Living with a secret is a hardship no teen should ever have to go through," reveals older Amara.

With the wave of her hands we are transported to another world. Nothing is recognizable in this new place.

"Where are we now," I ask.

"It's the land of the unknown. The land of anger. The darkest place you will ever be. You are slowly entering into it now. You have accepted the anger due to you not being your authentic self. Walking in this world will have a heavy burden on your mind. This world will filter you out and affect so many. Facing it is what you have to do, as to not run away or let it consume you. Feeling pain and rejection from emotions is a healthy thing," older Amara explains.

This world I wonder about only began not that long ago. The formation of the anger came from my secret. I became the Frost Princess to the cold and reserved to others because I fear being really just me. I will never be until the one that brought me into this world is willing to accept me for me.

How can I walk in the same world with my Mother who denies me the idea that I could ever marry another girl? How can I walk in a Church that doesn't want to accept people who are different even though the Church worships Jesus who always sought out those who were different. I'm broken into a million pieces by virtue of I just don't want to hide any more. Words have to be carefully crafted to not let on that I might think that a girl is cute. Girls can say to each other, you look super cute in that outfit. It doesn't mean they are attracted to them; I just worry and fear if I say something like that they will catch on that I am attracted to girls.

My body is flooded by my tears even though I can't cry but these are the tears that I want to cry out. I cry on the inside on the account of crying about the pain of hiding then I have to tell people my emotions. I took the sword through my throat and stomach, only to return with anger at all worlds for the reason that I am stuck in this dark angerful world. I live with this burden on a daily basis.

When I blink I'm back in the snow covered valley; which of course, I blanketed in snow from my own rage. My older self is nowhere to be seen. The sun peeks over the mountains to create shadows and reflecting bright surfaces. Light and darkness in the same existence. In the light areas I can see the glimmer of the snow crystals. There is almost a calmness in the glazed over snow that is touched by the light. Even though the light touches the snow it still creates a shift in colors of dark spots.

The shadows of darkness have always been my friend, even so I have never noticed with the light there are shadows that I can walk amongst too. I can walk in the light while blending in with the rest. The shadows are resting spots for the light which can help carry the burden. Blending light and darkness keeps the balances. There is no perfect light. Light can fade into darkness; however, darkness can fade into light too.

I know now that I can blend between the shadows and the light. I can use both to carry me through the hurt times that are coming. It's about dancing or waltzing through the people around you. What support team can I have? To be a leader I need a team. My team brought me back for a reason. It's not for my selfish ways. The isolation of being a leader will not help me, I need to dance with the blending of the light and darkness of me. The world isn't all that dark.

Chapter 29

Protecting loved ones and yourself is a natural instinct. Animals go to great lengths to protect their young. I see this with cows when they give birth. Some cows are very protective of their young, while others don't know what to do when someone enters the pen. On the farm we remove the calf from the Mother so early as you can see the pain the Mother is in when their young is taken from them. There are some cows that mourn, and call for their young for several days. It is heartbreaking like none other.

People say that animals can't feel like humans, but that is not true. Animals feel emotions, all humans do, nevertheless it's the reaction to those emotions that separate us. Society has accepted females to express emotions, while males to express emotions is considered weak in society. Men are supposed to be strong willed to handle anything that comes their way. Males that show and express their emotions are made fun of in school, communities, by their parents and society. Why do we strip away almost 50% of the population to not show their emotions?

This denies men to actually feel less alive as a human. Emotions are not weak, they are a sign of strength. Those who allow themselves to express; in addition to, be vulnerable with their emotions to others, are stronger humans than those of society who are denied to be vulnerable to express their emotions. This is the same heartbreak I see in our cows when we take their calves away.

How can I express my emotions of how I am feeling right now? I am heartbroken that I broke up with Zali. Who can I even express that besides Zali. I don't want to talk to her right now. The hurt is too strong; however, my mind wanders all through morning chores thinking about what I did, and why I needed to do it.

Heartbreak sometimes happens which makes us stronger. I have been in protective mode my whole life. I live in fear everyday someone will find out my secret. Doesn't that make me only half alive, if not even alive. I am denying myself to feel the emotions out of fear someone will find out that I'm a lesbian. I'm almost 16, plus I have a choice to keep feeling emotionless by hiding; or become vulnerable to the emotions of what I'm actually feeling. What is the first step? Do I tell my family or friends? Do I start changing how I live by not worrying about each word I say and my body language? Worrying is an emotion I have denied myself to express and in its place I express anger.

All my emotions have been masked, they are only being expressed by anger now. This is no way to live, it's no way for anyone to live. I'm sure there are others like me out there; heck, I was shown by my older self there are. It's time to be a leader in my community to give a voice to others who are also trying to protect themselves. I need to gather a team of support, since I know the support will be lacking at home.

Finishing up chores, I realize the only other person who knows about me is Adelaide. Why do I forget about her when I say I have no support. Maybe, it's because I have only talked to her about it once. People talk to their friends about a break up, since I can't talk to my Mom about it.

I decided to give Adelaide a call once I got in for lunch, she should be up by then. Before I could get to the phone my Mom asked me how the party was at Adelaide's house. Even though my emotions are all over the place at the moment I go protective again. I explained we hung out playing Jenga (of course I'm not going to tell her it was true and dare), twister and other card games. I told her we had different snacks to eat and it was a fun night. I added I wished I could have slept overnight with the other girls. My Mom reassured me there would be other sleepovers with my girlfriends.

"Isn't the snowball dance coming up soon," my Mom asks.

"Yeah, it's on January 19th," I responded.

"That would be a good day to have a sleepover with your friends," replies Amara's Mom.

My Mom is encouraging a sleepover on a Saturday night when we have Church the next day. I guess my brother has done it before, so why not me.

"I guess so. We are still trying to figure out the details," I state.

"Well let me know where everyone is going for pictures. Between your brother and you I will be driving all over for pictures," expresses Amara's Mom.

"Hey mom, can I call Adelaide and see if she can hang out today," I ask.

"Don't you and Zali hang out? Besides, you were just out last night," implies Amara's Mom.

"How is that fair since Markus can go hang out with Miranda," I suggest.

"Well, Markus has his license," responds Arama's Mom.

"I need driving practice, remember. This would give me a chance to drive to Adelaide's," I divulge.

"I guess for a few hours will be okay. Just make sure you are back in time for chores, if someone doesn't show up Dad will need help," Amara's Mom claims.

"Thanks mom!"

When I finish my lunch I call Aledaie. It's 11:45 am, I hope she is awake.

"Hello," says Mrs. Fischer on the other end of the phone.

"Hi, Mrs Fischer, it's Amara," I respond

Hi Amara. How was work this morning," Mrs. Fischer asks.

"It was fine Mrs. Fischer. I was wondering if Adelaide is there," I inquired.

"She is still sleeping with her friends, but I am more than happy to wake her up so she doesn't sleep the day away," states Mrs. Fischer.

"Thanks Mrs. Fischer," I replied.

I wait patiently for Adelaide to come on the phone. She is my only hope to talk to someone today. While I wait I head to my room and close the door. I have to tell her Zali and I broke up. I can't go into protective mode.

"Hello," Adelaide says groggily.

"Hey, Adelaide," I whisper back.

"Why are you whispering, Amara," Adelaide asks.

"I don't want my Mom to hear this. You are the only one who knows about Zali and I," I whisper.

"Yeah, so what's up," inquires Adelaide.

I can feel the tears building as the emotions are building.

"I broke up with Zali last night," I say sadly.

"YOU DID WHAT? What happened," shouts Adelaide.

"I can't say right now. I am hoping we can get together so I can talk with you," I express.

"Amara, you just need to come here, so we can talk. Just hang in there girl. I know you are crying. Wipe the tears and get ready. I'll see you in a little bit," asserts Adelaide.

"Okay thanks, bye," I responded.

I wipe my tears from my eyes, then take a moment to gather myself. I change my clothes, and tell my Mom we need to drive to Adelaide's house. My Mom tells me she will pick me up around 3 pm so I'm home for chores. Sometimes I wish we didn't live on a farm so I didn't have to be home for chores all the time.

This is a big choice in my story to talk to Adelaide about this break up. I have no one else to talk to so it has to be her. I knock on the door with Adelaide answering to give me a big hug before I can walk into her home.

"How are you holding up," Adelaide asks.

"I'm fine," I mutter.

"Girl, you just experienced your first break up," she whispers back.

"No, I'll be okay. I just need someone to talk to," I whisper back.

As we walk to the kitchen, I see to my surprise, Skylar, Nika, and Jade are still there. I turn to look at Adelaide with a surprise look on my face. How can I talk about my break up with the other girls around? I can't do this.

"I told Skylar, Nika, and Jade you had a crisis and needed to talk so we all agreed to support you in your crisis. That's what friends do," Adelaide says.

"Besides, we are going to make chocolate chip pancakes with whipped cream," adds Jade.

Adelaide places her hand on my back and rubs it gently to comfort me.

"So Amara what's the crisis," asks Skylar.

"Is it boy trouble," asks Nika.

"It can't be a boy, she said last night she didn't have a boyfriend," replies Jade,

"That doesn't mean anything. Remember Jade, she said she has winter formal coming up. It could be a boy," replies Skylar as she throws a chocolate chip at Jade.

"It's probably not a relationship thing. Why don't we let Amara talk," adds Nika.

I try to fight back my tears at the moment. Protecting and hiding has been my go to my whole life. How can I open up to them? There are so many emotions running through me right now. I fear what they will say. What kind of judgment will they bring? I can't handle the negative words of how terrible of a person I am. I feel shameful for being a lesbian in front of these straight heterosexual girls.

Anxiety fills my body, as I need to leave. I am starting to panic. I have no way to leave. I just need to lie by making something up. Protection is the only way.

In this moment of panic I remember my older self telling me I have a choice to go down the dark path, or choose a different path. Then I feel an arm wrap around me and pull me in close. Adelaide places her hand on my head to bring my head to her chest.

"This is a safe place, Amara. You can tell us anything and it will stay safe here," says Adelaide.

"It totally is," replies Skylar as she comes over to give a group hug.

The other girls come over so we have a moment together in a group hug. The heartbreak in the moment feels better. I feel vulnerable to share. My support team is reaching out. As a team leader I need to recognize where the support is. This is my new team. My hidden secret can't be protected by just me. My demons are way too strong, besides I need a team of support to help me get through this break up in my own personal journey.

"Awe girls. Look at you all," says Mrs. Fischer as she walks into the kitchen. "What's going on girls?"

We all break away from the group hug. I pull away from Adelaide and wipe my tears from my eyes to sit on the stool.

"Mom, can you get some tissues for Amara," Adelaide asks Mrs. Fischer.

"Ya sure thing sweety. Is everything okay," inquires Mrs. Fischer.

"Yeah, Mom it's fine. Nothing us girls can't handle," replies Adelaide.

Mrs. Fischer brings me a box of tissues for me, and leaves the kitchen to let us be. I wipe my tears and blow my nose. My vulnerable emotions and protective armor softens. I have trusted Adelaide since our friendship started. She has kept my secret so if she says this is a safe place then I should trust her again.

I lift my head to the girls to state, "I broke up with Zali last night."

There was a pause in the room while they processed the information.

"Like, Zali from last night," asks Nika.

"Yes," I confess.

"See I told you it wasn't boy trouble," replies Jade as she slaps Nika's arm.

"We had no idea you two were dating," states Nika.

"Oh my god, I kissed your girlfriend. I'm so sorry I didn't know. That isn't the reason you broke up," states Skylar as she places her hands on her face in shock by what she did.

"Oh no Skylar it's not because of that," I affirm.

"Was it Adelaide then? She kissed Zali a few times too," replies Nika.

"Hey don't blame me. I knew they were together," replies Adelaide.

"Wait what!? You knew and you still kissed Zali. You are such a bitch Adelaide," says Jade.

"Look who's talking Jade. You kissed Amara. Maybe it was you," says Nika.

"No, no, no, it wasn't because of all the kissing and who kissed who. I just couldn't keep hiding the secret of our relationship. Adelaide is the only person besides Zali who knows I'm a lesbian," I come out with my secret.

"What's wrong with being a lesbian," asks Jade.

"Everything! My family is super religious as well as my community. Being a lesbian is a huge sin. I can't come out to my family and friends in my community," I respond with angst.

"Why did you tell Adelaide then? You trusted someone," Skylar asks.

"Well she never actually told me. We were back in middle school, and Amara tried to kiss me. I have kept her identity safe this whole time," Adelaide confesses.

"Wow this is getting to be a crazy story," Nika says.

"The pressure of hiding who I am, while hiding this relationship just has broken me. I can't be myself around anyone in public. I just couldn't do it anymore," I disclose.

Jade places a hand on mine for comfort to state, "it is very brave of you to share your true self with all of us. You and I have more in common than you realize."

I am confused by Jade's response.

"What do you mean," I ask.

"Well, tell her Jade. She needs the support," states Skylar.

"I'm bisexual," Jade states.

I am surprised by her response. I guess I'm not as alone as I thought I am in this world.

"Don't take this the wrong way Jade, but does that mean you are like Zali, as in dating boys and girls," I inquired.

"Yes it does. Also I didn't know Zali was bi-sexual. When you said she was your girlfriend, I figured she was a lesbian too," Jade responds.

I started to explain my story of how Zali and I started talking during the summer and how it turned into a romance. I filled them in on as many details as possible, pouring out my heart and tears to the girls. It really felt great after to now have three other people know I'm a lesbian. They are all super supportive and have no judgment. I guess I have misconceptions about all people. I figured with my upbringing that no one would be accepting of me. I thought I would have to move out of the small town USA to finally be able to be me and accepted. Having friends who I can connect with to be myself around is refreshing. Also knowing Jade is bi-sexual gives me someone to talk and connect with. For the first time in my life I don't feel lost, plus trapped in the darkness. A new light now shines on my life.

Chapter 30

My heart is broken by my break up with Zali, so why did I hurt so much when I ended the relationship? Maybe the fact that she was my first girlfriend. The hurt comes from knowing someone else will be spending time with her and not me. The difficult thing is I still have to work with her, which becomes awkward at times. Instead of flirting and sneaking in a kiss, my body is filled with anxiety around her. This is not the same anxiety of excitement when the relationship first started, this is pain. My chest and shoulders are tight, plus filled with anxiety. How do I act around her? What do I say around her? I have become hyper vigilant around her to not express any emotions, or body language that would show my attraction towards her still. Managing these emotions is extremely difficult. I am trying to be civil as much as possible with Zali. Can we be friends moving forward, I have no idea what the future holds.

I dwell on the past on how I could have done things different. These thoughts are like torture to me. Why does my conscious want to torture myself with these thoughts? I wish the thoughts would leave my consciousness even though they don't. There is nothing I can do to change the past, but learn from it. I guess that is easier said than done.

I cry at night in my room alone with the pain bringing an ache I have never felt before. I can't even talk to my Mom about the break up. I would love to seek out some advice from her, nonetheless that would require me to open up about my true self. My attention turns to my new friends I have made. Adelaide, Jade, Nika, and Skylar are the only ones that know about my true self. I spend more time on the phone in my room talking to them. I live in isolation in my room feeling alone, yet I have my girlfriends to talk with. They are the ones helping me through this break up.

My school's formal dance is now just eleven days away after a week has passed since Zali and I have broken up. Zali and I briefly talked about Snowball, which is the name of our winter formal, besides never getting around to making plans. I think the fear of navigating the dance with my girlfriend gave me some extreme anxiety. As much as I was trying to tell myself everyone will think Zali and I are just friends, I couldn't shift those hyper vigilant thoughts of my secret being in jeopardy.

Jade and I have really connected after the party on new years eve. She has openly shared things about herself; by all means, I have too about myself which has been very helpful navigating my break up. It also paints a new perspective for me. Jade's parents know about her sexuality and are accepting of her. I am surprised and really happy for her. She knew in middle school, and came out to her parents then. Jade was very nervous as well as scared to tell her parents as a consequence there was also fear of rejection on her part. That fear was shattered when she told her parents the truth about her authentic self. Her parents reassured her they loved her and supported her no matter who she liked or dated.

Relying on friends is the only way to get through this break up and possibly helping with life's journey as a lesbian. What I have learned is to be grateful for the friends I have who are supportive. My nights are filled with restlessness and nightmares. Maybe not all nightmares, even so dreams that are troubling and sad. The nights range from the break up, to my parents finding out about my secret. There is an underlying fear my parents will find out; however, the strange thing is I actually feel better now that others know about me, so there might be a slim chance of hope after all. Even though they don't go to the same school as me, I can just be myself around them if I want. I don't have to worry about my secret slipping out because of something I say or my body language. I don't have to be hyper vigilant causing anxiety for myself.

It is amazing what a little support can do for a person, even though the break up is sad and it hurts daily, there is healing in this process. I was able to tell someone, well not just one but three others which gives me five total people that know I am a lesbian. That's quite a lot more where I began in the summer. The hurt and pain of the break up is difficult because all I have is my four friends to talk to help me get through it. The isolation in my room during the week is not helping. I try to hang with Skylar, Jade, Nika and Adelaide on the weekend for a distraction. All distractions are welcome to stop myself from overthinking.

I decided to ask Jade to my winter formal. I thought about Adelaide, but there is something about Jade's spirit and confidence I admire. Maybe that's why we have connected so well. She understands the struggle I am going through. Besides, they all asked me to come to their winter formal at the end of January. They know I need to be around people to help with a break up; heck, I have no one else to talk about it with.

I'm kind of lucky that Jade also has her license so she can drive us to the dance even though I just got my license two days prior. My parents didn't want my first big solo driving experience to be the school formal at night. Since I could only bring one guest from another school, I just felt more comfortable going with Jade to the dance. I know Zali will be there and to have someone who also has a secret like me will help me get through the dance.

The day of the dance arrives and I have nerves of anxiety. This is supposed to be my chance to get all dressed up with Zali, and now that is not happening. It will be difficult to see her hair beautifully done in her pretty dress. I guess that's the hard thing about break ups, my mind wonders about every possible scenario that might have been. How do I get through the pain of this heartache? The best thing is going to the dance with some friends. My friends will be there, yet I chose not to go with them. Skylar, Adelaide, Nika, Jade and myself were going to go out to dinner then Jade and I were going to attend my school dance.

My Mom took me to get my hair done in the morning. We had small talk at the salon with the beautician. Typical questions for a school dance conversation: did a boy ask you to the dance or are you going with friends? I still have the anxiety of my secret when these questions are asked. It definitely is eating away at me. My dance nerves are also hard to keep under wraps. I slowly get ready as the day passes, still it's hard to stop my mind from wandering. Someone make these thoughts stop.

There is an urge in the late afternoon to pick up the phone to ask Zali if we could go together to the dance. I am missing her more than I thought, even though that must be common when you can't have what you want. I definitely took her for granted when I withdrew from her. Why can't people realize that at the moment. Why does it take some heart aching moment to have the realization you miss someone.

I try to stay focused on the night ahead. I put on my strapless black glittery dress. I do love color but the silver glitter is so cute I had to get the dress. It has a slit up the side leg too. Jade and the other girls arrive at my place to pick me up. My Mom wants a few pictures of the friend group before we head to dinner.

Jade has a stunning bright pink spaghetti strap dress with a flower design from the breasts to the waist on it. Her hair has curls that are hanging while part of her black hair is pinned up. She looks super cute. We take our pictures to enjoy the moment then head out to dinner. My nerves calm some at dinner while we all laugh and enjoy each other's company. This is my few moments of distraction before I see Zali at the dance.

"Are you nervous about tonight," Jade asked while we drove to the dance.

"Extremely nervous," I responded.

"It will be okay. We are going to have an amazing time," proclaims Jade.

"It's just, Zali will be there. I'm not sure how to navigate the night after being in a relationship with her, and now I have to act like we never dated because I fear I will show some kind of emotions more than friends towards her. I can't do this," I profess.

"Yes you can. You have me here with you for support," states Jade as she reaches over to squeeze my hand, as she can tell I'm starting to have an anxiety attack.

"Zali is just a friend now just like any other friend. You can do it. Sure will you see her, most likely, but doesn't mean you have to talk to her or dance next to her," exclaims Jade.

I squeeze her hand back from her words of encouragement. I have never navigated these uncharted waters. This is a brand new journey with an ex-girlfriend. That awkward feeling builds as we get closer to the dance. My heart aches because my ex-girlfriend will be there, which I just want to give her a kiss and hug. I want to hold her close on the dance floor, yet all my desires can not happen for multiple reasons, the pain is too real.

"Girl you got this. You are cute, beautiful, stunning in that black dress. Let's go dance the night away and have fun," Jade verbalizes.

"Yeah, let's do this Jade," I affirm.

My stomach turns upside down and side to side as we enter the dance. I feel like I'm going to puke with nerves.

"Amara, look at me, you got this. Deep breath in! Now let it out," Jade conveys.

Jade holds out her arm to lead me in.

"My lady shall we dance," Jade says smiling.

I slip my arm around her to state, "why yes, lets dance,"

Music is blaring from the dance floor. Most people have arrived by now and we hand over our tickets to Mr. Cruise and head in. We walk in locked arms. Why am I not hyper vigilant about this? Jade is a friend, yet I'm not worried what people think of me with my arms locked with her. As we walk in I catch Zali across the room from the corner of my eye. She looks amazing in her dress. Then that heartache attacks me like a lion attacking its prey.

I turn to Jade to whisper to her, "I think I'm going to be sick. I just saw Zali. I can't do this. My heart hurts too much."

"Okay let's just go to the restroom first and collect ourselves. I get it, break ups are difficult. Remember she is also struggling with this break up too," affirms Jade.

We head to the restroom so I can collect myself. The last thing I want is to start crying and my makeup gets ruined. There are several other girls also in the bathroom. I'm sure the boys restroom isn't as crowded as the girls. Jade and I stand next to the sink and mirror to check our makeup, especially my eyes as my eyes are teary.

"Just breathe Amara," Jade whispers to me.

I breathe in and close my eyes to collect myself. Then I let out a deep breath and opened my eyes.

"Wow, you are so beautiful in that dress," exclaims Kelly.

I turn my head to the right to see Kelly standing next to me.

"Where did everyone else go," I ask.

"It's just you and me, my princess. I am not going to miss your dance to see you this beautiful," expresses Kelly.

Kelly gives me a kiss on the cheek and holds my hand.

"I know you are in pain my love. Heartache is no fun. Heck I'm stuck in a marriage I hate, but I love my child, nevertheless can't be with who I want to be with. You are a Universe away from me and that sucks," Kelly denotes.

"I can't keep going forward Kelly. I'm so lost. I have lost my girlfriend, my will to live and lead. I have gone cold," I responded.

"I can tell you have gone cold. You are in more pain than just the breakup. You want to be free. Look at you now, you have more freedom than you did the last time we saw each other. Life will get better. I just don't want you to go down the wrong path. I fear for you Amara," insists Kelly.

"My reality sucks. I will never be free," I proclaim

"That's why your armor has changed to the Frost Princess. Don't let the cold consume you. Amara, you are the strongest girl I have ever met. Go out there and show the world who Amara the Frost Princess is. I would love to stay and have just one dance with you, but I can't," states Kelly.

"Please don't go Kelly. I need you to help get me through tonight," I confess.

"You can do it. You are strong and beautiful. Go and be that princess tonight on the dance floor."

Kelly and I lean in for a kiss. Once we kiss I open my eyes as I pull away to realize I just kissed Jade.

"Oh my god Jade I am so sorry. I should not have done that," I divulge.

Jades smiles at me and replies, "don't be sorry," then kisses me back.

Chapter 31

Standing in a plain of existence of time that transcends in a multitude of directions. Time is consuming my inner thoughts. Why is the question that circulates my consciousness all about time? Time seems so linear to humans. I keep moving forward since that's all I can see. The present moment as reflecting on memories of the past is all I have to understand time. Humans can make predictions for the future, still it is unknown, but is it really unknown to us? The brain is a very complex organ that people have a hard time understanding. There it is again the concept of time. In some way all humans are obsessed with time at some point in our lives. Children that want to grow up fast are obsessed with time speeding up. Little children want for their birthday or Christmas, they wish time would speed up so it comes quicker. The waiting or anticipation of time to pass is difficult for all of us humans.

There are moments when I want to get lost in the moment of time because the joy is so great. I wish time would slow down just so I can be in that moment a little longer. A shadow creature of sadness lurks in the corner while joy fills the room. The sadness just makes its presence known, nonetheless never interferes. Even the joy of a moment ends while the next emotion and feeling takes its place. Time is constantly changing even though I see it as linear with that is where the struggle comes from. The unexpected changes that time brings is difficult for any part of my consciousness to understand.

There are moments humans wish they could go back in time to have another chance to spend more time with a loved one, or they want to amend a mistake they made. Focusing on the past that they can't change drives them into an emotional state that is different for everyone else. The emotions that circulate from the past drive human behavior of the present which affects their future. In some extremes it's like a snowball effect. People obese about the past which creates some sort of tension or issue in the present. That action seems to alter our future thanks to people thinking about the past again and saying to themselves, "if only, should, could, would of," even though time moves on in linear motion.

What if our thoughts as humans of the past as how things could have been different or trying to predict outcomes of the future events is a way for our consciousness to see the past. The linear time stream we as humans are experiencing the events. Is it possible humans have the ability to tap into an alternate time stream of parallel worlds? What if our physical selves can't travel through time, but our consciousness can? What would the possibilities be like? The possibilities would be endless; however, the understanding of our conscious time travel might be too complex for our brains. That is where I stand now; time is either my friend or enemy. What if I could control time? I could change the events, or live in a world that is accepting of me. I want to be in a world where I can just be my authentic self.

There is a mixture of cool and warm breeze swirling around me in this plain of existence. The invisible line of cold front and warm front can not be seen, even though it is felt. I now feel like I am stuck in the middle of this front. Time is flowing forward and backwards all at the same moment. It is creating vortexes throughout this plain. The past, present, and future are a three front system that has generated these time vortexes. This plain is a rocky barren place with melting clocks that are slowly warping into the time vortexes.

Time slips from these clocks as they slowly warp into the vortexes with the ticking of the clock going silent. It's a constant Tic Toc by the thousands of clocks in this plain. My only protection is my Frost Princess armor. My defenses are stronger with this new armor. I am still getting used to it. When I have the armor on I feel cold; not withstanding the cold temperature feeling, but cold hearted, defensive, and angry. It's the ultimate protection of not letting in many emotions or feelings in. I feel like it's strength and power that will help me overcome anything. I feel unstoppable with the Frost Princess armor on.

Being emotionless is really not being human. What am I doing, besides protecting myself some more, but am I really protecting myself? I bury my emotions in this new armor and begin to explore this plain of time. The mystery unfolds with each step I take as my feet crunch on the rocks beneath me. The grinding and crunching sound drifts and floats away in the air through the vortex to be lost in time. My sense is I am not alone here. Something or someone is here with me. Proceed with caution as I draw both my ice swords from my back. More defense for me.

"Come on let's go dance," Jade says to me as she pulls away from kissing me.

"Yeah, let's go," I say with a smile, yet the fear reflects in the bathroom mirror of what just happened.

I just kissed Jade in a public bathroom at a school dance with other girls in the bathroom, then she returned a kiss to me. The fear and panic crawl at me to make my heart race. My hands begin to sweat too. The feeling of the moment of joy is taken away by the other element that is standing in the corner; fear, anxiety, panic, and worry. I became vulnerable in a moment of weakness. It is uncharacteristic of myself. I am so conscious of everything I do to make sure I protect myself. This is a moment I wish I could go back in time to alter what just happened. Yes the kiss was enjoyable, in spite of that now I am regretting it out of fear of who saw me. What have I done? How can I enjoy the rest of the dance? My life is over.

The music is loud and it's hard to hear anything Jade is saying, yet she takes my hand and pulls me to the dance floor. Why do I let her take my hand? What are people thinking of that? I want to scream, even though my face puts on a smile to enjoy the moment. My insides are screaming in a panic. I just want out of this situation, We all can fake our emotions to deceive others to make it look like we are happy. I'm a pro at creating an illusion so things are perfectly fine.

My mind slips in and out of reality the rest of the night. I struggle seeing Zali on the dance floor and I try to avoid her as much as possible, besides it seems like she is doing the same. There are moments when I make small talk with other friends, however I stay close to Jade. I am scared and panicking that people know my secret now due to Jade and I kissing in the bathroom. I just want this dance to be over to be out of this situation; however, there is a part of me that wants one slow dance with a girl. Zali isn't an option as much as I stare at her throughout the night.

"It can't be easy seeing your ex-girlfriend here. I'm sorry," Jade whispers into my ear, then gives me a shoulder bump.

"Thanks for coming with me tonight Jade. It means so much to me to have you hear. You are right, it isn't easy," I mutter back.

I begin to tear up. I try wiping my tears away without ruining my makeup.

"Do you want to go," asks Jade.

"No, it's fine," I reply as I wipe more tears from my eyes.

"Whatever you want to do, I'll do. This is your dance lady," expresses Jade.

What I want I can't have. I want to hold a girl close in my arms around her beautiful dress and slow dance. I want her arms around me holding me close as we slow dance. I want to rest my head on her shoulder as I tune out everything else. I want to get lost in the moment with her on the dance floor. I want to be a normal girl without judgment from others because I like girls.

"Then you should just come dance with me," exclaims Kelly.

I look up to see Kelly standing in front of me in a beautiful green dress with gold flower design on her dress.

"You came back," I state as I wipe more tears from my eyes.

"I couldn't pass up the opportunity to dance with you. So let's go, Amara. Let me give you that dance you want," asserts Kelly.

Kelly reaches out her hand to me and I extend my hand. Our fingers touch and that spark melts my heart. My breath is taken away as our heels click walking to the dance floor. Kelly spins me around as the DJ's lights on Kelly's dress give it a shimmer and shine. This is the moment I have been waiting for. I am just a teenage girl, still the moments that we as humans crave in time are so precious.

After my spin, Kelly pulls me close as we wrap our arms around each other to gaze into each other's eyes. There is music playing and others on the dance floor, however for this moment of time I am lost. This feels like a good lost in time moment. I'm with someone that makes me feel complete. She doesn't judge me for anything I do. I feel her skin with my arms around her shoulder and neck, it's soft and delicate. I close my eyes and lean in close to her to rest my head on her forehead. The warmth of her forehead fills my heart with a sense of calmness. For just a three minute song I get to experience something I have desired since I danced with Adelaide at the roller skate rink. At the end of the song I give Kelly a kiss on the lips.

"Thank you for the dance," I exclaim.

"You are welcome," replies Jade.

My reality has been distorted by what happened. That three minutes of time is gone, and the fear pours in as I look around to see people staring at us.

"Amara, look at me. Look at me! It will be alright. I'm not going anywhere," Jade affirms.

"What do I do? What have I done to myself," I come out with a panic.

"It will be okay. Let's just slowly leave the dance floor, then leave the dance. Clearly this was too much and that's okay," replies Jade.

"Oh my god, Jade," I say in a panic.

"The more you panic the more you draw attention to yourself," affirms Jade.

We had to find our coats so we could leave. I just want out of this situation. What have I done? I let my guard down. Now my secret is out. I am not ready for this. Tears fill my eyes, and Jade wipes them away as she hands me my coat.

"Look there goes the two dykes," an unrecognizable voice calls out to both of us from a boy standing next to his buddy.

Those words pierce me like I am just shot by an arrow. Jade pauses and turns her body to them. I don't see her face, but she puts her middle finger up to them. I'm sure her facial look was not a pleasant look along with her middle finger.

"Let's get out of here," Jade tells me as she ushers me out.

"FU too, you dykes," The boy's voice calls out.

Jade pushes the door open and we step outside into the cold. My secret is out, plus how do I manage my life going forward. My hands are shaking while tears pour out of my eyes and down my face. Those boys used hurtful words towards me and Jade. My worst fear is happening. How do I escape from this moment in time?

This is a moment of time I wish I could go back in time to change what just happened. How can I even describe this kind of panic I am experiencing right now? What are my choices going forward? I'm sure if those boys know my secret most of the school also knows now. I will be the talk of the school all weekend. How will Monday look at school? I can't enter school on Monday.

Fear is the driving force for my next decision in my life. I am not ready for my secret to be out to the world tonight. The fear is accompanied with worry that the events of the kiss, and slow dance will get back to my parents. Oh Shit, my brother. When he finds out, if not already, he will definitely tell my parents to confront me about it.

The time stream that I have now created is unpredictable tonight. If I could control time I would change this moment. Tonight is not how I wanted to come out to the world. The negative reaction leaving the dance is hurtful. I wish the reaction was the same as it was with Skylar, Nika, Jade and Adelaide. Coming out to the world to be my authentic self was never going to be easy and there is no road map for what is to come. Will there be any support in my school? What will Zali do moving forward? Will she come to my aid and support me?

These emotions are intense. I am not mentally ready for this new journey in my time stream. My defensive protective mode is no longer there. I am in uncharted territory. What time stream do I create going forward? I wish there is a better sense of direction than the panic I'm feeling. Life will be different going forward as a new chapter in my life has begun. I feel like I want to freeze myself in time right now so I don't have to face the future. The future is more terrifying now that more people know my secret than when I was hiding. My next choice in time will ripple through thousands of lives. This is new pressure I have never felt before. I am scared, terrified, fearful, worried of the unknown future that lies ahead as the world now knows Amara is a lesbian.

"Hello Amara! Looks like you have a problem on your hands? I have been watching you for the past six months," proclaims Kumari.

I draw my swords up in defensive mode ready for an attack by her.

"Kumari, what are you doing here," I replied.

Chapter 32

We all fear what we don't understand or fear the unknown. It's like a creepy horror film where every corner is terrifying. Maybe you have a flashlight so you can see in the dark but you are too scared to use it because whatever is lurking and stalking you in the dark you don't want to give out your location. In that moment one feels safer to not have a light to guide oneself through the dark. Maybe whatever is terrifying you it will not find you; nonetheless, it seems in every horror film that thing still finds you in the dark. Helpless, hopeless, and despaired are the feelings that are whispered in my ear. I am the one now trapped in a horror film.

"Amara, Amara, Amara! Tiss, Tiss, Tiss! Look at you feeling sad and wanting to be vulnerable but you can't. Is that new armor you have? It's catchy. I would give it a seven out of ten. I don't know yet if it shoots you," Kumari states as she slowly steps in a circle around me dragging her sword into the ground.

Kumari is a tall warrior, approximately six feet to six foot-two. She has vibrant orange hair to go along with her body warrior markings. I call them tattoos, yet Kumari says they are not. Her warrior paint around her eyes is beautifully blended colors of a sunset, heavy on the orange in close view. It's almost like her warrior paint changes colors with each step as if the lighting that touches her face causes time to pass as if her face is an actual setting sun.

Kumari's armbands are bright golden yellow with ancient symbols on them that I don't even recognize. Her breasts/chest plate is a darker orange with thin black lines swirled around in an intricate design; and extends just over the shoulders almost like hands gently being placed on Kumari's shoulders. Her abdomen is bare; however, covered in symbols which once again can I please call them tattoos, however she has always instant they are not. These warp around her entire body. The colors flow from black to orange to yellow and back to black. With each step she takes the colors on her body flow as if they are a river always changing. Kumari also has close to a hundred orange and yellow gemstone piercings across her abdomen hugging her side to embrace her back.

Kumari wears a pleated black leather, or is it a hide material skirt? We have never exchanged fashion advice or tips. We don't hang out at the mall to go shopping. Around her waist are vibrant golden yellow chains that are attached at the waistline and create hanging loops that overlap each other. Her boats have a metal-plated glimmer as an orange and yellow reflection similar to a reflection on a claim lake. Where she hides all the weapons she possesses is a mystery to me. Kumari is a mystery even though she and I have a long history.

"What brings you here, Kumari," I inquire.

I slowly rotate with my swords still drawn, while Kumari ever so slowly stalks me almost like I'm the prey and she is the predator.

"I can't make a visit to my oldest and dearest friend, Amara," declares Kumari with a spicy attitude.

"We are not friends," I confess.

Kumari always has a sassy tone when she talks, almost like she is overconfident.

"Tell me Amara, how are you feeling that your secret is out," Kumari asks.

What is with her and the twenty questions?

"What secret are you talking about," I reply.

"Oh please, you didn't think I would not find out," proclaims Kumari.

"Enough with the questions Kumari and cut to the chase," I snapped at her in some frustration.

"Well, well looks like someone wants to fight," Kumari states as she fakes a lunge at me.

Kumari's lunge startles me, putting me in a more defensive posture.

"Oh there is no need to fight, I just want to see the struggle you are going through. You have been through so much, and this new armor is definitely masking something. What could it be," claims Kumarit.

Kumari places her index finger on her lips to give me a puzzled expression.

"What the fact that I died and came back to life," I responded, trying to cut to the point already.

I figured that is what she was referring to. Kumari laughs at my response.

"Is that how you got your new powers? Awe that is so sweet the Universe gave you a gift on your resurrection, but NO," Kumarit signifies.

Confusion sets in my mind as this was the only major event that has taken place. Word travels fast for some reason, so what is she talking about? Kumari pauses her circling around me and stares directly into my eyes like she is looking for an answer in my mind. Then Kumari cracks a smile at me. I'm even more confused. She is just trying to get into my head. Suddenly I feel a shift in the air as my hair on my arms stand up.

"Now you feel it Amara," states Kumari.

Kumari gets a serious look on her face. The energy of the environment we are both standing in has shifted like the change of winds as a storm rolls in. I feel a sickness coming over me as my stomach begins to ache.

"What have you done," I say to Kumari.

"It's the same question I want to ask you. What did you do Amara? Cause there is this sick feeling across the Universe," Kumari says in a serious tone.

"I have no idea what you are talking about," I reply

Suddenly a searing pain hits me like a full-on impact like diving into a pool all sprawled out. I drop both of my swords and drop to my knees. The pain is so intense. Worse than any period cramps I have ever felt. My head drops down so I can curl into a ball because the pain is so intense. I try to lift my head up to look at Kumari, but all I see is her boot being thrust at my face.

I let out a scream in the car as Jade presses the brakes to slow down and pulls over.

"Are you okay," she asks.

"No," I reply as I continue to wipe the tears off my face.

Jade unbuckles her seatbelt and leans in to embrace me with a hug. She just holds me as I cry in her car parked on the side of the road. Soft music plays on the radio, even though I'm not focused on the words. It feels like several minutes pass with no words being said, Jade just holds me as I continue to cry.

I slowly lift my head off Jade's shoulder as I turn my head to stare out the front windshield with the headlights beaming brightly into the night sky with the snow covered ground. Jade begins to rub my tears back while no words are exchanged. I feel she understands the situation that I am now in. She is out at her school, for all that her school has like 1500 students, mine has like 300. I want to feel comfort in this moment with her, however the shock just gives me a blank stare with tears.

I can feel Jade's eyes locked on me bringing with them concern for my emotional state. Something off in the distance catches my eye through the shining headlights. Is it an animal? Did someone follow us? I can't remember whether a car passed us or not while we sat stationary in the parked car. I want to say something to Jade if she sees what I am seeing, but I think the shock of everything has made me speechless. The object's shadow becomes clearer in the headlights revealing it is walking upright, so definitely not an animal. A person?

"Who the hell is that," Jade expresses loudly as it shakes me out of my trance. "Do you see this Amara?"

"Ah ya," I reply

"I think we need to go," Jade replies and puts the car into drive.

"This is really creepy, like a horror film creepy," claims Jade.

"Go Go Go Jade," I state.

I feel the panic in my voice as well as the panic on Jade's face. The person is continuing to walk toward us as we begin to drive. As we pass the individual who was walking towards us, they pause to stare at us. Jade and I both look at her standing on the side of the road.

"Is she in some kind of costume? Damn she must be cold and looks the part of a serial killer," states Jade.

Even though it's dark I can tell who it is. We lock eyes as we drive by Kumari. How is this possible? Jade can see Kumari? I know I have slipped into my imagination before while dealing with some sort of issue, but Jade can see her!

Chapter 33

I lay floating on my back in the cool lake staring up at the stars. There is no moonlight so the sky is dancing with white lights. My hair falls down as it floats on the surface of the water while my body slowly moves up and down between the gentile ripples. There is a claiming piece of mind as I float. There is no one else present with me, just me and the stars. I am far enough out in the lake that the sounds of the shore and night bugs are a faint sound. How did I become lost in this particular moment? I don't feel alone or sad, just content at the moment. Perhaps this is my calm before the storm. My mind needs to be prepared for what will be unfolding in the coming days.

It's the meeting of the minds this morning as Nika, Jade, and Adelaide are at Jade's house. Skylar was unable to attend because of a family event she was attending. We are all having breakfast together to game plan the crisis I am in after Jade and I kissed on the dance floor with my secret out now. I can hear the other three girls chattering while I stare at my blueberry pancakes. Nika places some bacon and eggs in front of me too.

"Try to eat something," Nika states to me as she places her hand on my shoulder.

My ears begin to tune into what Jade is telling other girls.

"Ladies, get this, last night while we were parked on the side of the road so Amara could collect her thoughts. A strange lady dressed in some kind of warrior Halloween costume appears out of nowhere. She was walking towards my car," exclaims Jade.

"What!?!?! That is really creepy," Adelaide replies.

"Ya, like right out of a horror film," rebuttals Nika as she bites a piece of bacon in her hand.

"That's what I was thinking too. I thought we were going to be chopped up into little pieces and never seen again," replies Jade with an elevation in her voice showing concern for the situation.

"I'm glad you two are okay from that situation," states Nika.

"Do you think you know who it might have been? Someone from the dance playing a prank," asks Adedaide.

"Her name is Kumari," I reply as I look up now fixated on the refrigerator while still having a blank look on my face.

"Kumari," Jade replies with confusion.

"Is she from your school," Adelaide asks.

As all three of them stop what they are doing while crowding around the island countertop I am sitting at in the kitchen. Well one secret is out so why not share this secret too. It has never turned out well for me sharing my imagination with people; however, Adelaide is here and she knows a small part of my imagination.

"No, Kumari is not a classmate, she is from my imagination, and I don't understand how Jade was able to see Kumari here in reality last night," I proclaim.

I waited for a response from one of the girls to say a nice joke to laugh it off as a way for me to lighten my mood and the mood in the kitchen, yet they didn't. The three girls seemed hooked by what I just said. Look at the events that happened in less than 24 hours. I kissed Jade in the bathroom, we kissed on the dance floor, had an intimate dance with Jade, and Kumari appeared out of nowhere in my own reality. Why not add this to the craziness?

"What do you mean she is from your imagination," Nika asks with just the right amount of curiosity to show she is taking this seriously, but maybe a little skeptical too.

My eyes roll up to the right to give Adeladie a look. She gives me a little nod to proceed.

"Wait, what was that look between you too," Jade says while pointing back and forth at both of us.

"Spill the tea," replies Nika.

Adeladie lets out a sigh to explain, "I know about Amara's imagination."

"You were going to withhold this information from us while I am telling you about some crazy murderous woman approaching my car," shouts Jade.

"Jade and Amara could have been killed," replies Nika.

"I didn't know Amara's imagination would come to life. She never told me that part," Adelaide barks back.

"Oh great now there's some crazy bitch out to kill Amara, and Jade as an accessory," replies Nika.

The hysteria is building in the room and I have no idea how to respond. This never happened before. Everything in my imagination stays in my imagination. That world is my escape, except now it's becoming real! I slam my hands on the counter top of the island to stand up to make an explanation.

"Ladies, there is way too much going on right now. I can't think straight or process anything. I have too many crises. My school, family, parents probably all know I'm a lesiban. Now my greatest foe in my imagination is wandering around somewhere in my own reality, and not in my head anymore. I don't have the power to stop her, so ya we are all dead," I exclaim.

I can feel the panic setting in as my heart begins to race and breathing becomes shallower.

"Whoa, Whoa, Whoa you have powers Amara? THAT'S AWESOME," Nika shouts out.

"No, I don't have powers. Only in my imagination world," I reply

"Wait, if Kumari is here then maybe your powers from your imagination are now real too," says Jade.

"Dude," Nika backhanded Jade's stomach, "your girlfriend is a super hot lesiban superhero! How cool is that," states Nika.

"OUCH," shouts Jade, as Jade hits Nika back on the shoulder.

"Okay it just got really awkward in here with that comment," Adelaide declares.

"What? Jade likes Amara. Amara likes Jade. They kissed. They are practically dating," determines Nika as she takes a sip from her mug.

I can see Jade's face get a little red and I could feel my cheeks get hot and red. Definitely some awkwardness as well as a few things Jade and I probably should discuss at some point.

"Timeout ladies. What if Jade is right and Amara can use her powers outside of her imagination," mentions Adelaide.

"Does Kumari have powers," asks Jade.

"Yes," I reply profusely!

"Perhaps Kumari used her powers to escape your imagination. This is totally out of a science fiction movie," rejoinders Jade.

"Look, even if it is true, I could use my imagination powers that aren't going to solve problem one. I am no longer hidden as a lesbian," I counter back.

"What kind of powers do you have," interrogates Nika as Adelaide slaps Nika on the shoulder.

"What, I'm curious about her powers," Nika professes.

"Amara is right, we need to help her with how to communicate to her family and navigate school. We will worry about crazy bitch later," voices Jade.

Ring! Ring! All of us are startled by the phone ringing.

"Maybe it's crazy bitch," riposte Nika.

"Hello! Hi Amara's Mom, yes she is," Jade answers the phone.

Oh no! My stomach drops what feels like ten floors in less than a second. I become instantly hot, almost like someone cranked up the heat in the house. I scan my eyes at Adelaide first, next Nika, and then Jade who is holding the phone. Every single bad outcome thought has come racing in my mind about a million times the speed of light. All three girls have the oh shit look on their faces, still no words can be said. I proceed to get off the stool to walk toward Jade to talk to my Mother. This is definitely not going to go well. My hands begin to shake in terror as I grab the phone from Jade and place the phone to my ear.

I feel myself losing my ability to stay afloat as I slowly drift under the water with each passing moment. I feel the change in the temperature of the water. The cool temperatures on the surface fade quickly to shear ice cold as actual ice passes me by floating to the surface. The twinkling of the stars have vanished to complete darkness. There is no more contentment. I try not to let panic set in, nevertheless it's really hard to resist and block it out. I feel alone at this moment. There can't be anyone possibly understanding the feeling I am experiencing at this moment. Is this what the feeling of drowning is like, because I am feeling like the breath of my life is exhaling from me. The life I have known is drifting further away as I sink to the bottom of the lake. Lost to time itself with no help to pull me back to the surface, my existence is buried in the depths of the lake.

Chapter 34

My greatest fear has come true at a time I feel like I don't have any support. Will my parents kick me out? No they wouldn't do that. An intervention with the pastor and youth pastor for sure. I'll probably never be able to go anywhere again. They won't trust me with any of my girlfriends. This panic is overwhelming as my chest gets heavier and heavier with each breath I take. I feel there is no hope for me. My Mom will go all religious on me while my Dad will follow suit, but with more frustration behind it. Dad will be stern in his response while my Mom will try to use her loving support only through sheer disappointment. It feels like people are tearing each of my organs out one by one as the breakfast I didn't really eat might come back up. I want to be positive right now, even though there isn't anything. It's just all negative going forward for me.

"Hi mom," I say.

"Amara, you need to come home this instance. What is Jade's address so I can come get you," declares Amara's Mom.

"Mom, I will be home in time for chores if that's what you're worried about," I reply.

I try to deflect my worst fear and maybe see if she did or didn't know yet.

"We have something to talk about, so you need to come home now," commands Amara's Mom.

"What is so important to talk about that it can't wait," I inquired.

Now I'm really trying to stall to see if she knows what happened at the dance.

"Amara, what is Jade's address? What we need to discuss will be discussed at home with your Father and me," replies Amara's Mom.

"Why don't I just get a ride back from one of the girls," I respond

It was too late when I realized what I just said. That will probably not help my situation.

"No one is going to bring you home. I am coming to get you," declares Amara's Mom.

"Mom, seriously, why can't someone just bring me home? What is the big deal anyway," I assert back.

What is this attitude of mine coming out of? I'm not usually like this being assertive, it's definitely not me.

"You know what exactly is the big deal, and now is not the time to discuss this. I need the address so I can come get you," exclaims Amara's Mom.

"The big deal is I'm hanging out with some friends. I don't understand what the problem is," I assert back.

I fire back at my mom, which I never do. Sure, I have been upset with her, but my tone is different this time.

"Don't you take that tone with me young lady," states Amara's Mom.

"Ugh, Mom, Seriously! I have friends that I am hanging out with," I profess

"Ya, and one of them you kissed," declares Amara's Mom.

Boom! There goes the explosion as I drop the phone to the ground. The other girls are all frozen at the cracking of the phone hitting the floor. I hear a faint whisper from one of the girls.

"Amara, are you okay," whispers Nika.

I am frozen by what my Mother just said. I want to move, but my muscles won't work. I want to start crying, yet the river of tears has been dammed up by boulders of shock. My mind wants to spiral out of control with the millions of thoughts now racing through my mind. I feel cold creeping in on my limbs. This is my end...

Everything's a blur after I dropped the phone on the kitchen floor. All I had to offer anyone was a blank stare. What am I going to do moving forward? My secret is out and as a teenage girl I am going to get slammed with bullying at school, nonetheless my parents won't care to do anything for their lesbian daughter. All my parents will want me to do is repent my sins and pray 24/7 to take this devilish act out of me. I am better off dead like I was in my imagination. I don't want to be brought back from this death. What I want to do is run away from all of this to never come back, but where would I go? The only place I feel safe at the moment is here at Jade's with my friends which I won't be able to see anymore.

Jade, Adelaide, and Nika all sit on the kitchen floor with me as the river of tears flows down past the ridges of my face and drips on my clothes. I don't even care to wipe my tears at this point. Jade tries handing me a tissue, but I'm completely zoned out. It feels like time could be standing still, but it could also be racing by like stock cars on a race track while I'm late for work.

"Come here Amara. I am so sorry you are going through this," utters Adelaide as she drapes her arm around my shoulder to bring me in for a hug...

Ggggzzzzz, hmmm (buzzing-electric shock) "Aaaahhhhhh!" I let out an intense scream as I am woken with volts of electricity being conducted through my body.

"You know Amara, what is better than torturing you while I have you chained up is watching you torture yourself in your friends kitchen. In the corn field with Zali and Aurora. In the theater and when you were with Darius," asserts Kumari.

"Kumari, you are such a bitch," I declare.

I try to fight the chains, but my strength is too weak and my arms are chained above my head.

There is faint light shining through the cracks in the walls. I really have no idea where Kumari brought me. The last thing I remember was her boot to my face. Most of the light that I do see is coming from what appears to be barrels of fires. I try standing to at least release the tension on my shoulders. My arms have gone numb from the blood having to work harder to pump against gravity.

"For being in your situation Amara, I don't think you can call me a bitch," states Kumari.

Kumari rams a cable right into my breast plate sending a violent electric shock through my muscle fibers as they twitch my body in all directions.

"AAAAHHHHHH!!!" I scream in agony.

Heavy breathing takes over as Kumari pulls the cable off my breast plate. I struggle to catch my breath as my heart rate has been elevated while my feet drag on the floor with all my weight pulling on my wrists that are chained up.

"Do you think you can cheat death a second time? I'm pretty sure your comforting session will end soon and you will have to face Mommy dearest," Kumari rebukes.

"How did you do it," I softly reply with the little strength I have left.

"Come again Amara? Your voice seems to have a little static in it," Kumari laughs.

"How did you get to my reality?"

"This is your reality," Kumari shouts and slaps me across the face and sends me spinning.

I let out another scream, but my strength is so depleted in this moment it's more of a moan. The pain surges through my body like the pressure of turning on a shower with the quick burst of water. My shoulders and wrists go from a numb feeling to a sharp jolting pain as I spin. Both planes of my two Universes seem to be crumbling at the same time. In the cross hairs of sitting on the kitchen floor, to the force of gravity taking their hands and pushing me down while my wrists are chained above my head; I feel the sadness of being flooded by the depressing waters. However, what is presently walking in the waters behind the dam I sink to the bottom in, is me as the Frost Princess. She is raging cold and freezing those flood waters to solid ice. The inner cold anger of the Frost Princess embracing this new power has arrived. What does this mean for me? What does it mean for others as well as the Universe?

"Cold dark days have arrived," I state as I crunch my feet on the ice I just created.

Chapter 35

Tic Toc, Tic Toc, goes to the clock as my parents and I sit in silence at the kitchen table with the only sound being heard is the analog clock on the wall behind me. Is my Dad waiting for me to start, or for Mom to start talking? The silence is deadly and terrifying enough without talking, what is it going to be like to actually break the ice. Huh, perhaps that's a pun intended as I crack a smile.

"Is there something funny about his situation," my Mom asks in a serious tone.

"No," I responded sarcastically.

"Then explain why you think it's appropriate to kiss other girls, because it isn't," Dad fires back.

"What? I didn't do anything wrong," I responded with my defenses lighting up the room as if someone tripped the alarm system.

"I can't believe this from my own child. How could you, Amara," my Mother says in a grief stricken tone.

I want to rage at my Mother across the table right now. I can feel the guilt and blame from her coming out with how this is my fault. My Mother's shadows of disappointment creep out as if her shadow of disappointment of me is cloud hopping when the sun is hidden behind a cloud. What does my Mother know about hiding anything?

"You will not be hanging out with any girls anytime soon," Dad says sternly.

"That's totally unfair," I say.

"What is unfair is what you are doing to this family. Your actions have consequences. It affects everyone in the entire family," exclaims Dad.

"Your Father is right Amara," declares Mom.

I can not hold back anymore tears as they trickle down my face as I wipe my face clean of the tears to hear my Dad say...

"What are you carrying about? This isn't something to cry about. You did something wrong," shouts Dad.

His presentation of his question is careless of his daughter's own feelings. I feel at this moment like my own Father just stabbed me with a sword. What kind of parent do I have? I want to run from the table but where do I even go? I broke up with Zali. My parents won't let me go anywhere. I'm trapped in this hell hole which I just want my friends, or somewhere to escape.

"Amara, look at me. Do you know how disgusted I felt when I heard you kissed a girl? That is so gross," Mom confesses.

I reply basically in a whimper as the beating of emotional pain continues from both of them, "I make you disgusted, Mom?"

"Not you, your actions do," states Mom trying to reach for my hands, but I pull away.

"Thanks mom! It's the same thing," I declare.

My eyes water to blurriness before the tears fall to the ground. I stand up in anger and slam my chair in.

"We are not done talking yet. Sit down Amara," shouts Dad!

I turn around to my parents with a sniffle with my tearful eyes, stare them dead in the face as I place my hands on the table to say, "You know what, it was always going to be hard to tell you this. I have been terrified to do this, but I guess it isn't on my terms anymore. I like girls, so ya I'm a lesbian."

I make another sniffle and wipe my tears from my face with both my hands to storm off up stairs to my room where I slam my door.

This is pain no daughter or son should experience, unfortunately I just did. I don't want to be here anymore. My Mom thinks I'm disgusting. My Dad is angry with me. The two people that are supposed to love me unconditionally have turned their backs on their own daughter and thrown her to the wolves. What love and support can I get from anyone at this moment? The ones that support me are at a different school. I am truly alone. I wish I never went on that stupid movie date with Zali; then I wouldn't be in this mess...

Throughout the night time chores my Dad and I don't speak or even look at each other. I figured he can't stand to look at his lesbian daughter right now; of course, it didn't stop my brother Markus from throwing jabs at me when Dad wasn't around. He knew I couldn't do anything about it. I would pass Markus in the barn and he would fake cough "dyke."

When I would return from getting cows in he would call out "the dyke has returned."

I tried to fight the tears the best I could.

I hid so well for 16 years and now there seems like there is nowhere to hide. Every square inch of the barn seems detectable. If my own home and farm are this harmful, what will school be like tomorrow? There is no way I can face any of them. I am better off dead.

After chores are finished on this Sunday evening, I grab my swords to head out on a great escape. The house is not the place I want to be right now. I walk past Markus kissing his girlfriend Miranda goodbye after chores. At least she didn't say anything bad to me during work like Markus did.

"Hey dyke, where are you going? I'm pretty sure Mom and Dad want you back in the house," states Markus.

"Fuck off Markus," I shout back and raise a middle finger back at him, as I continue to walk to the back of the barn where my solitude is.

I faintly hear Miranda state, "Markus stop it."

At this point I really don't care how cold or wet my clothes are from chores tonight. I can either sit in my room to continue to get lectured, or scream outside in my imagination. My heart rate increases with every step as frustration from the day. Tears are not the first thought anymore, its rage and anger. Why did the Universe, or what I have been taught to believe in God, created me so wrongly. Not only did I think that thought, but I shouted out those words... "Why did you create me so wrong?"

Chapter 36

Remember back to the volcano of lava erupting, and sudden cooling with ash falling from the sky, then turning into snowflakes. Well, that fallen ash has become my warrior paint as I take my fingers to drag them across the cooled ash on the ground. The black ash covers my right hand fingers as I place my middle finger at the corner of my right eye and begin to press hard enough to feel the skin on my face slowly pulling down by all four fingers on my face. The black ash marks my face as I am preparing for battle. I repeat the same process with my left hand to mark the left side of my face too.

There is no feeling of any kind to describe the emotions as I cover my entire Frost Princess armor in black ash. This is my mourning process as I feel like I lost my parents as well as everything in my world. A blackened heart is what I feel on account I will not be able to walk through those school doors today without other students staring at me, words being said about me behind my back, and then to my face. My pain is real and it feels like it is slowly paralyzing me from the toes up. How can I love anyone in this community let alone myself? Remember I am a disgusting person according to my own Mother. Bring on the darkness, or should I say the Dark Frost Princess.

The fateful morning has arrived to face the world I know outside my imagination. It feels like the winter formal dance was weeks ago even though it was less than 48 hours ago. My Mom makes small talk while all four of us siblings get ready for school. Mornings are always hectic in our house with three girls getting ready and Markus who seems to take longer on his hair than me in the morning.

On this particular morning I stay silent like a ninja to be undetected. Perhaps this should be my approach for school too. Dress in all black to be a ninja unseen. Wait, that wouldn't work because I would stand out since I would be wearing all black and that's not me. I do not need to draw more attention to myself at school than there will be, even though I feel all dark and black inside. I want to wear my black mask-covered armor out in public to protect myself. I know the black is only a magnet for attention today.

"Amara are you okay? You seem sad," my littlest sister Aurora asks me while standing in my doorway.

"I'm fine," I reply

"You're lying," Aurora responds.

"Aurora, I don't have time for this right now. I have to get ready for school and so do you," I snap back.

There I go to the dark angry tone again coming out at my baby sister. She didn't do anything wrong.

"Amara, you've changed, and I don't like you like this," Aurora protests.

I pause and look over at Aurora as she leaves my door frame. The thing about Aurora is we have always had a special bond. I would say if we paired up my siblings, Markus and Zoey bond better together; while me and Aurora bond better together. Aurora has an active imagination while her intuition is always spot on, besides being nine years old I don't think she fully understands my situation of liking girls.

When Aurora was about four she would tell stories very similar to me playing in my imagination. This was our way of bonding and spending time together as sisters. We would create our own sister world playing telling stories; but I wouldn't share too much of my world with Aurora just more so staying in her own world. Five years seems like a long time ago, and people can really change in that time. I really don't know how much story telling Aurora does these days; however, I do know her creative mind has turned to her artwork with it showing in her drawings.

My mode of transportation has changed since I have my license now and my own vehicle. At least my parents haven't taken my vehicle away yet. I don't have to ride with Markus, and get bullied by him on the way to school even though it's only like a three minute drive to school. What I find myself doing before I leave for school is writing Zali a note to apologize for what happened at the dance. I have no idea what she saw, but I'm sure she heard about it. My intention was never to harm Zali at the dance. I just took Jade as a friend, and we ended up kissing. Wow, I guess I haven't had a chance to process this all yet.

"Dear Zali,

I want to say how truly sorry I am for how I acted at the dance on Saturday. I was a jerk who ignored you because you are my ex-girlfriend, and it has been hard to get past that to be friends now. Part of me wanted you to be jealous of me walking in with Jade, but at the same time it was just darn right mean by not saying hello, spending time with you on the dance floor with you, or just talking. One thing we have always been good at is the two of us have been able to talk about anything. That is how our friendship started. I didn't expect our friendship to turn into a romantic relationship, yet it did. I ended it in a weird way, and we haven't really talked at work or at school, which is something I do miss.

I have no idea if you know this already or not, but I wanted to tell you myself regardless. Jade and I kissed on the dance floor, but we first kissed in the bathroom at the dance. Of course, after realizing I kissed Jade on the dance floor as everyone was staring at us, we left. I'm sorry if you saw this and it hurt your feelings. That was never my intention. The kiss just happened. Yes, I like Jade; but it doesn't matter now because my parents found out about the kiss, and won't let me hang out with any of my friends in the near future. My parents are disgusted with me as well as I told them I like girls before I stormed off. I hope we can salvage a friendship like we had during the summer, but I completely understand if you never want to talk to me again.

Amara"

I leave early to be one of the first students to arrive at school so I don't draw attention to myself walking into a classroom or the halls. I question the note I wrote Zali too while driving my short route to school. Maybe I shouldn't give it to her. What if she doesn't know at all, but wait she is going to find out, and she should find out from me.

Screech! I slam on my breaks as my body jolts forward from the momentum of my car coming to a sudden stop. My eyes widened in disbelief to see Kumari standing in the middle of the road, and now walking towards my car.

"What the hell is going on," I shout.

I quickly lock the doors and throw my car into reverse.

"Hi Amara," I hear Kumari's voice next to me in my car.

I turn to look and see a fist rocketing towards my face...

231

Chapter 37

My face jolts backwards with the impact from Kumari's fist hitting my face. I have no time to react when Kumari grabs my hair tightly,

"Aaahhh," I let out a scream.

She thrust my head and forced it onto the steering wheel causing the car horn to sound. Well, this definitely is going to draw attention to the quiet neighborhood on this Monday morning.

"Aagghhh," I let out another scream after my head bounces off the steering wheel.

Kumari jabs me with her left elbow into my ribcage as my pain reaches a full on ten on the scream scale. With a quick cut, her blade cuts my seatbelt as I fall to the driver's side door leaning against the door in complete agony. I moan in pain as everything is happening so quickly I have no time to process the all on assault by Kumari let alone counter back. Hands grab the shoulders of my coat to begin pulling me from the driver's side over the middle console and out the passenger's side door.

I want to fight back even though I am so dazed by what just happened my brain feels like scrambled eggs at the moment. Kumari drags me out of the car, and hurls me into the Monday town trash pick up bins. A loud thud of thunder rings out as my body collides with the trash bin taking the bin to the ground with me. Is no one seeing this right now in the neighborhood? Is no one calling the police as I get my ass kicked. This is a full on assault in the street, and no one is coming to my aid.

"Amara you are weak, pathetic, and a piece of trash, which I am rather enjoying this moment of kicking your ass in your own reality," declares Kumari.

Kumari starts walking towards me as I try to figure out what the hell is happening.

"Wait, wait, Kumari," I beg.

I stumble while pushing myself up with my hands off the frozen grass and concrete as I also try to gesture with one of my arms the universal stop signal.

While I pick my bruised body off the frozen ground, still holding up my left arm for the universal sign for stop, an energy surge flashes around my left wrist as a metal shimmering crystal blue bracelet clamps onto my left wrist. Without my brain even sending a signal to my right arm, it raises to have the same energy surge form around my right wrist to clamp on another metal shimmering crystal blue bracelet. I draw my elbows into my side by turning my wrists to face me with my fists closed to examine these bracelets on my wrists. I cannot believe my own eyes, these are my Frost Princess bracelets I use to activate my powers in my imagination. There is no time to think about how this is possible since I have been getting my ass kicked by Kumari, I just know the playing field between Kumari and I has just balanced out.

I smile at Kumari as I still have my fists closed as if I am looking at the bracelets, in spite of that now staring right at Kumari who has stopped dead in her tracks. I cross the bracelets at the wrists to pull them apart to activate my powers. No, this is not the time to worry about the logistics of how this is possible on the account Kumari is here again and attacking me. She wants to fight then let's fight.

The entire Frost Princess armor energizes my body, as if it heals my body instantly, as each section of my armor appears connecting with the next while my weapons all appear too. Now I feel like the Universe is balancing out in this fight.

"How is that even possible for you to have your powers," utters Kumari.

"I'm not here to talk to Kumari. You want to fight, now it's a fair fight," I exclaim.

I blast an ice spear out of my shoulder cannon right at Kumari, but she rolls out of the way. Unfortunately my ice spear hits my car to encase it in a block of ice.

"So you want to fight cold, and with dirty tricks," Kumari declares.

"Nope, just distractions," I call out.

I reacted while she rolled out of the way to run and jump then punch her when she stood up.

Bam! A direct hit as I send her tumbling to the ground. With a quick glance up I now notice an audience of people gathering around us. Great, now they show up, and I have to make sure they don't get harmed either. Mistake number one by me, taking an eye off my opponent. Kumari responds with her ninjutsu on me. The great thing about these powers, it's that they're psychically connected to the Universe, even though I have no training in the ancient arts of fighting. I know skills of the ancient arts while I have the armor on.

The crowd seems to be growing as the police arrive, however not sure what they are going to be able to do with two ancient powers battling it out. Kumari and I exchange blasts of our powers as the area has turned into an ice rink from my blasts, which is an advantage for me.

"You know your secret is out now. Look at the attention you brought to yourself. Both of your worlds are crumbling, almost like a black hole is pulling both realities out of existence," Kumari shouts.

We both have two swords drawn and even though the police are shouting on the megaphone to drop our weapons, there is no stopping this fight.

"My secret may be out, but I am not going to let you terrorize this world," I declare.

"Oh, honey you have no idea what I am capable of doing outside your imagination," professes Kumari.

"Aaahhh!" I attack Kumari.

Mistake number two as I let my emotions get the best of me. Our swords clang together multiple times before Kumari draws back to slice the taser cords that are attached to her back.

"You shouldn't have done that by getting involved in our business," Kumari exclaims angrily.

Kumari turns to the police officers who shot the taser, and holds out her hand to have a gold like dust of light begin to form on her palm. I notice the police officers try to draw their guns but it's too late.

"Kumari, NO," I scream at her.

Kumari blows the golden dust light towards the two police officers, and it vaporizes them in front of everyone watching. As screams from the crowd vibrate through the air; I quickly flick my arms and shoulders to activate my wings to blast right at Kumari to grab her in flight. She struggles to get free from my grip while we travel hundreds of miles per hour, smashing through trees, homes, buildings before I turn my direction to the sky. I am just going to drop her to her death for what she just did.

While reaching the height of near space of the atmosphere of the Earth to drop Kumari, I feel a presence of a touch on the back left side of my mind. It is a warm gentle touch, almost like a Mother's touch singling me not to do what I want to do. In all my rage and anger I want to die and kill my arch nemesis, but what will that accomplish? Kumari wins on both those fronts. People are getting hurt from me by hiding in two secret worlds. My sister Aurora said I have changed. I pushed Zali away. My parents don't even accept me. Mistake number three, letting my guard down again.

An orange energy blast that has a direct hit on my breast plate sends me spinning into a plunge back to Earth. Kumari can really pack a punch with her powers too. Her energy blast must've knocked me unconscious for a few seconds in the high altitude as I come to with no sense of direction as my body tumbles, spins, and swirls from the free for all from the gravity.

"Stabilizers! Wings activate," I shout.

I'm thrust up into the air as my armor stabilizes my whirling gravitational plunge to the Earth.

Boom! A sound wave cracks through the air molecules in the atmosphere as Kumari tackles me at sonic speeds to drive us crashing through dense branches as they crack and snap off. Dirt explodes into the air at our crater impact into the Earth. Kumari kneels over me as she has me pinned between her legs to begin throwing right and left punches at my face. Even though my face is shielded with my Frost Princess armor, my neck, face, and brain are rattled back and forth with each of her punches.

Vroom! Hum! Zing! Ding! The sounds of thack, thunk ring out as Kumari falls off me. Kumari rolls in the crater to her side to pull out four arrows out of her shoulder, arm, abdomen, and breastplate. Each arrow she pulls out she lets out an agonizing scream of pain and tosses the arrow out of the crater. Where did those arrows come from? Better yet, where did we land?

Kumari says an ancient chant as her markings (can we please just call them ancient tattoos already) glow in an orange and yellow light to heal the wounds of flesh cut open by the arrows on her body. The blood recedes back into her body as the glow brightens to heal her.

"That was not a smart choice to get involved in our business," Kumari states angrily as she climbs out of the crater.

"When it involves my friend, then yes, I will get involved to aid her," the Forest Huntress responds, as she pulls back the arrow on her bow.

Vroom, hum, zin, vroom, hum, zing! The Forest Huntress is on an all out assault on Kumari. Right hand, left hand, grabbing arrows while switching the bow from each hand to the next. Kumari uses her powers to deflect the arrows, but at what point is the Forest Hunt firing quicker?

Ding! Direct shot on Kumari's lower leg as she drops to one knee. Kumari draws her sword in the moment of the rain of arrows being shot, to send an orange energy blast through the ground at the Forest Huntress.

Zap! Kumari's energy travels across the Earth to blast the Forest Huntress.

"Kelly," I shout.

I jam my two swords into the earth to freeze the surface around us, blocking Kumari's energy blast.

Swishing of my swords as I pull them out of the ground. I have no idea how any of this is possible, but it is all happening in real time. Kelly is standing behind me with her Forest Huntress armor on. I have my Frost Princess armor on and Kumari is several feet in front of me. My two worlds have collided in a massive collision that hasn't been seen since the asteroid that destroyed the dinosaurs impacted the Earth millions of years ago. When I woke up this morning the biggest concern I had was that my secret is out, and how am I going to face my reality at school. I guess now my other secret is out too, so it's time to face both my secret worlds!

Chapter 38

Collision of reality and imagination is like the collision of consciousness and unconscious mind, or perhaps the battle between the Ego and the ID. The Superego boundary that separates my Ego and ID, or conscious and unconscious might be my armor; or not even at all in this case. Boundaries of my two secret worlds have been crossed like the plane of water beneath, and the air above that plane of water. Two different worlds of existence with life in both, but it's hard for one lifeform to exist in the other's environment.

I can put on protective gear like a scuba suit, or just dive down in a submarine. Those can only protect me for so long beneath the surface of the water. If I dive too deep I get crushed by the pressure of the environment I am in. The same similar pressure I am experiencing now with my two secret worlds. I dove too deep into depths of pressure, as my body can not sustain the pressure, making me feel like this is too late to resurface, as my oxygen is running low. If I surface too fast I will end up getting the bends which are nitrogen bubbles that cause decompression sickness, which I would compare to high stress, panic attack, or high anxiety. Which are all symptoms I am experiencing at this moment. Some of the symptoms are similar: headache, dizziness, difficulty thinking clearly, and weakness in the arms and legs.

On the other end of it, the surface is filled with life. Escaping to the depths of the ocean isn't the option, then climbing to new heights must be. As I escape in hiding my panic sets in, which makes it harder to breathe. This is similar to climbing to new heights in altitude to escape in my journey of hiding; but it creates the illusion of a panic attack. My chest tightens with tension in my shoulders. My breathing becomes shallower as though I am gasping for air, yet I keep climbing to avoid my problems, only I have created another entirely new problem I must deal with. This is altitude sickness. I have climbed too fast to escape my problem making myself sick to the point of a headache, vomiting, insomnia, and reduced coordination.

One extreme to the next to hide in two different worlds. The surface identity has been my sexual orientation (or in this case my conscious or Ego); while the depths of the ocean has been me hiding my imagination (unconscious or ID). The surface is more visible which makes hiding my sexual orientation more difficult; while the depths of the oceans are harder to visually see making it easier to hide my imagination.

In high altitudes it's an extremely low air pressure system with air molecules spread far apart from each other. The ocean depths create new atmospheric pressure for every ten meters of ocean depth. This creates an extremely high pressure system. Where might I be going with this concept? When high and low pressure systems collide in the atmosphere it creates rain or storms. In rare situations two systems of extreme pressure (two low pressure systems) attract each other when they normally would repel each other to create an extreme tropical cyclone called the Fujiwhara Effect.

My two secret worlds that have normally repelled each other have combined to create the Fujiwhara effect of secret worlds. The outcome of the Fujiwhara effect is hard to predict, and the destruction it will cause could be catastrophic. What I do know is I'm the cyclone and I have to run my course along with running out of fuel without causing too much destruction.

Rain begins to fall as rumbles of thunder can be heard in the distance. The storm that has been building has arrived in full force. There might not be strong winds like a cyclone, in spite of that it's about to get nasty out.

"You two honestly think you can put up a decent challenge for me? Amara has never defeated me," claims Kumari.

"How can I defeat you when you run away everytime," I profess.

"It's not me who runs away, Amara. You have always run from any problem and never confronted it. That's why you are weak," Kumarit declares.

"Don't let her get under your skin Amara! You are strong, besides I'm right here by your side. Together we are stronger," replies Kelly

"Nice speech Huntress Kelly, but I believe you also tend to disappear and abandon Amara in her time of need. You are never there for her. You're not her friend," responds Kumarit.

Clink, cling, ding! The rain drops intensify as the earth beneath our feet turns from a loose soil to a muddy top. I glance to my right side for a quick second at Kelly after what Kumari said.

"Don't listen to her. She is trying to divide us," Kelly responds to my glance.

Kumari begins to motion step to her left, like she wants to stalk us as her prey. Lightning flashes and shimmers a reflection off all three of our armors. In the bolt of lightning Kumari charges us to make the first move. Kelly and I both step in a defensive tactic from Kumari's double sword attack. Kelly is able to block Kumari's sword with her bow, creating a loud vibrating thud on contact. In an instant reaction Kumari slices the second sword onto my sword creating a loud clunk vibration through the forest.

The rain has made the soil muddy with our footing which Kumari seems to have no issue with. Lucky for Kelly having the Forest Huntress armor is very adaptable to this environment; however, for me it is not. I get knocked to the ground and slide in the mud. Freezing the mud is my only option. I launch two ice spears while laying in the mud at Kumari's feet to freeze the ground from her to me. I jump up to skate across the ice while Kumari in her frustration sends an orange energy blast to break her feet free. I pack a spinning heel kick that sends her crashing into a tree. I give Kelly a hand to lift her off the ground. This battle is only just beginning.

"Aahhh," Kaumari shouts as she blasts a massive orange beam from her diamond in the center of her breast plate.

The blast sends Kelly and I sailing through the air several feet. That felt like a supernova impact on us both, or at least me. I let out a moan in agony.

I call out, "Kelly."

My call is not loud enough with the rain falling and lack of strength. Kumari chants some sort of ancient phrase as she uses telekinesis to lift us both up into the air. More thunder rumbles as lightning lights up the sky too.

"You two just don't get it," states Kumari as she holds her arms out, controlling us in the air.

"I know too many ancient powers. My resources are unlimited to be defeated," announces Kumari.

"What do you possibly get from all this by killing us both? Have you ever thought that far ahead," I called back out.

"I bring about a new age," exclaims Kumari

"An age of what," rebukes Kelly.

"Only if you two really knew," states Kumari.

"Well enlighten us," I ask.

"I would rather not," replies Kumari.

Kumari waves her hands together to collide Kelly and me together then launches us deep into the forest.

"Now let's play the hunting game," laughs Kumari.

"Kelly," I called out.

"Amara," Kelly calls back.

"Kelly," I responded.

"Amara," Kelly replies.

I can hear Kelly calling out my name but finding her as I stagger to my feet is another question. If anything happened to her, I don't know what I would do. Kelly is someone I fell in love with in my imagination, for all that now that she exists in my actual reality I don't know what to think of it. None of this makes any sense as I'm actually still in the bathroom at the dance because I'm just imagining all of this. No Amara, stop lying to yourself. I am here fighting for my own existence, in my imagination world, in my own reality, while my secret of liking girls is out to my community. I guess both are challenging in their own way. I can't run away from either one.

I deactivate my helmet and stagger from tree to tree calling Kelly's name. Eventually I stumble upon her pinned under several large fallen trees. I fall to the ground as tears water my eyes after I have found her.

"I can't use my powers to get the trees off me. Whatever blast she hit me with really did some damage," mutters Kelly. "It will be okay, I will get you out of there. Maybe if I freeze the trees I can shatter them and get you out," I affirm.

"Okay try it," replies Kelly.

"It's going to get cold, just hang on," I claim.

Kelly gives me a facial expression when she is ready.

Sparks fly out of my wrists as my powers of my armor aren't working either.

"No!" I scream out.

I try lifting a fallen tree off Kelly with all the strength I have but nothing moves. I begin to sob in frustration.

"I don't know how to help you," I utter.

"You won't always be able to help everyone," Kelly utters.

"But it's you Kelly. It's you! I can't lose you. Somehow here you are in my reality," I whisper.

I reach to hold the arm that is free to hold her hand while I take my other hand to brush the hair from her face and any debris.

"Help yourself right now, Amara," Kelly professes.

"What do you mean," I ask.

I lean in closer to her as tears continue to fall from my eyes.

"It's not always about everyone else and trying to protect them. Being you is what protects them without you even having to try to protect them," expresses Kelly.

What is Kelly even talking about? Protecting people is who I am... that touch is back in my mind. Someone is trying to reach out to me. Ugh there is too much happening right now, I can't concentrate. My mind goes blank with comfort from whomever is reaching out to touch my mind. The touch feels soft and gentle on my mind, almost like a Mother in nature. Deep breath in, 1, 2, 3, 4. Exhale 4, 3, 2, 1. I open my eyes to find myself kissing Kelly on her lips. I slowly pull back and gaze into her eyes.

"Wow, What was that for," Kelly whispers with a smile.

"Because I love you Kelly. I may never get another chance to say it, and it's possible we both don't get out of this alive. I want to say it out loud to you since you are in my reality. I love you," I confess.

"I love you too, Amara," Kelly confesses.

A bright blast of light shines on my breast plate. I push away from Kelly to make sure it doesn't harm her. I can feel an energy surge from the Universe as I begin to float above the ground. My arms are extended and my legs too to form a starbody formation.

"Amara, Are you all right," shouts Kelly.

As the energy light begins to fade I am lowered to the ground. I have this wicked ice staff in my left hand and a similar diamond to Kumari's in the center of my breast plate except mine isn't orange, mine is a crystal blue color. There is no time to waste by admiring what just happened. I take my ice staff, spin it to blast to freeze the trees that have fallen on Kelly. Then leaping into the air to land my ice staff on the trees to shatter them to free Kelly.

"What just happened," I state while my helmet deactivates as I help Kelly up.

Kelly gives me a kiss on the lips, "I think you did something for you and faced a fear from both your worlds. I am proud of you Amara!" Kelly gives me another kiss.

"Thank you! I would love to continue this chat, but I bet the bright light gave away our location and Kumari is already on her way. Oh no, your armor needs a recharge too," I proclaim.

"No sweat girl, I have my old armor too," Kelly states.

Kelly raises her forearms and snaps her fingers on both hands to change to her Amazon warrior armor.

"I think the Forest Huntress just needs a rest. Besides, I like this outfit better since it's from my native Universe," declares Kelly.

Chapter 39

It's one thing to slip between my two worlds when my anxiety reaches its threshold, which I will say I have been doing more of lately since I started dating Zali. Before Zali, I had the shadows as my friends to hide. No one knew my secret about who I liked. Heck, I kept it from myself even trying to just "fit in", whatever that means. Look what happened during cross country with Ted. Hiding and trying to "fit in to be normal" only gets people hurt. I have also tried being myself with friends while sharing my imagination in middle school. That didn't turn out so well either. Adelaide has been the one true friend who has stuck by my side and hasn't dismissed my imagination. Unfortunately, we just grew apart until recently. Why does life have to be so complicated when it comes to making friends, trusting friends, being yourself through who you like, your identity, skin color, or anything that pertains to being a human?

Amber and I have been friends since elementary school, except I have never told her about my imagination. I'm sure she knows about my kiss with Jade. I wonder how Amber will react knowing I am a lesbian? Will she treat me differently? Maybe we will start talking again. I do miss hanging out with Amber as well as talking to her. It hasn't been the same since homecoming between us. I feel like there has been one loss after another with the intensity of the pressure to keep my secret in addition to Zali and my relationship secret.

Then there is Jade, who I have a crush on, but if Kelly is really here in my reality then Jade and I wouldn't work out just like Zali. Heck my parents would put a stop to any relationship with Jade too. Jade is sweet and brings out a different side of me similar to Kelly. I guess I made my love life a complicated one, and confusing on my emotional side. Let me be real with myself, my parents won't let me go anywhere now that I told them I am a lesbian nor go near a girl until I go away to college.

"Amara watch out," shouts Kelly.

I am pulled away from the path I am walking and down towards the ground as an orange energy blast collides with the ground we were walking on creating a massive explosion. Dirt, branches, leaves, and any other parts of debris go flying through the air. Some of the debris falls on us covering our armor as we roll over from our face dive to the ground.

"I think Kumari found us," I state.

"Are you all right, Amara," responds Kelly.

"I'm fine. You," I ask.

"Peachy," utters Kelly.

"Come on, let's find Kumari," I exclaim.

I reach my hand to Kelly to help her on her feet, instead she pulls me down while tucking her legs to flip me over right as Kumari lunges her sword downward where I was bent over to help Kelly up.

"Ughh!" Screams Kumari as her sword swishes out of the ground into the air.

Kelly springboards to her feet, and draws out her two daggers to engage in fighting with Kumari. Clang, cling go the swords and daggers as the blades clash with immense force against each other. One quick blow is countered with a defensive tactic to return an attack on the other. It's almost like an intricate dance with deadly blades of steel.

"Huntress, you are always coming to Amara's aid. Are you ever going to let her fight her own fight," questions Kumari.

"She doesn't ever have to do this alone," reputes Kelly.

Swoosh, Swoosh, Swoosh! I spin my ice staff, readying myself for another battle with Kumari. I swing my staff at Kumari's blind side where her defenses are most vulnerable while she fights Kelly. Thawk! Kumari clutches my ice staff between her arm and body as though she anticipated the attack.

"No, No little girl," utters Kumari.

Kumari spins with and lunges at me with her sword. I dodge with a right backwards bend to avoid her sword. This is a two on one fight, yet Kumari is strong, moreover a split second faster on every move we both make. Even though Kelly and I attack both her sides, Kumari is lightning quick to defend.

"Ladies, I am getting tired of this little dance of ours," states Kumari.

Kumari drops to the ground with a quick roll, including a touch of her hand to her diamond on her breast plate, an orange energy blasts out at me and then Kelly.

The impact of Kumari's energy blasts propels us backwards in the opposite direction. My body feels broken on the impact with the tree and the energy blast. Kumari's diamond is her energy source, and the only way to slow her down. We have to get it from her.

"Poor Amara, now she has to learn to fight on her own. What happens when you see the Huntress get choked to death," professes Kumari.

Kumari drags Kelly over near me, then wraps her hand around Kelly's neck to lift her in the air.

"I wouldn't do that if I were you," I call out to Kumari as I try to pick myself off the ground.

Kelly is a more dangerous fighter when she is not planted with two feet on the ground. Don't ask me how that is possible. She claims it's something about how she was trained in her Universe and the gravitational forces are different between the two Universes. Kelly swings her legs up onto Kumari's arm that is extended, and locks her legs around Kumari's shoulder while applying force to Kumari's face. Instead of choking Kelly, Kelly has used her own weight to counter Kumari to pull on her shoulder socket.

"Aaghh," Kumari lets out a scream.

I lunge at Kumari with my shoulder (in wrestling terms it's called a spear) to take her to the ground. All three of us are on the ground momentarily, which I still am trying to process the chaos of everything that has happened since this morning. My adrenaline is still running high since slamming on my brakes when Kumari stood in front of me in the middle of the road on my way to school.

Okay, Amara, concentrate like this is your imagination; but it's now my actual reality. Focus! What is Kumari's motive for being here besides being my arch nemesis? Do our conflicts end with me running away? That is what she keeps saying. I'm always hiding from her; but wait, is that what this is all about, hiding? It can't just be me hiding. There is always a balance in the Universe, so what is she hiding, or protecting? Come to think about it, we aren't too far off from being mirror images of each other. That's exactly what a nemesis is, the complete balance opposite in the Universe. The opposite has to fit the slot like a puzzle piece, or to balance the scale to not tip the Universe scale to one side. Good vs evil are mirror images of each other. Positive and negative charges. It took two negative charges technically to make a positive charge. In a sense the negative and positive charges are similar. What makes Kumari and I similar to each other's Yin and Yang?

"Amara, now is the time to strike her," Kelly shouts with an arrow drawn on Kumari.

"Hahahaha," Kumari laughs as her hands begin to glow as she is powering up for another strike.

Swoosh goes Kelly's bow as she releases the arrow to zing toward Kumari. With a swipe of Kumari's glowing orange and yellow hand, the arrow ricochets off her energy blast, then a return swipe with Kumari's left hand sends an energy blast at Kelly to knock her to the ground. Hmm, buzz, as I blast an energy blast for the first time out of my diamond in the middle of my breast plate. My energy blast has a light crystal blue and white color to it. The blast from me is a direct hit on Kumari's back, thrusting her forward like a long jumper in mid-air on their jump before she collides with the ground.

I can hear Kumari let out moans of pain with a tone of frustration of what just happened. "What are you hiding, Kumari? You keep saying, I keep running from what I'm hiding from, which is being a lesbian; but what are you hiding from me," I question.

My feet crunch on twigs and squish in the mud as I approach Kumari.

"You really think I'm hiding something from you," Kumari utters back as she picks herself up off the ground.

Zing! Ding! "Aagghh!" Zing! Ding! "Aagghh!" Zing! Ding! "Aagghh!" Kumari screams.

Kumari drops to the ground on her knees as three of Kelly's arrows impale Kumari's body.

"Aarrhh," screams Kumari as she rips the arrows out of her body.

"Let's find out what you are hiding. There is an imbalance in the Universe, so what's your secret," I ask.

I throw a right punch, left punch, then a right knee to Kumari's face. She falls over after my knee to her face. I gesture to Kelly to pause her movement as Kumari is mine as I know she is hiding something from me.

"Come on Kumari, what's your big secret," I inquired.
    I spin a kick with my leg this time as Kumari blocks it from her knees. She slips a blade out of her wrist and throws a left punch with the blade at me. I counter with a forearm block. The fight is now on! Kumari draws her swords as she stands, and I return by drawing both of mine.

Cling, clang! Swoosh, go the swords as the metal smashes against each other with every strike we take.

"Amara, you are hell bent on I have a secret, but it is your secret that has caused the imbalance in the Universe," claims Kumari.

"Ya, I don't remember you having some of these powers in my imagination, so something is up," I divulge

We continue slashing our swords at each other in our conversation.

"You are the one living with fear," rebukes Kumari.

"Why did you leave; or should I say how did you leave my imagination which is in my own mind, to be here? Something must have driven you out? Fear Perhaps," I question Kumari.

"Ugh," sighs Kumari.

Kumari rage attacks as I counter with my own rage. This is the Fujiwhara effect in full force. Two extremely pressurized systems colliding, with each strike on each other emerges the two systems into one massive storm. Both our rage is toward each other, with mine fueling from my parents, and living in hiding due to my community, adds energy on my side. What energy is fueling Kumari is the mystery, and the secret I believe she is hiding.

The energy behind us intensifies the more we engage in our fighting. Sparks of energy are being released with each clash of our swords. There definitely is a bright glow illuminating from both of us, and the center point of the light is coming from our diamonds. We both dodge, duck, jump, and spin to avoid each other's swords.

"Wait, you showed up after Jade and I kissed. I haven't seen you in quite some time. What does the kiss have to do with an imbalance," I ask.

We both pause as both of our breathing is heavy from fighting.

"You really are clueless of any imbalance," responds Kumari.

"So, there is a secret," I state.

"I never said that," responds Kumari.

"You didn't have to say it directly, but you said you were clueless. There is something you are hiding and I'm going to find out what it is," I declare.

I quickly place my swords back in their holsters on my back as Kumari gives me a look back of suspicion as to what I'm up to.

"Let's go find out, Kumari," I announce.

I snap my arms to activate my wings to blast off to the sky.

Chapter 40

Every story must come to an end at some point. There is a beginning point to the story, but sometimes the beginning gets debated by humans. For example, the beginning of time. One side of the debate is the beginning of the big bang theory. It all starts with atoms and a massive explosion. Sorry, I'm not an expert in this field. The other side of the debate is some divine being created the Universe. They are two very secret worlds that have more questions than actual answers. Perhaps, my story of two secret worlds isn't too far off from this concept. The big bang and a divine being both generate the Universe from nothing. What there is then has to be something that came from nothing, and nothing came from something. Of course, the end of the story of the big bang and the divine Universe will all end someday. That means something will become nothing again. For anything biotic their story will come to an end, just like mine will.

What if, in those two secret worlds there is the same piece of origin? Then it wouldn't be a what if, it will be a what then. If the big bang came from nothing in addition so did the divine being; but only to be separated in their stories. What event would it take to bring those two secret worlds together before the story ends? Another question, what happens once the two secret worlds merge together, does the ending change, and does the story begin again?

My molecular structure of my own identity exists in a microcosm point in the Universe. In those micro points in the Universe there is enough negative charged energy to repel my molecular structure thanks to my atoms identifying differently than those around me in my environment. If you send a strong enough electric current, which is negatively charged, through a metal, it will magnetize it creating a north and south pole. This creates two different environmental worlds from one object. Only opposite poles can go together, so the same environmental poles will now always repel each other, never to be in contact with each other again.

I have been magnetized by my community, and their negatively charged ions. I repel myself into two secret worlds always causing conflict with each other like a north and south pole of a magnet. The more negative energy from my community's ions the stronger my north and south poles increase creating a bigger barrier of force between them. My two secret worlds were ending just like any other story, however for some reason my molecular structure in a microcosm part of the Universe has changed to demagnetize my worlds as it merges them into one story. This story is not ending, it just has a new beginning.

As I soar to the sky to begin my search for Kumari's secret, my mind is pulled back by the soft touch that has been reaching out to me.

"It's you or should I say me, who has been reaching out this whole time," I claim

My mind is in a bedroom with my older self again.

"Yes it has been me," replies older Amara.

There is no armor on, just regular clothes. I reach out my arms for a hug as my older self embraces me like a Mother would hugging her own child after not seeing them for a long period of time. It's a comforting feeling I have been longing for for quite some time from my own

Mother. The words you make me disgusted really take away from those comforting hugs from my mom.

"Where's your baby," I ask.

"Oh, she's in the other room playing. As you can see, there is no more crib. She is in a big girl bed," responds old Amara.

"Wait, last time I saw you she was a newborn," I claim.

"Time is a funny thing. You blink and they are walking," states older Amara.

"Why have you been trying to reach me," I ask.

"Something has changed on our paths. Let me correct myself, your path now," declares old Amara.

"What do you mean," I inquired.

"I stayed hidden until after I graduated high school, and came out to everyone when I graduated college. I knew then I wouldn't need my parents' support anymore as I could live on my own. For some reason that has all changed now. We or you coming out happened way earlier than it was supposed to happen," older Amara exclaims.

"I don't understand. How is that even possible," I question.

"Unfortunately, I don't have the answers for you," responds old Amara.

"This would explain why my imagination is now real. My powers are real. Kelly is here in the flesh. Oh, Kumari too," I profess.

My older self takes my hands to state, "Amara, listen to me you have a longer journey ahead of you than I did."

"You look happier, and more joyful than the first time I saw you. There is hope for me, right," I ask my older self.

"I have done so much healing in my journey and so will you," replies older Amara.

"I don't even know where to begin to heal. I just kissed Jade on the dance floor practically in front of the entire school, then told my parents I'm a lesbian when they confronted me about it," I confess.

"Who is Jade," older Amara asks.

"Remember, Adelaide's friend. They go to the same school together. Jade was my date for the winter formal," I probe.

"Your timeline has completely changed. I never knew Jade in my timeline, let alone kissed a girl on the dance floor. As far as the winter formal when I was 16, Zali and I went to the dance together," responds old Amara.

"I broke up with her about a month before the dance," I state.

I see a confused look on my older self's face, when I ask, "What is it?"

"This is why it is so dangerous talking to yourself from the future and the past. Your journey of healing begins now. Letting the anger and rage take over will not help. Let the pain in so you can feel it. I know it will hurt at first, but it will help you become who you are meant to be. You will be tempted to go into a deeper hiding. Validate the feeling and be Amara," expresses older Amara.

As my mind drifts back to whatever reality I am actually in, my challenge going forward is going to be scarier than ever before. I can't tell if I feel like I'm back in the dark forest again, and I jumped off the cliff into the water to escape. Part of me feels like this is the moment the ground is cracking open around me with my Mother being angry at me. My consciousness is being pulled by different emotional feelings, even though at the same time those feelings are trying to go in opposite directions of each other. There is this pressure force that is containing those feelings too. The glass is going to break as those magnetic forces seem to be all applying the repelling force on me. Somehow I need to do this. I need to find out what Kumari is hiding from me. She has answers, and is unwilling to share.

CRASH! Kumari directly collides with me as we both tumble through the sky. Our storm is now airborne. I restabilize myself as Kumari sends an energy blast at me. My body is hurled in a spiral backwards across the skyline. I stabilize myself again to observe Kumari zooming towards me.

"Wings retract," I shout.

As gravity grabs me and pulls me from the sky while I look up towards the Earth's sky. "Aahhh," I scream out.

I send a blue energy blast from my diamond up toward Kumari, and hit her in her left leg, sending her into a flipping spin.

Our diamonds are both our power source, and I have to take her diamond to stop her. I return to flight to launch four ice blasts at Kumari, which one of them hits her to freeze her right arm.

"Kumari, this ends now," I shout.

While latching to her, I reach for her diamond in the center of her breast plate.

"Hands off," declares Kumarit.

Kumari whips her iced arm across my face, rattling me from reaching for the diamond. "Let me return the favor," I protest.

I grab her wrist as she tries to take my diamond.

"No you can't have it," Kumari shouts.

I let go of her wrist to grab her orange diamond at the same time she grabs mine.

BLAST! BOOM! A massive energy wave lights up the sky, and the shock wave jets us apart.

"What the heck just happened," I proclaim.

"These diamonds have way more power than I perceived. I am going to need yours now, Amara," exclaims Kumari.

However one might call it, destiny or fate, this is my glass shattering. I'm not helping myself, nor helping others. I have no clue what I'm doing. My outcome and Kumari's outcome could be already predetermined, or by chance it is still unknown. What I do know is I have been given this gift, of my imagination powers being real, just like my identity as a lesbian from the Universe. No more running. No more hiding. If this is the new world I live in with powers with my sexual orientation known to the world then so be it. I'm not going to let some crazy as bitch like Kumari dictate my future.

"You want my diamond, Kumari, then come and get it," I shout at Kumari.

The Fujiwhara effect of two extremely pressurized systems are on a collision course for each other's power source. There is no repelling of these magnetic forces, just a tidal wave of energy expelled from the Fujiwhara effect. I close my eyes and take a deep breath in, as I feel the surge of my energy from my blue diamond circulating my armor like a heart pumping blood through the arteries and veins. I blast off towards Kumari, as Kumari glows in a stream of orange and yellow light towards me. Tic Toc, Tick Toc goes the clock, but the speed at which we are traveling it's only a second or two before our collision. Is this what death really feels like as my events of my 16 years of life race faster than I am traveling toward Kumari, rather each image is a clear memory. Our energy forces explode on impact with each other creating a massive BOOM! BLAST! CRACK! SMACK!

Chapter 41

Click, click of my shoes is the only sound I can hear in this dark empty space I have awoken in. I feel like there is nothing here, just complete emptiness. There is no light filtering in, just a void of darkness. So then, where is here? I don't feel any presence of my consciousness or unconsciousness in this void.

"Hello," I called out.

My voice echoes several times as though it is traveling farther and farther away from me while softening in volume each time it vibrates back to me. This is no small dark void, it's an endless one. The only direction I am aware of is down because my feet are grounded, well that is an assumption in itself too. I guess up is when I tilt my head up, yet it all looks the same no matter what direction my observations explore. Complete darkness swallows me whole, which not even my eyes can adjust to without any filtering light. I am as good as blind in this environment.

"Is there anyone else here," I called out.

Why would I ask such a question, even if someone or something else is here with me, I wouldn't see them anyway. Is this the darkness of death, and my soul is waiting to move on? How long will I be here?

Six months after Amara and Kumari's collusion in the sky...

The night sky begins to be painted with brush strokes of pinks, oranges, and golden yellows as dawn breaks over Lake Michigan creating a beautiful ambience reflecting off the waves rising and falling. The mid July morning is still warm from the scorching heat of the day before as the seagulls have their morning chatter. Whoever took the liberty to wake in the early morning light, 4:44 am; and stroll the shoreline of Lake Michigan has a shocking surprise to find a girl lying face down unconscious at the edge of the wet sand with the waves crashing ashore. Her legs continue to be padded by the incoming waves as calm morning waves gently flutter her clothes and legs. Whoever has stumbled upon the mystery girl has done the right thing and called 911 to report they found a body.

Thump, long pause. Thump, another long pause.

"She has a pulse, but it's faint," officer Darius McKinley calls out to his partner.

"Jen, radio the paramedics, we have a pulse. She is alive," states officer Darius McKinley

While officer Jen takes a few steps away from the girl, officer Darius drags the girl out of the wet sand and water and lays her flat on the dry sand. Little known to officer Jen, officer Darius whispers something into the girl's ear while laying her head down into the sand.

"Amara you are going to be okay. Help is on its way," whispers Darius.

"We have a female, Jane Doe, unresponsive. Approximate age 14-18 years old. Faint pulse. We are monitoring breathing and pulse until paramedics arrive! What's your ETA," announces officer Jen.

"Jen we need prints on our Jane Doe to run a missing person to see if there is a match out there," exclaims officer Darius.

"I'm on it," replies officer Jen.

The sun begins to rise over the lake's horizon while the paramedics attend to the girl who is still unresponsive. Straps are tightened as the paramedics and first responders carry the gurney across the sand to the concrete path where the ambulance is parked. Officer Darius and officer Jen finish up their questioning with the civilian who made the call. The mysterious Jane Doe would have to wait until any fingerprint matches come back.

Two days later...

"Hey we just got a match on the prints for our Jane Doe. You aren't going to believe this," states officer Jen.

"Who is it," responds officer Darius.

"It is Amara Vanderwahl. The girl who mysteriously disappeared 6 months ago on the same day those two officers got vaporized by that creature," exclaims officer Jen.

"Jesus fucking christ, Jen, how is that even possible," announces officer Darius.

"I don't know," replies officer Jen.

"How does Amara just show up one day on the shoreline of Lake Michigan after 6 months," questions officer Darius.

"Maybe whoever kidnapped her was done using her for whatever purpose, and was hoping to just dispose of her body," responds officer Jen.

"The leads started as a possible hate crime investigation when it was found out she just came out as a lesbian, nonetheless there were no leads linked to that. The trail just went cold," expresses officer Darius.

"Wasn't there a second ice creature of some sort too? Then they just flew off to never to be seen again," states officer Jen.

"Whatever it was, we have our work cut out for us now as well as the department. Let's go, Jen, we need to inform the parents," declares officer Darius.

"It's almost twenty hundred hours," states officer Jen.

"That doesn't matter when a loved one is found," replies officer Darius.

"I will notify the Cap," replies officer Jen.

"I will call the hospital and tell them we have an ID for the Jane Doe who came in two days ago," replies officer Darius.

"This is officer Darius of the North Point Police Department. We have an identification for the individual "Jane Doe" who arrived two days ago. I am the officer on duty with my partner officer Jen Gracia who filed the report for the "Jane Doe," deviluges officer Darius.

Officer Darius listens to the nurse on the phone, and waits for the next instructions.

"Her name is Amara Vanderwahl," states officer Darius.

"Yes I can spell it for you. A-M-A-R-A. V-A-N-D-E-R-W-A-H-L. Date of birth is 01/17/1986. Amara's parents' names are Patricia and Kenneth Vanderwahl," states officer Darius.

Officer Darrius makes sure the nurse is informed with all the important information the hospital needs before Amara's parents arrive.

"You are welcome. We are going to notify the parents next so they should be there shortly," declares officer Darius.

Where does one's conscience depart when either it is in a coma, has amnesia from dissociation, or even just sleeping? One moment I feel like I'm trapped in this void of darkness, then there are beams of light filtering their touch on my closed eyelids. The sense of sound vibrations are picked up traveling through the air molecules to my eardrums. Between the mixture of the two senses brings mass confusion from the feeling of disorientation. My eyelids feel like fifty pound weights have been attached by hooks to each one to hold them down making it difficult to open them.

As the river of feelings begins to flow from the peak of the mountain of my consciousness down the river of nerves, there is sensation of movement within my fingers. This particular feeling I would rather be in the void of darkness because it feels like I have been drugged. Why would I be drugged? My senses become more aware with each passing second. Beep, beep goes a heart monitor as I slowly tilt my head to the left to squint at the sound for recognition.

"Hey there," a nurse speaks softly to me when she enters the hospital room.

"I'm glad you are awake Amara, I am just bringing you a new ID bracelet because we finally found out who you are," states the nurse.

"Where am I," I mumble out, while the nurse attaches the ID bracelet to my right wrist.

"You are at Memorial Medical. We are going to take care of you. If you need anything just press the red call button that I placed next to you."

The Universe is mysterious, clever, and a little bit witty. There are moments in life that make you laugh uncontrollably with a friend or a partner. Even in the darkest moments the wittiness of the Universe can shine through. Perhaps, you have been in my shoes and asked yourself, can I really feel happiness and joy when I'm sad and depressed right now? Maybe, it's guilt or shame of feeling the positive emotions while in the negative emotions. In the same moments the Universe is being witty, the Universe can be clever too. Is it possible the Universe can learn? Well if it is always seeking homeostasis; then yes, the Universe is clever in those moments of darkness.

Which leads to the mystery of the Universe. Being a farm girl and my Grandpa Ed who taught me everything I know about plants; it still is a mystery that wheat seeds must be planted before a hard freeze and not in the spring. However, once the wheat sprouts (mind you they need to before the hard freeze) they are a lush green amongst the earthy browns of later fall. Wheat is a plant similar to garlic that needs to go through the dark days of winter. In science this is the wintering process. If the plant doesn't winter, it will not survive. No matter how harsh the conditions are during the winter the wheat and garlic will flourish in its spring growth. It is a great mystery to me how much the plant or seed gets beat down by the elements of the Universe, nevertheless it finds a way to bring the growth during the spring. The plant still produces crops for harvest.

Wintering is part of time itself; moreover it can be amazing, mysterious, or whatever you want to call it. Nevertheless, sometimes the

Universe gives you the time you need or others to prepare for the next season. There lies the mystery of the Universe. Some might call it, they were moved by the Holy Spirit, or a divine intervention of some sort. Your beliefs are your beliefs, and that is what makes us all unique and special as humans.

Being only 16 years old I can not say how it feels to see your daughter alive after missing for six months. Joyful, euphoric, exhilaration, exuberance, gratification are a few words that come to mind. When I opened my eyes to see my parents sitting in my hospital chairs in the early morning, I saw tears in my Mother's eyes; along with for the first time I lay witness to my Dad crying. There are no words exchanged during this moment, just a warm embrace from a Mother as she sobs while holding me tight. This is a moment words can not be expressed. These are the powerful words of the nonverbals that can move mountains; a moment of a Mother and daughter bonding over love for one another.

My Dad is a tough, rugged, emotionless man, but all that imbalance of him tipping the scale of the Universe has to break at some point. Daddy's first of three baby girls is home, and for Dads in the world might not express their emotions well; but they will do anything for their daughter. My Dad is a man of few words, however when he speaks, he means business. This is different by the virtue my Dad doesn't have words to say; but the length of the hug as well as not being a one armed hug like he usually does, brings a nostalgic feeling of memory lane of just him and I playing together when I am younger.

As the earlier morning hours flow into late morning I have been overwhelmed by detectives, therapists, doctors running tests on me all to find out answers to where I was, and what happened. To my surprise

I am unaware six months have passed. I knew I couldn't go into details about Kumari and I fighting with our powers so I said the last thing I remember was driving to school. It wasn't a total lie. Sometimes leaving a good mystery for others to solve is good enough. I had enough on my plate trying to understand how six months went by, let alone the questioning, and family continuing to visit me. Still I am waiting for someone to bring up the elephant in the room which came from the most unlikely visitor.

The nurse wheels me into my room and waiting there for me is my grandfather. He had his blue flannel short sleeve shirt with suspenders holding up his khaki pants. It is the usual Grandpa Ed look.

"Looks like you have seen some better days," chuckles Grandpa Ed.

"Grandpa Ed," I say with excitement as the nurse helps me to my bed.

"No driving tractors for fall harvest for you anytime soon," Grandpa Ed exclaims.

"Grandpa you can't keep a farm girl with a broken leg and broken ribs off the tractors for fall harvest. I guess I'll just have to learn how to use the combine finally," I reply with a smile.

My Grandpa Ed and Dad are like twins when it comes to body language and looks. The apple didn't fall far from the tree with these two. Seeing my Dad cry is one thing, but seeing my grandfather tear up is something out of this world.

"Ah, I guess we could just attach one of the dual wheels from the tractor to your leg. Then you can haul the wagons with your running speed," remarks Grandpa Ed.

"I missed you grandpa," I tell him, tearing up, and opening my arms for a hug.

"I missed you too, Amara," Grandpa Ed says, getting all choked up.

"So how's your garden, grandpa," I ask.

"Well better than yours this year," Grandpa Ed chuckles with a smile.

"Aaa, I wasn't around to plant mine. Apparently I have been missing for six months and I have no memory of it," I express.

"I just figured you were just out for a run," jokes Grandpa Ed.

Grandpa Ed has the wittiness I need in this moment, and the Universe provides those moments when we need them the most. This is a conversation that is way more enjoyable than the million questions of my disappearance. My grandfather even tilled up my garden for me in hopes that I would return.

He kept joking, "I knew at some point you were going to come home from your run, and when you didn't I just did the next thing with your garden."

My grandpa also planted my crops for me.

Like I said, the most unexpected visitor is the one who recognizes the elephant in the room first.

"Ahem, I just want to make sure I tell you this before I go because I don't want you disappearing on one of your runs again without hearing this from me," Grandpa Ed declares.

"Grandpa, I promise I won't go for another run," I smile at him.

"What is it," I ask.

"I just want you to know I don't care if you like girls and date them. You are my granddaughter, and your happiness is more important than anything else. I just want to let you know that," professes Grandpa Ed.

Joyful tears fill my eyes as I can only say in a whisper, the words of thank you to him.

"What I have realized when you were on your run, there are more important things in life than fussing over you liking girls. If that's what makes you happy, then that's what I want for you," delivered Grandpa Ed.

"That means the world to me, grandpa. Thank you," I gracefully utter back as we hug good-bye.

This is the moment the Universe finds the balance after the turbulent highs and lows in the past year. Fear of the unknown is what kept me hidden, even though it is also something that has helped shape who I am in the Universe. I started off with two secret worlds, nonetheless now the questions are; is it just one secret world, and where is Kumari?

Epilogue

I remember the strenuous emotions of hiding my own transgender identity as a teenager growing up on a dairy farm in a Christain family and community. I created my main character Amara, in "Two Secret Worlds," to live vicariously through Amara's experiences in the book. I applied and adopted my desires I repressed based on my own emotions, feelings, experiences of hiding my transgender identity. I grappled with years of emotional conflict between my Christain family beliefs, morals, values, and trying to understand my own gender identity as a transgender woman.

Growing up in the 1990s and early 2000s there was no language I was exposed to that generated what the word transgender meant. I just knew I was different between the ages 7-9 years old. Some of those thoughts were feeling different while spending nights staring out my window at night looking up at the stars pondering if I belonged on this planet or to this family. Something just never felt right being in my physical male body. I just didn't know how to express it at the time when I was between the ages 7-9.

I wanted to be a girl so badly, but the messages I received in my Church, these thoughts and desires of wanting to be a girl between ages 7-9, were considered sinful in my Church teachings. The torment of micro aggressions on myself started at a young age conflicting how I felt inside, and my outside environment I was being exposed to. I was being taught in Church to love thy neighbor, and treat others how you want to be treated. However, the other messages of homosexuality are a sin while God will condemn those practicing homosexuality behavior to Hell. I prayed as a young child, and as a teenager to take these thoughts and desires away, nevertheless my inner identity desires only grew stronger as I aged.

When I heard the message in my Church, God doesn't make mistakes, and God knows who you are before you are in your mother's womb; that confused the hell out of me. I questioned this concept of the Church for decades. It took accepting myself as a transgender woman before bringing myself closure. I couldn't trust my parents, youth pastor, or friends with my secret of wanting to be a girl as the older I got. I continued to hide and repress all desires and emotions deep in my creating a shadow self. That shadow self began to follow me around from an early age until I came out to my ex-wife in June of 2020. Finally, I felt free of the weight of the world off my shoulders in August of 2022, when I came out to my entire family, friends, and the world. My shadow self of repressed thoughts, emotions, and feelings had grown for almost 30 years, creating a new path of healing as I live my authentic transgender woman self.

I started writing *"Two Secret Worlds"* in July of 2022 a month before I came out as a transgender woman to my family and the world. This book was a way for me to heal in my transgender journey from my hiding for thirty years, and especially from my teenage years. I created Amara, from my personal experiences hiding as a teenage girl in a Christian community. Amara is a mirror image of me, as though I were born a biological female and not transgender. This was my way of fulfilling my innermost desire.

"Two Secret Worlds" differs from other books because the emotions Amara experiences in the book are my own personal emotional

experiences I felt and repressed as a teenager. Also, I applied the healing emotions I felt while writing *"Two Secret Worlds"* to the character Amara. When I journal to process my feelings and emotions for self care, my writing is filled with metaphoric writing to allow myself to connect with the Universe plus nature to understand my emotions better. I find the Universe is always seeking to balance the negatives with the positives and vice versa.

It took me until I was 34 years old to come out to my ex-wife, but at that moment I didn't accept myself as transgender, that took time, in addition to I had to process the new flood of emotions I was experiencing. Any identity a human is grappling with creates a shadow self to balance out society's "justifiable norms." In 2025 the rhetoric is heavily based round anti-transgender policies, racial profiling, persecution of religious beliefs and many more. I want to make this crystal clear to all the readers, a human being's personal identity whether it's transgender, gay, bi-sexual, non-binery, or etc; are concepts having nothing to do with conflict with theology or choosing to be like that. Period! What it has to do with is living as an authentic human being. A living, breathing, human who wants to be a part of society to express their inner self. I have friends who are religious who have accepted me as a transgender woman, and family who are religious who do not accept me nor see me as a human. Fear of the unknown plus differences continues to divide humanity; however acceptance and closure will be the uniting factor of humanity to bring about its greatest potential.

My fear from June of 2020 until August of 2022 was my family, parents, siblings, and other family members casting me out of the family. I wish I could say my story has a happy ending with my blood family all supporting me with open arms; but sadly my blood family used their Christian beliefs to cast out their own child, sibling, and niece from all family functions and gatherings. There are different stories of those who tell their families they don't want to be a doctor, or a lawyer like everyone else in the family. Maybe the situation is that the parents want the child to attend an Ivy League School or a certain University because the parent attended, and it will look good on a resume. There is a story about why they fear not to speak up to share their inner desires. The environment a person is in needs to be accepting, affirming, and a growth mindset.

My story and journey is hiding my transgender self for nearly thirty years. Every human has their own story and journey to share, it's not just humans in the LGBTQIA+ community. My journey is my own uniqueness, besides I can take this journey as fast or as slow as I want. Society doesn't get to tell me how to live my life and my authenticness. Society doesn't get to tell me I chose to be transgender. I will let everyone in the world in on a little secret, transgender people didn't choose to be transgender, it is who we are. We were born this way similar to there is no choice in the color of skin one is born with. The difference between being transgender and color of skin is it is an internal concept of identity. What someone can't physically see is hard to understand and creates fear.

I was raised with the concept that religion requires faith in something that can't be seen. Have faith in those who are transgender, homosexual, heterosexual or any part of the spectrum because all those identities and orientations humans created are internal and will never be able to be measured quantifiably or quantitatively. Having faith in a higher power can't be measured by quantity or quality either, so let all humans be who they are. That is the lesson I have learned in my journey. Another person will never be able to consciously be in another person's consciousness to understand them. That is why empathy, compassion, and grace are important.

I end with this, my journey is still writing my unique authentic story. I will not let anyone else narrate my story with their voice. My voice will not be silent as I will narrate my story. I am a tree in the Autumn showing her true authentic colors, bringing vibrant beauty to the world. If the world fears authentic beauty then they only have to look in a mirror to find the shadow self haunting them with the fear. Being authentic like nature gives the world authentic beauty to all of us humans. People take in the beauty of the world, and sometimes people forget to stop to be in the moment with the authentic beauty. Have empathy for yourself, self compassion for self, give yourself grace, and remember to love yourself. If you don't love yourself first, you can't give love to someone else. Be true to who you are; and always look for the positives in the negatives, because if you look for the negatives in the positives you will get electrocuted.

Glossary of Symbols & Motifs

1. **Underneath the water/Underwater:** Humans tend to take the first observation of new people they encounter, and make subjective observations (opinions, feelings, emotions or previously acquired biased knowledge) to formulate an opinion of the individual. The true beauty of the individual isn't what is on the surface, it is the character of the person. Think about the expression "Don't judge a book by its cover."

2. **Darkness overshadows:** Darkness overshadows the light of the water for the true inner beauty is referencing how new things can be fearful and scary while people forget how beauty is still there. An example is a cherry tree blooming in the spring is beautiful to look at with the sunlight shining on it; however, in the dark of the night the same cherry tree blooming might cast shadows that create fear in people's minds. The beauty is overshadowed by the darkness.

3. **Squash plant with a male and female orange flower:** Transgender and intersex individuals are nothing new to this world. Nature is filled with these natural concepts. This was a transformation from one gender binary to the next. A squash starts off with male flowers close to the roots, but as it grows it realizes it has to be a female in order to survive and reproduce. As a transgender person myself, in order to survive and stay alive; it was important for me to grow and transition to the other gender I identify with.

4. **Eyes deceiving in the darkness of beauty:** A shifting of perspective or narrative happens in the conscious mind once a person is told something about a person, place, or thing. The example here is someone coming out as transgender, bi-sexual, or gay. A friend, family member, or co-worker had one perspective (daylight) before, and now they have a different perspective of the person with this new information (darkness). Another example is food. A food tastes really good (daylight) until someone finds out what ingredients are in it, and suddenly they don't like it (darkness).

5. **Artificial Light:** Artificial light is any light that is produced not by the sun or a source of fire. In this context I am meaning someone is trying to change another person to be something they are not. Someone wants to change another person's personality, religion, beliefs, foods they like, sexual orientation, or gender identity.

6. **I'm only a shadow:** The true authentic self is hidden from the world, while it comes out in one's personality, people might reject, judge, bully, make fun of another person's true authentic self. A person stays a "shadow self" hidden by fear of what others might think of them. This concept can also be known as the looking glass self.

7. **The ground calls out/cracks in the ground:** This is a metaphor for mental health. People show signs of mental health crises in the most subtle ways. It might be metaphoric, cryptic messages, changes in behavior, isolation, and many more. The cracks in the ground are the pain someone is going through while no one else is paying attention to it. The ground calls out,

is the person in a mental health crisis who is calling out for help, yet no one is really listening or hearing. The inner authentic beauty goes unnoticed with the feeling of being ignored adding fuel to that mental health crisis.

8. **My crack:** This is the confusion I had growing up with my gender identity. I hid my gender identity from everyone including myself. My religious beliefs, who I desired to be, and knew who I was caused a perfect storm of pain of mental health. My hiding ability was so intense I created this internal crack that slowly became bigger over time.

9. **Gold and silver armor:** The gold and silver armor represents the hypervigilant awareness of my surroundings to make sure no one would ever find out my secret of wanting to be a girl when I was a teenager. The demons were all the microaggressions I caused on myself from religious beliefs, walking past the girls section in the clothing department, tone and reflection to comment on a female classmate's outfit, and many others.

Reflection & Discussion Question Guide

1. How does Amara's relationship with faith evolve throughout the story?

2. What does the concept of "Two Secret Worlds" mean to you personally?

3. Where do you see yourself reflected in Amara's doubts or discoveries?

4. Who is the true personality characteristic of Amara?

5. How did fear of Amara's secret being discovered contribute to who the real Amara is?

6. How do your fears or greatest fear contribute to who you are as an individual?

7. Analyzing the relationship between Amara and her mother; how did this relationship affect Amara's development through her journey between the two secret worlds?

8. Analyzing the symbolism of the relationship Amara has with Kelly in her imaginary world, what impact has it had with Amara in what kind of relationship she is seeking in reality?

a. What impact does it have on Amara's personality throughout the book?

9. Reflecting on Amara's point of view of humanity, what is your sociological perspective of humanity recognizing, accepting, and supporting human diversity? (Note: culture, race, gender, sex, personality traits, clothing, economic status, etc.)

About the Author

Harper DePagter is also the author of her children's book *"I'm a New Mom."* She published her children's book in 2017 under her deadname before she came out as transgender in 2022. An educator, small business owner of HARPS The Handy Mom, and proud LGBTQIA+ community member. Harper speaks as a leader for transgender advocacy and rights. She is a proud Mother of two children.

The Acknowledgement

I find it ironic I am writing my acknowledgement at my place that brings a sense of calmness, comfort, and reflection. I am at the beach on this hot summer day with my two wonderful, beautiful, and supportive children. They both are my pride and joy in life. They are my first acknowledgement I want to recognize for helping inspire me to write "Two Secret Worlds."

In my journey as a transgender woman, transgender Mother, and a divorced parent; my children have risen through each obstacle that has come their way. That tenacity I needed to sprinkle in my character Amara, and the support she has around her. My children inspire and motivate me every single day. I lived in fear and confusion in my identity growing up; however, living my authentic life creates a life for my children I wished I had growing up and inspiration in my character Amara.

At this time of writing my acknowledgement my children are young and still trying to understand the environment and world they are in. They both bring a smile to their face when they tell someone they have a Dad who is their Mom now, but they can still call me Dad. That is their world they are trying to make sense of and live in. My children are my motivation for everything I am doing in my life. To my children, I love you with all my heart and through the multiverse. Keep being your amazing authentic selves, and thank you for the daily inspiration.

As a transgender woman author, this entire book would not be possible without my own life experiences I used to create my character Amara. My next acknowledgement is to my Deadname self. To write "Two Secret Worlds" I was able to channel His (pronoun usage for deadname) emotional trauma hiding the transgender identity from family, friends, community, and the world. I appreciate everything He endured for me so I could live my authentic life, and be able to write "Two Secret Worlds." His story can now live on through Amara's character and be told in a unique way He always wanted to live as a teenage girl. I love Him for everything He had sacrificed for me so I am able to live my authentic life. Thank you Nate (deadname) and enjoy your eternal retirement. I hope this is a way to honor you for everything you did for me.

I want to take a moment to acknowledge my two best friends who inspired me to develop the friendships Amara has in "Two Secret Worlds." I have been friends with Ms C. for over twenty-four years. We have periods where roads crossed paths and went the same direction. Then there have been moments when roads have crossed paths and went in different directions. Ms C., you have always been there to support me as I have always returned to support you. In the ultimate trust in 2020 I came out to you as transgender, and you instantly switched to using my correct she/her pronouns. Then in 2021, when my name Harper came to me, you immediately changed my name in your phone contacts. Thank you Ms C. for a quarter century of friendship and the inspiration for friendship development for Amara. I appreciate the love and support in my journey. Thank you and I love you.

To my second best friend Ms N. She came into my life in 2023 during my darkest hour. Ms N. you were the first person to give me a hug after my discharge from my suicide attempt, even though I only met you twice prior. My experiences I missed out on as a teenage girl were dreams fulfilled by Ms N. when she hosted the girls night out. We all did our hair and make up while Ms N., you took the time to style my wig for the night out on the town. She is the one who gave me my dreams I hoped for as a teenage girl, but I was hiding Harper while I was presenting as a teenage boy. Ms N., you inspired moments in "Two Secret Worlds" I created for my character Amara to experience because I finally was able to experience them as a transgender woman with you. Thank you for being the best friend a girl could ask for to give me my first inner teenage girl moments I so desperately desired to experience for decades. Our roads in our journeys might not always go the same direction; however, I want you to know you have been an inspiration to me. I am truly grateful to have you as my best friend. I love you Ms N. and thank you for all the encouragement, love, and support in my journey.

My acknowledgements are coming to an end, and this is for all the past and present supporters in my journey. To all who have supported me in the past, and who are not currently actively involved in my life supporting me in my journey, I want to say thank you. You all played an important role in my journey when I needed your support in my journey at that current moment. I appreciate you, in addition I am grateful for your love and support.

For those who are currently actively involved in my journey supporting me, I want to also say thank you. You all are providing positive encouragement when my positive energy is at its lowest. That is when you all stepped in just at the right moment to lift my spirits. All of those encouragements help me to keep going to finish writing "Two Secret Worlds" with a sprinkling in a character who pops in just at the right time who will encourage Amara when her spirits are low. Thank you for the current support in my life and journey. I appreciate all of you. I love you all. I am grateful you are in my life.

One final note to Harper. Thank you for sharing your bright, vibrant, authentic self with the world. No matter how challenging or difficult the environment or situation is as a transgender Mother, you continue to find the positives in the negatives. Keep voicing your authentic beauty to the Universe. I love you.

"Amara and Kumari will be back for another adventure in an upcoming sequel."